HIGHLAND ECHO

WILLA BLAIR

OLIVERHEBERBOOKS

Copyright © 2023 by Linda Williams

Published by Oliver-Heber Books

0 9 8 7 6 5 4 3 2 1

To Laird Peter, who has always believed in me.

ACKNOWLEDGMENTS

I am eternally grateful to my Beta reader, Laura G., for making me slow down the action and show what my characters feel. My books are better for her insights. And to my friend, Bev W., for her excitement when a new book is on the horizon. It's more encouraging than she knows to see a reader's anticipation in real life. To my editor, Kim, who catches what I and others missed, and whose insights are always welcome. And, finally, to my publisher, Tanya Anne Crosby, for taking many of the burdens off my and her other authors' shoulders, freeing us to do what we most love to do—write.

1

SCOTLAND, EARLY AUTUMN 1539

"**E**ilidh! I didna expect ye to be here."

Eilidh Lathan frowned up at her eldest brother, Drummond, who seated himself across from her at her table in the Aerie's great hall and signaled to a serving lass for his evening meal.

"Where else would I be at this hour of the day?"

"Sleeping until tomorrow morning? Ye need a few days to recover from the clan lairds' Gathering, especially after what the attacks on Donal MacNabb put ye and Mother through."

"She does look more tired than I ever recall," Eilidh admitted, her concern reflected in the frown on her brother's face as he gazed aside to where their parents sat.

"Ye, as well," Drummond said, turning back to Eilidh. "I saw ye helping her both times he was hurt."

"'Tis what I am meant to do," Eilidh reminded him. "Ye once called me Mother's Echo. I am going to take her place someday." She hoped, like an echo, her talent was not a weaker version of her mother's that would fade away over time. "And Tavish helped, too."

"I shouldna have named ye so," Drummond admitted. "Ye are

as strong a healer as she. And she has taught ye things she spent years learning for herself, so with experience, ye will someday be even better than she."

Someday.

Eilidh hoped he was right. Both their brother Jamie and sister Lianna, triplets with Drummond, had married away from the Aerie, taking their healing talents to their new homes. Eilidh had lived most of her life with the expectation of remaining at Lathan as its healer. While having her future so well laid out for her was comforting, the certainty of it also made her wish for far horizons.

Drummond seemed to lose interest in their conversation as soon as his food arrived. They ate in silence, the rumble of voices in the hall muting as more people turned to filling their bellies.

At first, Eilidh thought nothing of the cool breeze that wafted across the hall, then she realized someone must have entered from the bailey. Bhaltair and his men? She turned in time to see a lone stranger approach Uncle Jamie, her brother's namesake. He wasn't really their uncle, rather a cousin and their father's life-long best friend. But to Eilidh, he'd been Uncle Jamie her entire life.

Disappointed that the man she wanted to see had not entered, but still curious, she watched the stranger pull a missive from inside his léine and hand it over. Uncle Jamie read, his expression darkening as his gaze moved down the page. What could have happened at Fletcher that the laird would send a courier all the way to Lathan? Was this an urgent summons for Uncle Jamie to return home?

He set the missive aside, spoke briefly to her mother, who nodded to the courier, then summoned a serving lass to lead him to the kitchen to seek a meal. From there, Eilidh knew, he'd be given a place to sleep before carrying Uncle Jamie's answer, if one was required, to Fletcher. The man bowed his acceptance of their hospitality and trailed the lass from the great hall.

By the time her gaze returned to her parents and Uncle Jamie, they were deep in conversation, and none of them looked happy.

"Ach, I wonder what news that man brought," she said, catching Drummond's attention with a tap on his hand. His gaze was also fixed on their parents.

"Naught good, I'd guess," he muttered. After a moment, he added, "They keep looking this way. At me? Or ye?" He turned his head to look at her, his brow crinkled.

"Me, I think. I'll go find out..."

"We'll both go," Drummond told her, stood and helped Eilidh up from the bench. "This looks like something to concern all of us."

Uncle Jamie and their parents stood as they approached.

"My solar," their father Toran said and lifted his chin in that direction.

Drummond frowned, worrying Eilidh. This could not be good news. But she held her questions until they were alone in the laird's solar, seated around the long worktable in the middle of the chamber.

"Jamie, tell Drummond and Eilidh what news ye just received."

"'Tis our granddaughter. Some ailment our healer has not been able to relieve. Wee Orla is getting worse, and Caitrin begs Aileana to return with me to help. But," he said and held up a hand to forestall any comments, "she also warns of trouble near Fletcher. Lowlanders."

He and Toran exchanged a frown, no doubt thinking back to the Lowlander invasion twenty-three years earlier that brought Eilidh's mother to the Aerie. Aileana met her daughter's gaze, her expression unreadable.

"'Twill not be an easy trip," Jamie reminded him. "Toran, we'll need a large contingent of warriors to act as guards."

"Ye will have them."

"Mother? Ye canna go." Drummond leaned forward and pressed his lips together.

Only minutes ago, he'd expressed his concern for their mother. Eilidh knew such a journey would only compound her exhaustion.

"She willna," Toran said before Drummond could explain why he advised against it, and before Aileana could answer his heir. "She's worn down from saving Donal's life—twice—not to mention all the other bloodshed she and Eilidh dealt with during the gathering."

Earlier today, they'd bid goodbye to her father's other close friend, Donal MacNabb, and his wife Ellie, the MacKyrie Seer. Their daughter Yvaine had just married Eilidh's twin Tavish. The newlyweds were away, celebrating their honeymoon. They would return to the Aerie well before Samhain, but Yvaine's parents couldn't stay that long. They needed to return to MacKyrie before autumn snows closed the passes into their remote glen.

"Toran—" Aileana interrupted him, putting a hand on his arm. "I'm no' so weak as that."

"Wife, ye are at yer limits. Ye need rest. Anyone can see it. I forbid this." At Uncle Jamie's sudden intake of breath, he added, "But Fletcher needs help only Lathan can provide. Eilidh will go. Her skills near match yer own. And she is nay so depleted as ye are."

Eilidh's chest swelled with pride. He really felt her skills were nearly a match for her mother's? But what of the Fletcher's warning?

"Toran, I can..."

"Eilidh will be able to help, I'm certain," Uncle Jamie broke in when it appeared Aileana would continue to argue with her husband and laird.

"I will do my best," Eilidh said and nodded, anxious but excited all at once. The quiver in her belly threatened to force her to her feet. This was her chance to prove herself without her mother standing over her.

"Ye will travel with Bhaltair and enough of his men to keep ye safe on the journey," Toran continued, pinning her with his gaze. Bhaltair had escorted Eilidh's elder brother Jamie to care for an injured clansman. He'd taken her sister Lianna, now married to the MacDhai laird, to care for ill MacDhai horses. Soon after, he'd gone with Drummond on the journey where he met his wife, Morven.

Lately, Bhaltair seemed rarely to be in residence at the Aerie. Eilidh felt the lack of his presence each time. What good was a chief guard never within the Aerie's walls? She knew her father sent him because he was the most formidable warrior in the clan —and Toran wanted only the best to keep his children safe.

Now, it was her turn.

At that, a thrill ran from Eilidh's chest to her fingertips. A journey with Bhaltair, even if accompanied by a host of others, might give her time to make him notice her as a woman, and not just as the laird's youngest daughter, a presence he had dismissed as long as she was safe with her family inside the Aerie's walls. Outside, he would have to pay attention to her. She nodded. "I will go, Mother. Uncle Jamie," she added solemnly. This was her rite of passage, from being seen as simply the youngest daughter and future healer to acceptance as a responsible adult in her own right. "And gladly. I look forward to being of benefit to Fletcher, just as ye have meant so much to Lathan over the years."

BHALTAIR LATHAN PREFERRED the silence that lay over the forge like a warm blanket after Edan, the clan's blacksmith, left for the evening. That was when he could inspect the stacks of weapons Edan was making, to ensure that the clan's armory remained well-stocked. Above them, hammers and tongs hung from pegs on the walls. Nearby, finished horseshoes, nails and iron strapping filled barrels. All manner of household items needing repair, such as Cook's pots, knives, and skewers were piled in one corner to work on as time—and need—allowed. Weapons came first. Bhaltair was pleased that several weapon piles had grown. Edan had continued to work despite the disruptions during the lairds' Gathering.

Bhaltair wasn't the Lathan arms master—yet. But he hoped to be when old Duncan decided to give up the position. In the meantime, his men needed reliable, well-crafted weapons, and Bhaltair was an excellent judge of steel. This was a world he knew, a craft he understood. He'd learned it while fostered away, but had little call to use it now. He had become a warrior, not a blacksmith, as his foster father had predicted. He'd been better at fighting than folding steel.

Satisfied at Edan's progress, Bhaltair sat on a barrel to sharpen his own blades. The uninterrupted, rhythmic slide of steel against a whetstone soothed him, letting his mind rest, absorbed in the simple, repetitive motion. The lairds who had signed Toran's treaty over the years had recently come to renew ties with him and each other, but the spirit of the event had been sullied by violence resulting from a long-held grudge. Now that all of the Gathering visitors save Toran's cousin and best friend, Jamie Lathan Fletcher, had gone, Bhaltair could indulge in his version of a peaceful pastime.

He'd been born to fight, it seemed. His mother birthed him soon after receiving the news that his father was one of the men killed at Flodden Field along with the old laird. He had no memory of his father save his mother's tales and her wish that he avenge him. He'd grown up with Toran as Laird Lathan, and after his mother died suddenly, Toran sent him to foster with Donal MacNabb at MacKyrie, where Toran sent his most promising—or troublesome—lads. Donal's training had made Bhaltair the man he was now. He owed him nearly as much as he owed the laird, and had been proud to put a stop to the plot against him during the Gathering.

He hoped autumn and winter weather would bring an end to conflict in the Highlands until spring. But he'd heard a courier arrive as he neared finishing one of his blades. This stage was critical for honing an edge that was sharp but strong. Whatever news the courier brought would wait. If he was needed, Toran would send someone to find him.

Before long, footsteps approached and he knew his respite had come to an end.

"Bhaltair? Are ye in there?"

Toran! The laird had come himself? That did not bode well.

"Here, Laird." He wiped his blade with an oily rag and stood.

"There ye are." Toran approached, outlined by the dim glow of the hearth. The banked fire still warmed the space, as did the slowly cooling anvil. "How ye can work in near darkness is beyond me."

"It helps me to focus on the feel of the blade rather than the shine, Laird."

"That seems a clever solution, but tell me, how often do ye cut yerself?"

Bhaltair chuckled at that. "More often than I like. What do ye need me to do, Laird?"

"Ye saw the courier arrive?"

"I heard him."

"I must send Eilidh with Jamie to Fletcher. There is an ill grandchild—"

"I will ready my men."

"And the messenger and yerself. I willna trust my youngest daughter to anyone save ye and Jamie."

Bhaltair's heart thumped against the inside of his ribs at the idea of traveling with Eilidh. He rubbed his chest to tamp down his sudden eagerness. She was not for him. He forced his attention back to his laird. "Jamie was yer best scout. I ken the tales."

"I doubt ye've heard all of them, but Jamie can fill ye in on the way. Aileana is helping Eilidh prepare. There is some urgency."

"We'll leave at first light."

"Ye ken me well, Bhaltair." Toran turned to go, then turned back. "Get some sleep before then, too."

"Aye."

Toran nodded and headed back into the keep.

Bhaltair swung his newly sharpened blade a few times, testing its heft and balance, and nodded with satisfaction. He hoped not to need it, but it would serve him well if he did.

He had escorted each of the laird's bairns on lengthy trips, all of which had ended in a hand fasting or a wedding. Now it was Eilidh's turn. Whom would she be introduced to, he wondered. And how did he feel about delivering her to meet another man?

He pursed his lips and stepped out into the star-filled night. He'd always been more at ease with her brothers and older sister, Lianna. And he had no business lusting after the daughter of the laird. It had never been an issue with Lianna. She'd been in love with David MacDhai since he fostered with them, and even after he left her broken-hearted, it was clear she was not interested in Bhaltair.

He suspected Eilidh feared him. She spent most of her time training with her mother, but when they did cross paths, she avoided his gaze. And he'd always believed she would make an alliance outside Lathan, even if she brought a husband back here. She would follow in her mother's footsteps and take over as Lathan healer when the time came. It didn't matter what he thought about that. There was no alternative. Certainly none that paired him with the tall, beautiful, and shy healer.

THE NEXT MORNING, Eilidh yawned as she stepped out into the bailey. She'd slept but a few hours, her dreams filled with fleeting images of Bhaltair astride a horse or stalking through the keep as she'd often seen him. Even in her dreams, to her, he was not just a man. He was the warrior, the guardian the laird called upon again and again to keep safe not only his family, but the rest of his clan. Eilidh could not find a way to make him hers, even in her imagination.

And there he was, quitting the stable, leading his warhorse and another. Hers! Did he mean for her to ride beside him? The thought made her heart beat a fast trot in her chest. What would she say to him? Or would he demand her silence as he kept his sharp gaze on the area around them, looking for hazards, listening for sounds that didn't belong, or the absence of normal forest sounds that signaled trouble.

He saw her and lifted his chin, beckoning her over. His hands were occupied with the reins of both horses. His danced about, eager to be away, forcing Bhaltair to keep tight control over the great beast. A dozen of his men waited for the signal to leave. They were already mounted near the wagon filled after a hurried flurry of packing with clothes, food and extra weapons, along with herbs, tinctures, and potions from Aileana's herbal.

Behind Eilidh, the keep's door opened and her parents walked out.

"Bhaltair is ready early, as usual," Aileana remarked as she came down the steps and put an arm around her youngest child.

"Has anyone seen Jamie?" Toran followed her down the steps. Just then, Jamie left the stable leading his mount, the Fletcher messenger following behind him. "Ah, everyone is here. Are ye ready, Eilidh, lass?"

Was she? Nerves had her belly aflutter and her palms damp, but the solemn expression on Uncle Jamie's face recalled her to the reason for the trip. "Aye, Da." She nodded toward Bhaltair and the pack tied behind her mount's saddle. "My things are already in place."

"Let's get ye mounted up." Toran led her, still secure in the curve of her mother's arm, to her mount. Aileana kissed her cheek and released her. Toran put his hands on her shoulders. "Ye'll do as Bhaltair tells ye, aye? He will keep ye safe."

"Of course, Da."

"And Jamie, as well," he added with a glance at his cousin, who nodded.

"She'll be looked after as if she was our own. We are honored to have a healer so gifted at Fletcher," he said. "If only for a short time," he added after a pause.

Eilidh couldn't imagine why that made her father frown at his cousin. Thanks to Uncle Jamie, Fletcher would treat her as the little sister much as everyone did at home. That should make her father happy. She sighed and added her frown to his. "I'm no' a wean. I can—"

"I ken ye are a lass grown," Toran told her. His voice lacked any humor and his gaze captured hers as firmly as his hands held her shoulders, keeping her still. "Ye are a braw and a wise lass. But dinna mistake me. Ye must come home safe and unharmed, aye?"

A mist of tears clouded her view of his face and she blinked them back. He loved her, and he knew what her loss would mean to her mother, and to the rest of the clan. Even when she doubted herself, Toran, Laird Lathan, had always believed in her. She had always known it, and saw that in his eyes again now.

"I will, Da. I promise ye."

"Good." He glanced up and cleared his throat. "Keep her safe," he said to Bhaltair.

"As ever," the big man replied.

Her father lifted her onto her mount. She kicked a leg over to ride astride and took the reins Bhaltair handed her. She was ready. She nodded to his form, not able to meet his gaze with tears in her eyes, then to her Da. Her mother stood with hands clasped over her breasts. "See ye soon," Eilidh promised and gave her mount a gentle tap of her heels to get it moving.

Bhaltair kept pace with her, and they headed through the Aerie's bailey, out its heavy gates, and down the trail to the glen. She'd ridden this far many times, but never had she seemed to reach the glen so quickly, or the woodland beyond it. Uncle Jamie flanked her opposite Bhaltair. Three of the guards rode around them and took point in an arrow formation that put her in the middle of the riders, two others flanking Bhaltair and Jamie, and the rest of their company following behind or escorting the wagon, pulled by more horses. They would not travel quietly, but the size of the group, and the stature of the men protecting her, would discourage any troublemakers. If all went well, they would reach Fletcher late the next day.

As they rode, she wondered what Bhaltair's reaction had been to her father's words. A lass grown, he'd called her. If her father saw that, could Bhaltair as well? As she'd expected, he said little to her during the first day. She had hoped while they crossed Lathan land that he'd be more relaxed, but his attention remained firmly fixed on their surroundings. His other men, one of whom, Cole, she counted as a friend, took their cue from Bhaltair and spoke to her only when necessary.

They camped that night in a wee glen with clear sight lines to the trees on three sides and down to a burn on the last. Bhaltair posted guards and established a rotation before they gathered firewood and created the camp. Eilidh knew he would not tolerate a guard falling asleep, and his men were well-trained. She had no reason to worry. Yet she did. They were miles from home with a full day's ride yet before them.

Cook had packed plenty of travel rations, so making the evening meal fell to junior guards, leaving her with nothing to do but sit and think. If they were attacked, if anyone got hurt, it would be up to her to save them. She knew she could do it—her father's words still rang in her ears, comforting, but also challenging. In an all-out attack, how many Lathans would be hurt? How long would her stamina last?

Bhaltair approached the campfire, pulling her out of her spiral of anxiety and making her sit up straighter on her log. Uncle Jamie paced at his side, but her attention stayed on the big chief guard. He saw her, nodded, and settled with Jamie on the far side of the fire. His gaze tracked her friend Cole as he approached her with a wrapped packet of food.

She sighed, then smiled at Cole and accepted the meal, but not before she saw Bhaltair's expression sharpen as he regarded his man. The reason for his reaction interested her more than the bread, cheese, dried venison and apple that would fill her belly, or the fact that Cole gave her a wink and backed off without saying a word. Clearly, he and the other guards were under orders to treat her respectfully or face the consequences.

Bhaltair's steady gaze met her next glance across the fire, his attention not on his retreating guard, but on her. Something deep in his eyes told her he would fill her dreams.

2

Bhaltair did his best to listen to Jamie telling the tale of his first trip to Fletcher. Jamie had led an interesting life, and Bhaltair, to be honest, wanted to hear more about it. He was a good man, and had once been the Lathan's chief scout before Toran turned him into a diplomat and sent him out to collect signatures on his treaty.

As children, Toran and Jamie had known the Fletcher laird's daughter, Caitrin, until Jamie's sister was killed, and for her own protection, Caitrin was sent home from fostering at the Aerie. Jamie's story started there, and got darker as he told it. Toran had sent him to Fletcher to escort Caitrin to MacGregor to be betrothed. He kept his voice low, not meant to carry, but Bhaltair had to wonder if Eilidh could hear Jamie's tale from across the fire.

Bhaltair hoped not.

They were in the middle of the Highlands. By rights Eilidh should be tired and would sleep well, but with Jamie's tales of MacGregor's sadism ringing in her ears, she might lie awake the night through and fall asleep on her horse on the morrow.

That, he would not allow.

When Jamie next paused to take a breath, Bhaltair held up a hand, and tipped his head toward Eilidh. "I think the lass is tired. We should settle the camp for the night."

Jamie nodded. "Ye are a wise man. Aye, see to her while I bank the fire."

Bhaltair rose and circled the fire to Eilidh. She swayed where she sat, eyes heavy lidded. He was certain she wasn't aware of him standing before her, but had fallen asleep sitting up.

"Lass," he said softly. "Eilidh, 'tis time to lay down yer head."

Her chin lifted and she blinked, then looked up at him, craning her neck back to scale his height with her gaze. Seeing that, he crouched before her. "Ye're nearly asleep. Let me tuck ye in and—"

In the dying firelight, he saw the color staining her cheeks.

"Nay, I must..." She hooked a thumb toward the burn. "I'll be but a moment."

"I'll go with ye."

"What? Nay. Ye have men standing guard all around us. I'll be fine."

"Aye, ye will, because I will be nearby. With my back to ye, aye?"

She huffed out a breath, took the hand he offered and stood. "Keep yer distance."

He didn't bother to answer, but turned her toward the burn and kept pace until they reached the grasses and shrubs that grew along its banks.

"Stay here," she commanded, and moved forward into the cover.

He let her go, knowing if she got into trouble, he would hear and reach her in moments. With his back turned, he had a good view of their camp. Eyes beyond Jamie at the edge of the woods caught the firelight and reflected it, shining malevolently. Wolves!

With an oath, he called out, "Jamie, behind ye." Then he lowered his voice. "Eilidh, hurry lass."

"I will," she answered. "Go to him. I'm safe here."

Against his better judgement, Bhaltair ran for the camp and pulled his broadsword just as Jamie brandished a flaming branch and thrust it toward three wolves that dared the open ground before him. The wolves whined and danced aside from the flames, but did not retreat. Bhaltair swore. "I'll have to kill them," he said, "or they'll be on us again as soon as the fire is out. Where the hell are the guards?"

"Here," Cole said and limped into the clearing, blood coating his leg, his sword black with it. "I got two more in the woods. They're hungry and from the look of them, we're as good a meal as they've managed in a long while."

The wolves began to circle when the guard joined them. "That one's mine," Cole said, pointing at the largest female. "She gave me this," he added, nodding at the blood on his leg. "I killed the alpha. She's his mate."

"Take them," Jamie called as one rushed him. His flaming branch guttered, and wouldn't protect him much longer. "My sword is beyond them, on my bedding, damn it. So finish this."

Eilidh would not be safe with them near the camp. Bhaltair did as Jamie commanded, though it pained him to kill such magnificent creatures. But he didn't have enough men to protect the camp from a larger pack these might attract. In minutes, it was over.

EILIDH KNEW she should not have been surprised by Bhaltair's insistence on escorting her to the burn. He could not afford to allow anything to happen to her. Her father would... well, she didn't know what Da would do, but it wouldn't be good for Bhaltair or any of his men. And her mother would never get over her loss. Losing one of her children was Aileana's greatest fear. Seeing them marry away from the clan was hard on her, but she accepted it because it was expected. But never to see one of her bairns again? Nay, Bhaltair was right to stay close. Still, she heartily wished she had brought along a female friend. One of the maids. Someone to accompany her that was not Bhaltair Lathan.

Concern filled her when his attention was taken by the sudden threat to Uncle Jamie. Bhaltair was torn between two duties—her and her uncle's peril. For her, the choice was simple. She was in no danger. Not unless the wolves got past the men and scented her. Growling, snapping, and canine whining filled the air. She hated to watch, but her friend Cole had returned with blood on his leg, and if any of the others were hurt, they would need her soon. She hurried to finish, then moved quietly upstream a few feet to wash her hands and face. In moments, she realized the fight with the wolves had ended badly for them. She heard the men, but nothing else. Rising and drying her face and hands on her skirt, she heard someone behind her. "Bhaltair?"

Silence.

Eilidh's blood froze in her veins and she turned her head. Had a wolf found her? She flexed her knees, prepared to run and took a breath as she turned to face the creature. Nothing was there.

Before she took the first step back toward camp, something knocked her to the ground from the side. Her breath left her in a painful whoosh as a rough-bearded man pawed at her, hands tangling in her clothes.

"Where's yer purse? Give it, and I'll go," he hissed in her ear as he tore at her dress. "Ye wear no gold chain? Yer dress is fine enough. Ye must have jewels. Where?"

Cold air chilled her breasts and belly as he ripped the cloth covering them, searching.

"Naught? Are ye one of them? Ah, mayhap ye have more treasures," he muttered in a low voice, his hand brushing over her cold-peaked nipple, "but first I want yer coin."

His threat of greater physical assault broke the shock of his attack. She sucked in a breath and screamed with everything in her.

"Bollocks! I should gut ye for that," he swore as he rolled off her and lunged for the burn.

Bhaltair arrived seconds later, sword in hand, and dropped to his knees beside her. "Eilidh! God's bones, what happened?"

Her hands fluttered uselessly at her torn clothes. "Man... tried to rob..." Somehow she got control of one arm while she spoke and pointed with shaking fingers. "That way... the burn."

Bhaltair gathered her up in his arms and pulled at her torn clothes in a futile attempt to cover her. "Did he hurt ye?"

She shook her head, rolling away so that he would not see her breasts. Only then, when it stopped, did she realize his touch on her skin had awoken her hidden power, the empathy that went far beyond the healing powers her clan respected. She could feel his outrage that someone attacked her so close to the camp. He vibrated with a fury so incandescent that it shocked her. Was it directed solely at her attacker? Or did Bhaltair in some way blame her, too, since she had insisted on leaving the campfire, and on sending him to help Uncle Jamie? She clasped together the tatters of her bodice so he would stop trying to cover her. The heat of his hands seared her breasts, and his blazing fury made her want to cower away from him.

She was bruised, filthy, exposed, and mortified that Bhaltair had found her half-naked, and was appalled by her. That he saw her in this state. She could not bear that he would learn her body in this way and always associate it with this moment. The scant progress she thought she'd made with him today, getting him to speak to her, to look at her, was destroyed in this blaze of emotions. He would never see her as a lover, but as a victim.

She heard him shifting behind her. In a moment, he pulled her up and surprised her, slipping his léine, still warm from the heat of his body, over her head, covering her. She shuddered, her muscles reacting to the comforting change in temperature, and the fact that it broke the skin-to-skin contact that let her feel Bhaltair's raging emotions.

"I've got ye, lass," he said softly.

Given the fire she'd felt coursing through him, his tone was calmer than she expected.

He pulled her back against his chest and reached around her shoulders to tighten the laces in front, then took a breath and called for Jamie and the guards.

Grateful, Eilidh realized he'd hidden her from the men who ran up in answer to his summons. He'd left his sleeves dangling loosely over her chest, and she made no move to slip her arms into them.

"A man tried to rob her," he reported when Jamie arrived. "He ran toward the burn. Find him!"

"Eilidh, are ye all right?" Jamie's voice filled with concern and anger.

Eilidh shook her head, but kept her face averted. Bhaltair, holding her from behind, couldn't see her face, but Jamie could, and tears were starting to fill her eyes. She didn't want to cry. She wouldn't!

"Of course ye are not," he muttered. "We'll find him. He'll answer for attacking ye." He moved off with four other men, sent two at angles to search, two back to mount and search on horseback, and took the most direct path across the burn for himself.

Eilidh watched them move without really seeing them. Bhaltair's heat at her back both soothed and upset her. This was not the way she wanted him to see her mature body for the first time. For years, he'd seen her as a bairn or young lass. Now, she'd be a victim, and she'd never convince him she was a woman grown, someone he could desire—and love.

Lost in her thoughts, she shrieked in surprise when he gathered her up and stood with her in his arms. She squeezed her eyes shut and clung to his heavily-muscled shoulder through the fabric of the shirt he'd wrapped around her. He carried her back to camp and settled by the fire. She blinked at the brightness behind her eyelids, suddenly aware of being warmed front and back, by the fire and by Bhaltair's body heat. She blinked and cut her gaze from the fire to him. Only then did she realize without his shirt, he was bare from the waist up. The plaid normally draped over one shoulder was wrapped around them both. The arm over her belly was strongly muscled and dusted with light hair. She'd seen him shirtless before on the practice ground, sparring with other men, but admiring him from a distance and feeling his sculpted body hard and hot under hers made her feel two very different things, low and deep in her core.

Despite how she got here, she wanted to stay in his arms forever. It was a place she'd dreamed about for years. But she dared not tell him that, or any of what she was feeling. Despite giving him her heart, she did still fear him--just a little. He was a warrior of great renown, not a man cut out to be a husband and father, no matter what she might wish him to be. And she feared his reaction if she did reveal her heart. If he spurned her, or worse, laughed at what he thought of as her girlish infatuation, not understanding the depth of her feelings, she couldn't bear it.

THE FURY FILLING Bhaltair at Eilidh's attacker knew no bounds. He would gladly strip the skin from the man with a very small, very dull blade. But first, he had to care for the very shaken lass. The nearly naked lass, whom he could no longer deny was fully a woman. His attempts to pull her torn dress back together only resulted in his hands brushing her breasts, making things worse for her. In any other circumstance, he might have been able to enjoy the sensation against his fingers and palms, but never like this.

Eilidh was in shock from the attack. It was up to him to protect her, but his strength was useless in this moment. His own shirt was the best he could offer to keep her from the other men's gazes. He had covered her, then wrapped his plaid around them both and cradled her next to his chest, hoping the furnace of his body heat would stop the shivering that consumed her.

Holding her in his arms, feeling the rounded softness of her arse on his lap, should make him hard and hungry for her. But he would not compound the fright she'd suffered at the hands of a strange man. If she had not screamed, and he had not arrived when he did, she would have suffered much worse. The thought of that sort of assault happening to Eilidh, the lass he'd known for years and had watched grow from a wean to a lovely young woman, sickened him. He was grateful he'd been as close by as he was, despite the distraction the hungry wolves caused.

He reached for his belt, confirming his dirk was still there. He'd propped his sword on the log next to them, but he wanted more than one blade in reach. He couldn't be sure that in killing the pack alpha pair, they had driven the remainder away. But some of his men were still on guard around the camp while the rest searched with Jamie. If he had to sit on this log for the rest of the night with her in his arms, he'd make sure nothing would disturb Eilidh's rest. Tomorrow, she'd be safe and sound at Fletcher, where Jamie's wife could care for her. During difficult times, he'd observed that women sought the company of other women.

At his movement, reaching for his dirk, Eilidh whimpered, so he wrapped his arm around her again. She was calming, and falling asleep, the shock wearing off. He'd like to think sharing his heat, keeping her warm and holding her, caring for her, allowed her to find some peace.

He vowed to take care of her for as long as she would allow him to. As much as he would like to be the one to find the man who'd done this and avenge her, he would not trade holding her, cradling her softness against his chest, and feeling her relax in his arms, for anything. His men were on the trail of the attacker. He had to be satisfied with that, and with thinking up ways to torment the man when they found him and brought him back. He sat by the fire with her on his lap, rocking her until she finally stopped shivering, sighed out a soft moan, and fell asleep in his arms.

This was not the way he would have envisioned the first time he held her until she slept, but for now, he must be satisfied.

3

Eilidh roused slowly from slumber, blissfully warm and cradled in loving arms against a massive chest. She snuggled deeper against it, her fingertips stroking the hot skin that warmed her to her bones until a man's deep groan disturbed her semi-conscious state. Undeterred, she snuggled closer, inhaled his musky scent, and curious, touched the tip of her nose to his skin. That didn't satisfy her need to explore him, so she traced the tip of her finger along a firm ridge of muscle angling onto his belly. Before long, the rod growing against her hip woke her fully. Mortified, she realized where she was and what she'd done.

Bhaltair!

She tried to leap up, only to fall back, swathed in his shirt and tangled with him in his plaid. Memory of her attack came back to her, and of how he found her. Half naked and fighting tears. Now he was half naked. He must be nearly frozen, holding her like this for—how long had she been asleep? She buried her face against his chest. How would she ever look him in the eye again?

"Eilidh. *Dinna fash*. All is well now."

Bhaltair's deep voice vibrated against her cheek. Despite her chagrin, it lured her to accept the comfort he offered. "Is it?"

"Aye lass. Ye are safe. The sun will be up soon and we'll be on our way. Ye'll be at Fletcher afore ye ken it."

She nodded but made no further move to leave the circle of his arms. Instead, she rubbed her cheek against the fine, light hair covering his chest, curling like a kitten seeking warmth. She might never get this chance again. Once they reached Fletcher, or even before that, once Bhaltair deemed her recovered well enough to unwrap her and set her on her feet, he'd go back to keeping his distance, and she'd go back to living with half her heart missing, given long ago to him.

It made her sad. But that was how they'd always been, and despite being in his arms right now, she doubted this journey would change either of them. She inhaled his scent, trying to memorize it, to make that small part of him part of her as well. She wanted that much to hold onto, since he might never be willing to give her more. She nearly moaned aloud when he began stroking a hand up and down her back. She'd never known he could be so caring, so gentle. She'd only seen the warrior in him, though she'd long hoped he was much more than that. It gladdened her to discover she was right, at least in this small measure.

THE SUN WAS up when Jamie and the other guards who'd gone out to search brought back their quarry. Bhaltair murmured Eilidh's name and unwrapped his plaid to wake her from the doze she'd fallen into after they'd exchanged a few words before dawn, and before that when she had traced a questing line down his belly, where she never should have been allowed to touch him. She'd surprised him, and his body had reacted before he could control it. He shoved that memory aside before it happened again, and stood.

She leaned against him, fighting wakefulness. He wrapped his plaid around her to keep her warm, letting it cover her from her shoulders to her ankles. Then he gave her a little shake.

"Eilidh, wake up. 'Tis time to go." Could the lass truly sleep on her feet? Last night before the trouble started, he had thought she'd been asleep sitting up.

Her eyes blinked open and she gazed up at him. "Morning." It wasn't a question, but a statement by someone still trying to get her bearings.

"Aye, morning. I'm sorry to do this, but I must ask ye to look at that man." He turned her to look at the man held between his guards, Jamie at his back. "Is he the one who attacked ye?"

Her head came up then and she frowned, but she didn't speak while she studied their captive. "The beard, aye. He's dirty enough. Have him speak."

Jamie prodded the man. "Say yer name."

"What?" The man's tone was fearful but resentful at the same time.

"Speak yer name," Jamie repeated.

"Pritchard."

"Say ye should gut me," Eilidh spat, her voice gaining strength and resolve. "Say it."

The man hesitated and paled, but Jamie prodded him again. "I should gut ye for that," he finally replied.

"'Tis him." Eilidh's voice held no hesitation. "I didn't see much of him. He was on me too fast, too close. But he spoke. He wanted gold, jewels, a purse of coins. He's a poor judge of targets. I had none of those things."

"Ye had more treasure than that, bitch. I liked the wee sample I got, afore ye screamed."

Bhaltair had been watching with interest how bravely Eilidh dealt with her attacker, but at those words, his fury rose again.

"That threat will get yer cods cut off instead of just yer hands. Then I'll string ye up and watch ye dance as ye bleed."

Pritchard paled and his shoulders slumped, his bravado collapsing with Bhaltair's words.

Eilidh gasped, and her face, too, lost its color. Too late he recalled how her compulsion to heal might draw her to the very man who'd attacked her. The import of Bhaltair's words would sicken her. He couldn't imagine the agony of caring for someone with such damage, yet the graphic detail of the warning he'd given her attacker and the prospect of suffering those wounds as she strove to save his life would also terrify her.

Jamie was frowning at him and shaking his head. Aye, he knew better, but his fury had slowed his thought and let his words overreach. "I'm sorry, lass," he murmured. "I shouldna have threatened him in yer presence." Punishment would have to wait until they reached their destination and he could physically separate her from her attacker's fate. But how to travel another day with the man? Eilidh would be uncomfortable the entire time.

"Nor should ye do it," she scolded. "He did me no permanent harm. Look at him. He's half-starved and desperate."

Bhaltair was glad her shock had given way to anger—even at him. And that she'd kept her voice down. The man might not have heard her words. He didn't want her to give him hope. The Fletcher might set him free, but a few hours of fearing for his life would be the least he deserved.

"Dinna let his appearance sway ye, Eilidh. No' until we ken more about him."

"My point exactly," she insisted, finally meeting his gaze. "Ye dinna ken why he did what he did. I'm not excusing him. I dinna wish to look at him. But he doesna deserve what ye threatened."

"Ye are right. I'm angry over what he did to ye—no matter what may have driven him to do it. He will ride with guards. Behind ye. Ye willna have to see him. But he will pay for what he did. No man threatens ye or puts his hands on ye as he did and gets away with it." He had done much the same as he tried to cover her with her torn garments, but he accepted the irony and set it aside. He lifted his chin to Jamie and the guards. "Secure him on the wagon. Two guards at all times. Dinna let him out of yer sight." They moved to obey and he turned back to Eilidh. "Have ye more clothes packed where ye can get to them?"

She nodded. "In the bundle on my mount."

"Let's get them. Ye can change, we'll break our fast, and then we will go. Ye can forget this ever happened."

Not that she would. He wanted to bite his tongue for his thoughtless words. After the attack, the way she woke up before dawn exploring him, and his reaction to her, would she ever forget this day? Bhaltair doubted it.

Did he want her to remember? And what about his memories? He'd spent hours with her in his arms. She couldn't know it yet, but he had begun to hope she would remember that, too, and realize there was more to him than the warrior she thought she knew.

Eilidh could not stand to look at the man who'd attacked her. She distracted herself by doing as Bhaltair suggested, changing into her own clothes, though it pained her to return his shirt and give up something that carried his scent. Something she would have loved to sleep with the rest of her life, since the man it belonged to would likely never share her bed or her life.

While some of the guards prepared food and drink to break their fast and others set about breaking camp, Eilidh distracted herself by treating her friend Cole, the guard the wolf attacked. She cleaned the wound as best she could and closed it. "I'll need to check it every day for at least a sennight to ensure it doesna fester," she told him quietly. "I shouldha seen to it last night and not left ye with such a wound in the hours since the attack."

"I dinna blame ye for that," he answered equally softly. "Ye were—"

"It doesna matter," she insisted. "I shouldha seen to it last night. I dinna want to open it again to clean it out. Ye shouldna have to endure that because I didna help ye when ye needed me."

"I trust ye, Eilidh. Ye havena failed me yet."

He said it kindly, which only made her feel more guilty. "I hope I havena done so now," she told him. She worried, and she'd blame herself for every problem his wound might yet cause.

From his position on the wagon, bound and gagged, the prisoner could see much of what went on in the camp. She was careful to keep her back to him, not only to avoid seeing him but to keep him from observing what she did for Cole. She resented having to hide what she was doing from the stranger in their midst. "I'm going to wrap this again, though it doesna need it. But as long as we've a stranger with us—"

"Aye, of course."

She made quick work of it. When Cole again tried to thank her, she silenced him with a glance toward their captive. He nodded, understanding her.

She was grateful she didn't have to silence him with her other special ability, and wondered why it hadn't occur to her to use it when the man attacked her. She must have been in shock, too surprised or too breathless to touch his skin, summon the power her mother gave her, and force him to unhand her before he started ripping her clothes, searching for jewels and coin. Too bad for him, she'd had neither, and that Bhaltair, his men, and Uncle Jamie were close by. And that they were such accomplished scouts and warriors. The man had stood no chance to escape them.

She'd fallen asleep in Bhaltair's arms, so she really didn't know how long it had taken them to find the man, but he'd been bound and under guard by the time Bhaltair woke her and asked her to identify him. Even with the beard covering part of his face, she'd had no doubt. His smell, for one, evident from several feet away, betrayed him, as did the pitch of his angry growls that matched the tenor of the threats he'd murmured to her as he pawed her and tore her clothes. And if that were not enough, the words he repeated that he'd spoken just before he ran from her left no doubt. She realized she'd never really seen his face, only his shoulder, his beard, a hand and forearm, bits and pieces of her attacker but not the whole man. Seeing him under guard, smaller than the men escorting her, she realized he wasn't as tall as she, and he appeared rough, dirty, and desperate. Thin enough that he hadn't had any good meals recently. Was he a hunted criminal or simply a lost man from a broken clan?

She could almost pity him, but the moment her gaze dropped to his bound hands, her fear and anger returned anew. He didn't deserve her pity. No matter how desperate he might be, he had no excuse for attacking a lass. Her father would throw him in one of the lower caves in the Aerie's tor, lock the gate and throw away the key.

So why must her attacker go with them to Fletcher? Because they were so much closer to it than to the Aerie? Bhaltair could spare two guards to escort the man to the Aerie.

But Bhaltair was spoiling for a fight. When she glanced around at their captive, she'd also noticed him watching her with Cole. He knew she had to treat Cole's wound, so he couldn't object to seeing her close by him.

Perhaps seeing her brought what happened last night back to the forefront of Bhaltair's thoughts. He had threatened to do serious damage to the man for harming her, and that made her stomach roil. Had she succeeded in convincing him to wait? To discover more about the man before he exacted some brutal revenge? She worried that Bhaltair would do more damage to himself—to his own soul—than to her attacker by punishing him as he threatened to do.

Today's ride would be nothing like yesterday's. She considered speaking to him again, but didn't want to risk making him even more angry than he now appeared to be.

What a tangle her attacker had caused. Not just for himself, but for her, for Bhaltair, for all of them. And what would Jamie have his wife, the Fletcher Laird, do when they reached her?

4

They arrived at Fletcher just as the sun set behind the nearby hills. This time of year, the days were quickly getting shorter, the nights colder. Eilidh was glad of a safe, warm haven for the night. And a stout cell to hold their prisoner while Uncle Jamie, the Fletcher, and Bhaltair discussed his fate. Eilidh wasn't certain she wanted to be part of that discussion, though by rights, she should be. She should consider what she would recommend if she did take part, but hoped she didn't have to.

A striking brown-haired and brown-eyed woman met them at the door to the keep. Tall and with an air of assurance, Eilidh knew she must be the laird, Caitrin Fletcher, even before she spoke.

"Jamie, love, where is Aileana? Who have ye brought to help us?"

Jamie embraced his wife, then introduced Eilidh and Bhaltair. The other guards were taking care of the horses and overseeing the prisoner. The Fletcher messenger who'd fetched them walked past on his way into the keep, and accepted a nod from his laird.

"I shouldha kenned ye," Caitrin said when she learned Eilidh's name. "Ye take after yer mother, ye do. 'Twill be Fletcher's honor to have ye with us. And Bhaltair, welcome. Come inside. Let's get ye settled. Supper will be in an hour so ye will have time to wash the journey from ye, if ye wish."

"I do," Eilidh said, flashing back to the smell of her attacker and the feel of his hands and beard on her skin.

"Take care of the lass first," Bhaltair said. "I will speak to yer arms master and make arrangements for our prisoner."

"Prisoner!" Caitrin glanced, wide-eyed, at her husband, then turned back to Bhaltair. "Explain."

Eilidh recognized the tone of command, very much like her father's. Caitrin was laird here, and used to being obeyed.

Bhaltair gave her a succinct but complete version of events.

"Very well." She signaled to an older man. "Steward, if ye please, show Bhaltair and his men where to secure their prisoner. We'll discuss his fate after supper."

To Eilidh's dismay, Bhaltair left them without another word or glance at her. He followed the steward back across the bailey. After his recitation of the events, though he didn't mention his gentle care of her, she thought she might at least receive a nod of acknowledgement as he took his leave. She supposed she would see him at the meal, but perhaps not. He might prefer to remain with his men.

"Now, Eilidh, since I just sent the steward away, let me show ye to a chamber." She took Eilidh's arm familiarly, having missed, Eilidh supposed, Uncle Jamie's reaction to her touching a Lathan healer. Or not. Suddenly she released Eilidh's arm and apologized. "I was so surprised not to see yer mother, I forgot not to touch ye without yer leave. Of course, yer talent is why ye are here in her stead. I willna do so again."

Her tone was apologetic and kind. Eilidh could not take offense. "Ye did nay harm. I hope I can help as well as she would."

"I hope so, too. I ken from Jamie's tales that 'tis best if ye are rested and fed before ye take on the burden that brought ye here."

"How is the bairn? How urgently does she need—"

"Nay so urgent that I canna first show ye the hospitality ye are owed. Ye have had a shock."

Eilidh weighed her words. Was she being kind or had the child's condition not worsened in the last few days? Eilidh desperately wanted to wash the remnants of her attack from her body, but she was here because the bairn needed her ability. "I admit I would love a chance to bathe, but I dinna wish to delay—"

Jamie cleared his throat. "Laird, perhaps if ye introduce Eilidh to the bairn, she will be able to accept yer hospitality with a clear conscience. Let her assess for herself—"

Caitrin nodded. "Of course." She smiled at her husband, then turned to Eilidh. "Ever the diplomat, my Jamie. Would that suit ye?"

"Yes, very much. Please take me to her."

A woman rose and at Caitrin's gesture, left the chamber when Eilidh entered. A wee lass lay quietly in a crib more commonly used for bairns in swaddling. Eilidh's stomach sank. "How old is she?"

Caitrin had followed Eilidh into the chamber and stood near the door, a pensive expression drawing her brows together. "Nearly two. She was born on the winter solstice."

"She's too small for a lass that age. What has the healer recommended? What have ye tried so far?" Eilidh asked her questions as she moved around the crib, studying the bairn, who met her gaze with eyes that seemed to carry the knowledge of a lifetime. An old soul, was this lass. Without waiting for Caitrin to answer her earlier questions, she asked, "What is her name?"

"She's called Orla."

"Golden princess. The name fits." She had a crown of curly golden hair. Eilidh looked up from the lass.

"Her mother thought so." Caitrin's lips quirked into a brief smile, then fell. As if a cloud had passed over her face, her gaze turned sad and shadowed. "Her father, Aulay, had light hair. He died the following April, before his daughter was old enough to be given her final name."

"I'm sorry." Eilidh gave up her study of the wee lass and turned to fully face Caitrin. "Yer daughter must be sick with worry."

Caitrin sighed. "Kellina is also well-named. Strong-willed. She took Aulay's death hard." Caitrin paused, as if considering how much more to say, her hands clenched together in front of her. "She was sad for so long, I feared for her, especially when Orla's illness persisted and worsened. But she has fought ever since for her daughter."

"Where is she?" Eilidh thought it odd that the bairn's mother was not with her.

"Likely resting. She spends much of her time here, but I asked the healer—the woman who was just here—to keep her away until ye had a chance to meet Orla. I'm sorry, I should have introduced ye."

Eilidh nodded. "There's time for that later. And thank ye for the privacy. That was wise. Ye ken what I do to heal?"

"I believe so. Jamie has told me the story of yer mother's efforts to save him. Kellina kens, too. She was the one who suggested asking her father to return with the Lathan healer. She kens the tales of how yer mother cared for him. I'm glad for her to have children who share her talent, and I'm grateful to be able to call on her—and ye—and receive help so quickly."

Eilidh recognized the tone of a formal statement of appreciation. "Thank ye again, Laird Fletcher. I will convey yer words to my mother when I return home. For now, ye may stay if ye would like, but I'll ask ye to take a seat and not disturb me. Ye will ken when I am finished. I will address ye."

"Thank ye, Eilidh. I appreciate the trust ye place in me." She moved to a chair near the hearth but out of Eilidh's direct line of sight and sat down.

Eilidh nodded and turned to Orla. The lass's gaze was fixed on her. Even without touching her, Eilidh sensed her curiosity and deep regard. "Ye will be a wise woman when ye grow up, lass. Now, let me make certain ye get the chance."

Eilidh clasped her hands in front of her chest, closed her eyes, and took a deep, calming breath. Once she felt the stillness fill her, she opened her eyes and placed her hands just above Orla's too-small frame. Her pulse quickened and her breathing ceased for a moment, then resumed when Eilidh remained still. Yet her gaze never betrayed the anxiety Eilidh felt in her.

Eilidh touched her, gifting her with tranquility. Orla's eyes drifted closed. Eilidh reached deeper, sensing the blood flowing through her veins, the breath entering and leaving her lungs, the gentle pulsing of her belly. There!

Something had damaged the lass's viscera, and not just once, but again and again over time. No wonder she was so small. She could absorb only a small portion of anything she ate. Eilidh completed her survey, tracing her fingertips over the child's body and feeling the tingles in corresponding areas of her own. Orla's bones were weak, her blood thin, there were so many small things wrong with her, Eilidh wasn't sure where to start to treat her. No one thing pointed to the cause, but the mass of problems gave Eilidh an idea. She lifted her hands, opened her eyes and turned to Caitrin, not surprised to find her watching with hands clenched in her lap.

"What does she eat?"

"Do ye fear poison?"

"Nay. But ye must tell me what she eats."

"Mother's milk for her first year, both her mother's and a wet nurse. She had a good appetite and seemed to grow well."

"And after that?"

"Everything the clan eats, softened or mashed or stewed, of course."

Eilidh nodded. "I have an idea, but first I need to ask her nurse or her mother a few questions."

"Ye think 'tis the food? How can the food meant to nourish her have done this?"

"That is what I must discover, Laird. And I will."

In the meantime, she would be wise to accept the laird's offer of hospitality, and treat the bairn when she was better prepared. She told Caitrin so and followed her to a comfortable nearby chamber. A cheerful fire burned in the hearth and a tub sat steaming near it. "I will send a lass to help ye," Caitrin offered.

"Thank ye, but I can manage well enough on my own. I will enjoy a few minutes of solitude."

Caitrin smiled and went to the door. "After two days with all those men, I imagine so. Very well, but someone will be nearby in the hall. Call out if ye have need of anything." With that, she left Eilidh alone.

Eilidh was certain Caitrin did not realize how her words could be taken, given the attack on her. *Those men*. She forced the reminder aside and regarded the tub. A dish of soap and stack of towels sat on a table beside it. She had all she needed and quickly stripped out of her clothes. The water she sank into was blissfully hot. The stiffness of the last two days melted out of her muscles. She leaned her head back against the rim of the tub, cushioned with the folded edge of the sheet that lined it, closed her eyes and let her mind drift.

BHALTAIR OPENED the chamber door the steward showed him to and glanced over his shoulder to offer his thanks. But by then, the man had moved off toward the stairs, so Bhaltair let him go and stepped inside. Steamy warmth enveloped him, coming from the hearth fire and the tub in front of it.

It took him only a moment to realize the tub was occupied.

Eilidh.

What was she doing in his chamber?

He glanced behind him to ensure the hallway was empty, then pushed the door nearly closed. He did not want anyone walking past to be able to peer into the room, but he dared not close it completely. Instead, he stood quietly, taking in the view and fighting to control his reaction. His body tightened mercilessly.

Eilidh's head rested on the rim of the tub. Water covered her breasts, but her arms were draped along the top of the tub, leaving her upper body visible in the still steaming water. The heavy breasts he'd sought to cover when she'd been in shock from the attack were now displayed for him to see, and to recall the feel of them under his hands as he tugged her torn chemise over them.

He didn't move. Or breathe. He could only stare. And want.

She must have fallen asleep or she would have reacted to the door opening. He moved silently when he needed to, but he hadn't had a reason to as he entered the room, thinking it his. Obviously, there had been a mistake.

Should he try to leave without waking her? If she heard and woke up, would she know he'd been there or assume a serving lass had checked on her? He didn't want to reinforce the trauma of her attack, frightening her. A male presence in the place where she thought herself alone and safe would surely upset her.

Torn, he stayed still as a Greek statue by the door, hardly daring to breathe.

She moved. Rousing, if only a little, her eyes still closed, she pulled a cloth from the side of the tub, dipped it in the water and ran it over her shoulders and breasts.

Bhaltair's body reacted as it hadn't in years. Every part of him tightened, hardened, and vibrated with need. For Eilidh. The one lass he could not have.

Her hand trailed lower, pulling the cloth down her belly.

He couldn't take much more. His body betrayed how he wanted her. If she saw him, she would know just how much.

But her movements slowed, and her head rolled to one side. She'd fallen asleep again. Should he make some noise and wake her?

He should leave. And never tell her he'd entered her chamber by mistake while she dozed in her bath. If she knew, she'd feel humiliated, and she would avoid him all the more.

And that, he didn't want.

The knowledge washed over and through him like an onrushing tide. He wanted her to realize he was just a man, but not like any other. He was a man who cared about her. Who wanted her. Who would take care of her and love her for all of their lives. But she'd never give him the chance if she knew he stood staring at her right now.

He turned away and grasped the door handle, ready to step out and leave her in peace and privacy. But he couldn't resist one last glance. As he turned his head, she started to slip into the water.

She'd drown!

He had no choice. He called her name and lunged for her. She came awake at the same moment as her mouth went below the waterline. She heaved herself forward and up, shrieking and splashing water everywhere, eyes wide and panicked. She batted at his hands as he reached to pull her up.

"What are ye doing in here?" She grabbed for the sheet lining the tub and pulled it over her body as she slid down, hiding herself from his sight.

"Eilidh, I'm sorry. The steward led me to yer chamber. A mistake. I was about to leave when ye started to slip and I feared ye would drown."

"Drown? Drown! In a tub? Didna ye think the water in my face might wake me?"

"I... there was nay time to think. I had to save ye."

She let her head fall back onto the rim of the tub. "I thought ye were... him. That I was still on the ground by the burn. Or he'd come back to have another go at me." She jerked the sheet from the other side of the tub and draped it over the first one covering her, dismay and aggravation in every tense movement of her arms and shoulders.

Bhaltair sank to his knees beside the tub, careless of the water soaking his trews. Damn it. He'd done the very things he'd never wanted to do. He'd embarrassed her and he'd reminded her of the trauma she'd suffered. "God's bones, lass. I'm more sorry than ye can ken."

"I need ye to leave."

"Eilidh—"

"Now." She huffed out a breath. "I... please go."

He heaved a sigh of his own and forced himself to his feet. She'd never forgive him. And he'd never forgive himself. He'd always regret making this trip. If he hadn't come with her, he would not have just ruined every chance he might ever have had with her.

AFTER BHALTAIR LEFT, Eilidh stayed in the tub, replaying in her mind what had just happened. She'd never seen him look as dejected, as regretful, as he did trudging to her door. Perhaps he'd been sincere in his apology. Aye, he had been. She knew it, and had no reason to doubt him. But how long had he stood at her door staring at her before she started to slip beneath the water? How much had he seen? She could imagine how she'd looked.

She unwrapped the sheets covering her and looked down at herself. There was nothing wrong with her shape or size. Twice in two days, he'd seen her breasts. There couldn't be any doubt left in his mind that she was a woman grown. But he'd paid them no attention, focused, it seemed, more on his remorse for having reminded her of her attack. Rather than showing a man's interest in her, Bhaltair insisted on being her savior, protecting her.

She was tired of it. Tired of all the years they'd known each other with no hint of interest from him. If the last two days hadn't sparked some lasting desire for her within him, she might as well give up. Whether he meant to or not, he'd made it plain he didn't want her. She was only a job to him. A responsibility laid upon him by her father. A lass he needed to save—even from herself. And worse, a victim.

What a shame. She'd spent years of her life infatuated with him. Longing for the day when she would grow up enough for him to notice her. Staying clear of him when the violence of his chosen profession became too much for her to accept or called too strongly to her compulsion to heal, frightening her. When he came home bruised and bloody, needing a healer's care, Eilidh had made herself scarce. Her mother had seen to him every time. Perhaps if she had cared for him herself, she might know more about why she remained invisible to him. Unwanted.

Until after the attack, when he'd held her so gently. Almost lovingly. He had reacted when she nuzzled him. She'd known in an instant when his body betrayed him. But he was just a man, and she, still half asleep, had teased him as a lover might. Any man would have reacted as he did. It had nothing to do with her. With who she was. Or what she hoped she might become to him.

With an oath, she stood and grabbed a drying sheet from the table beside the tub. She'd managed to splash the surface, but the inner folds were dry. She stepped out of the tub, careful not to slip on any of the water she'd spilled, where Bhaltair had knelt delivering his apology. Once again, she'd managed to make him appalled, but at himself this time.

She toweled off and dressed, cursing herself the entire time for her naïveté. He was a man, with a man's appetites. And to him, she was just a lass, youngest daughter of his laird. Someone to protect. Firmly and forever off limits. Why had she never seen that before?

She was here to do a job, too. She'd best focus on preparing herself for the healing she came here to do, and forget about caring in any way for Bhaltair Lathan.

5

E ilidh had just finished drying and braiding her hair when someone knocked on the door.

"Eilidh? 'Tis Jamie. Are ye ready to go downstairs to eat?"

"I am," she called, grateful that Uncle Jamie had the courtesy to knock. And glad that she would not have to try his patience by forcing him to wait in the hallway for her. She'd had enough of men bursting into her chamber to find her undressed. Even if that man was Bhaltair Lathan. She went to the door and opened it. Uncle Jamie stood on the other side, an elbow extended, beckoning her out into the hallway. She pulled the door closed behind her.

"Ye must be hungry," he told her as she took his arm.

"I am." She realized those were the only two words she'd said to him since he showed up at her door. She really needed to be more open with him. He was her father's cousin, which made him hers as well. She'd called him Uncle Jamie since she was a small child, in part because one of her brothers carried the same name, confusing her. Uncle Jamie himself had suggested the label. "Ye must be, as well."

"Aye," he said as they started down the stairs. He inhaled deeply as the scents of the coming meal reached them. "I'm looking forward to supper. The Fletcher Cook is an artist. Not that the Lathan cook isna. Lathan was my home for most of my life, but Fletcher is home now, so 'tis most wise to appreciate what I have, aye?"

Eilidh savored the appetizing scents, too. Her stomach grumbled to be filled. To distract herself, she changed the subject. "Except for visits, ye have been away from Lathan most of my life. Was it strange to return and spend as much time as ye did during the Gathering?" They reached the bottom of the steps to the great hall while Jamie contemplated his answer.

"Strange? Nay. It will always be my home. Toran and Aileana —and ye and yer brothers and sister—will always be my family. I'm lucky, though, to have been given the chance to make a family with the lass I fell in love with when I was but a lad. And here she is," he added as they reached the head table. Caitrin had yet to take her seat, but much of the clan was already in place. "Caitrin, love, Eilidh is fainting with hunger. Shall we sup?"

"Uncle Jamie! What a thing to say," Eilidh objected, then saw the grin he shared with his wife, so she grinned, too.

"Is she? Or are ye, my love?" Caitrin patted the back of the chair beside hers. "Eilidh, come sit next to me. I want to hear all about yer family. 'Tis been forever since I was last able to visit. Ye and yer siblings were too young to remember me."

Jamie handed Eilidh to her chair, moved to his wife's other side and seated her. As soon as he settled beside her, servants began passing among the tables setting out trenchers of meats, fish, vegetables and bread.

Eilidh's mouth watered at the enticing scents wafting through the hall. Just when she thought she'd expire from hunger, a smiling lass placed a trencher in front of her and others set platters of bread, cheeses, and vegetables nearby to choose from.

"Help yerself," Caitrin said and nodded toward the platters.

"We dinna stand on ceremony here. Ye saw that the clan was served first, not this table. We take care of our own, then ourselves."

Eilidh took her at her word and served herself, noting as she did that Caitrin and Jamie did the same from platters placed near them.

More people filtered in to the great hall and found seats at the lower tables, but one headed straight for the high table. Eilidh surmised that this must be Orla's mother, Kellina. She had the same shade of brown hair as her mother.

Kellina didn't wait for introductions, but stopped below where Eilidh sat at the table and demanded, "How is my daughter? Can ye make her well?"

"Kellina," her mother chided, "Have ye forgotten yer manners? This is Eilidh Lathan, the healer come to help Orla. Eilidh, my daughter, Kellina."

Kellina had the grace to look embarrassed. "I'm sorry. I—"

"*Dinna fash*," Eilidh said, stopping her with a wave of one hand. "I understand yer concern. Ye needna apologize."

"Thank ye," Kellina said and took a breath. "What can I do to help ye help my daughter?"

"Come have something to eat," Caitrin demanded. "Let Eilidh eat. Then she can answer yer questions."

Kellina frowned at her mother, but nodded. "I do have questions."

"I hope I will be able to answer them," Eilidh told her. Kellina moved away and took the empty chair by her father, so Eilidh turned her attention back to her meal. She didn't think she'd have many answers, Not yet. She'd barely arrived, barely met Orla. Kellina didn't strike her as someone with a lot of patience, but then again, she'd been forced to wait and watch for months as her bairn weakened. Eilidh knew in the same circumstance, her patience would be exhausted, too.

A ripple passed through the hall as the Lathan guards

entered, amusing Eilidh. They were impressive to look at, all tall and well built. Handsome, too. She noticed several of the women and girls elbowing each other and gesturing toward the newcomers. The men ignored the attention. Cole caught her eye and smiled. Bhaltair's gaze avoided her as it swept the chamber. He nodded toward an empty table.

A glance aside showed her that Caitrin was also amused by the reaction the men elicited. Past her, Jamie ignored the commotion. But Kellina seemed entranced. She stared, a cup raised halfway to her mouth, her gaze riveted to the Lathans. At first, Eilidh assumed she was taking in all of them, but as they separated to take seats at the table Bhaltair indicated, it became clear that Kellina was watching him.

A fountain of molten jealousy erupted from Eilidh's gut and climbed to the back of her throat. She looked away, but that turned her gaze to the man who fascinated Kellina.

Bhaltair's gaze met Eilidh's and heat of a very different kind climbed to her chest and spread through her body, warming every part. He didn't smile. He simply gave her a quick nod to acknowledge her, or acknowledge that she'd caught him looking at her. He took a seat and accepted a trencher from a giggling serving lass. Other lasses brought drink to the table and food to the other men. They seemed to take an inordinate amount of time leaving the table, or perhaps Eilidh's perception had slowed as she, like many of the women in the hall, focused on Bhaltair.

He was certainly easy to look at. The broadest shoulders of any man in the room, hair mixing shades of blond from light gold where the sun touched it to aged honey underneath, and blue eyes that flashed in the sun. Or in the heat of anger. She'd never wanted them to flash at her, but she understood why any woman seeing him for the first time would be entranced. His jaw was square and as firmly muscled as the rest of him, prone to flexing when he became annoyed. Despite all the battles he'd fought, his nose remained straight as a blade, unbroken. And his lips—she shouldn't be thinking about his lips—but like any lass, she couldn't help herself. They looked firm and she wondered if they would be hard or soft when they touched hers.

A stray thought crossed her mind as the serving lass left the men's table, and she fought not to laugh out loud. That serving lass had best be prepared to bring him another trencher, and perhaps one after that. He was a big man, and a ferocious fighter. He trained hard, and he ate like he did, too.

That thought broke the spell and she looked away in time to overhear Jamie mention her name. She glanced aside to see if he'd addressed her, but his attention was on Caitrin.

"That's possible," Caitrin said.

What was possible? She resumed eating and did her best to listen to the laird and her husband's conversation, certain they thought the general hum of voices in the hall kept them from being overheard.

"Any man who weds with her will become a Lathan, ye ken that, aye? We'd lose him from Fletcher," Uncle Jamie said.

"Unless we convince her to remain with us," Caitrin said.

Eilidh's stomach suddenly seemed overly full. They were discussing making a match for her with one of their men. Convincing her to remain here. She'd just arrived! Did they expect to perform a wedding before she left? Had her parents asked them to consider a likely match for her? And did they know the Fletcher would try to convince her to remain, and not return to her responsibilities at Lathan? Now the heat of anger rose from her chest. Her upper chest, neck, and face must be reddening from it.

No matter what, she would not remain here once she'd finished what she came to do. Nor did she want a Fletcher husband. The man she desired was sitting across the hall from her right now.

Nay, she reminded herself, her appetite fleeing. He was the man she'd thought she wanted. The man who showed no interest in her as a woman, save for a brief moment when she surprised him. That hit her heart, reminding her he'd acted as though he'd never had any interest in her.

Perhaps there was a man for her here. A Fletcher who could come back to the Aerie with her. A man who would grow to love her and treat her as a husband ought. Yet, Bhaltair sitting quietly at table, ignoring the serving wenches, still drew her gaze.

ONCE HE ENTERED the Fletcher great hall, Bhaltair couldn't miss seeing Eilidh at the high table with the Fletchers. He ignored the ripple of conversation that erupted as he and his men found an empty table and took their seats. He acknowledged Eilidh with a nod since she was looking at him. So were most of the rest of the lasses in the hall. Eilidh must be amused by the attention her guards received. Next to her, the Fletcher laird smiled and shook her head, turned back to Jamie, and listened to whatever he said to her.

Bhaltair paid only enough attention to the lass on Jamie's other side to conclude that she was the Fletchers' daughter. That decided, he sat down and dug in to his meal. It was much better than travel rations. Very good, actually, he was certain, judging by the appreciative grunts and groans of the men around him.

He listened with half an ear to the comments made by the other Lathan guards, but his mind wasn't on them or the food. It was on a hunger of a very different kind. One that only worsened as he watched Eilidh at the high table. She sat with the laird and her "uncle" in full view of everyone in the hall. He wondered how she managed it. She was normally quiet, even shy, among her own clan, the people who knew her best. Being on display like that, among strangers, must be difficult for her.

His men ate with relish and flirted with the serving lasses. Other women in the hall seemed to spend more time staring at the Lathans than eating. A few came by the table on their way out of the hall and made offers to his men that Bhaltair tried to ignore. Many of them were directed at him. Quietly, his men complained that he was taking the attention of the lasses from them, and even if he didn't want to enjoy an evening's sport, why shouldn't they? He ignored them, too. Finally, only Niall Lathan was left and crossed his arms. "What has yer cods in a twist?"

Bhaltair gave him a glance from the corner of his eye. "What do ye mean? There's naught amiss with me."

"Ye are quieter and grumpier than usual. And if Eilidh was a man, I'd say ye were of a mind to kill her where she sits, ye frown so fiercely at her. Ye'd best stop, if ye dinna want the Fletcher laird to notice and throw ye out of her keep."

He thought he had fought down his impulse to rescue her and take her away from the attention she was being subjected to, but apparently his expression gave that the lie. She didn't need to be rescued. She was a woman grown. He'd seen the proof of that after her attack yesterday, and again after stumbling into her chamber while she bathed a little more than an hour ago. She was a laird's daughter. She could take care of herself. And if she needed it, with Jamie Lathan, nay, Fletcher, she had family to protect and care for her.

Bhaltair clenched a fist under the table. His job was to get her here and get her home again safely. That was all. While they were here, he and his men were guests of the Fletcher laird. He had no business making a scene with Eilidh, no matter how much his gut screamed at him to take her away from a situation that he knew made her uncomfortable. To get her alone. To... damn it, what he wanted to do with her would get him and the rest of his men tossed out. A Fletcher guard contingent would have to take her home. He couldn't imagine explaining that scenario to her father —or what Toran would do about it when they showed up at the Aerie without his daughter.

He drained his cup of ale and signaled for another. He would

eat, then he would bed down with his men—those who weren't
bedded down with a wench somewhere.

Eilidh would call for him if she needed him. If not, he'd see
her when she was ready to return to the Aerie, and not before.

To Eilidh, Bhaltair seemed to fill the vast space in the great hall,
and make everyone and everything else disappear. She kept
picking at her food, watching him from the corner of her eye,
then through her lowered lashes as she kept her face angled
toward her supper. He ate and drank quickly, without joining the
conversations around him. His gaze kept lifting to her, frowning
and fierce. Every time it did, she would drop hers, hoping that he
did not notice her watching him. Yet did it matter? He was
watching her. Because of what he'd seen the last two days? Had
he, at long last, developed a man's interest in her as a woman?
Did that realization anger him? What could make him frown at
her so? Or was he simply keeping an eye on his charge, ensuring
her safety?

The uncertainty would drive her mad before she ever got
away from here.

At least he hadn't left his table with a lass as others of the
Lathan guards had done. Before the night was over, the Fletchers
might need to make matches with several of her guards and their
lasses, not just match her with one of their men. She glanced
around the hall, but couldn't begin to guess which of the Fletcher
men they might consider for her. She knew none of them. They
all looked strange. And none of them were Bhaltair.

She gave up her useless speculations and finished her meal,
then addressed Caitrin. "I need a few minutes to prepare before I
care for Orla."

Caitrin nodded. "I will escort ye myself."

"I can find my chamber. Please, finish yer supper, and fetch me when ye are ready."

"Very well. I will come for ye. Take yer time. I willna hurry."

"Are ye certain ye can find yer chamber?" That from Uncle Jamie on Caitrin's other side.

"Aye, of course. I paid attention when ye escorted me here."

Jamie grinned. "Then go on with ye. If ye get lost—"

"I willna," she assured him and rose. To Caitrin, she added, "Thank ye, Laird Fletcher, for yer hospitality."

"Dinna thank me yet. Ye may still have cause to regret coming."

Eilidh glanced beyond Caitrin to her daughter, Orla's mother, who watched her with hope in her eyes. "Nay, I willna."

6

Eilidh found her chamber with no trouble, and took only a few minutes to take care of her own needs. She settled by the fire to sit quietly and clear her mind. A healer never knew what they would encounter when treating a new patient. Caring for a small child was even more fraught. They were unable to say what bothered them, and the families were understandably desperate for a good outcome, something that no healer could promise.

The talent Lathan healers wielded helped overcome a wean's inability to communicate. Eilidh's talent reached into an injured body or one plagued with an illness and she sensed the effects on her patient. Injuries were bad enough, but illnesses were much harder to understand and treat. She would need all her calm, all her focus, and all her strength this evening.

She dared not give up on finding the cause or Orla's sickness and healing the wean. Not only were a child's life and health at stake, Eilidh was her mother's representative at Fletcher. Though she was on her own for the first time, she could not fail, or she would always be seen as someone unable to accomplish anything without her mother's help.

Sometime later, a soft knock roused her. "Eilidh, 'tis Caitrin. Are ye ready?"

Eilidh stood and shook herself back to alertness. "I am. Just a moment." She took up the small bag that contained potions brought from Lathan that she might need in addition to her own skills, and opened the door.

Caitrin stood in the hall with an expectant look on her face. Eilidh nodded and gestured for her to lead the way. "Tell me more about the bairn and the illness."

Caitrin described what they had observed and what the Fletcher healer had done. "She will want to be included," Caitrin told her. "I hope ye dinna mind."

"I'm sorry, but I do. I need silence and stillness to... do what I do. This will be more involved and longer lasting than what ye observed before supper. The presence of another person, an unaware, untrained person, can disrupt my ability."

"So, I may not be there, either?"

"Not at first. Once I make a deeper assessment to determine what Orla needs, then perhaps. I make no promises."

Caitrin was silent as they turned into the crossing hallway. "I dinna claim to understand, but Jamie is confident in ye, so I am, as well."

Eilidh's heart sank. If she could not help, they would be left with no alternatives and no hope. The bairn would die. "Thank ye. I will do everything in my power..." Her fist clenched and she hid it in her skirts. She would! Not saving Orla would also ruin her whole future before she began to be independent. But the effect on her was nothing to what losing Orla would do to Kellina and the rest of her family. She would not let that happen.

They reached the doorway Eilidh had visited earlier, and Caitrin stopped. "She is in here. I will go in and ask the healer to wait in her herbal, if that suits ye?"

"Of course. Thank ye."

Caitrin entered the chamber. A few moments later, after some hushed conversation, the older woman exited, gave Eilidh an assessing glance that Eilidh returned with a nod, then the woman took herself off down the hall. Eilidh entered the chamber.

"Orla hasna had a nurse since she began to fall ill," Caitrin said. "Her mother or the healer or I spend the most time with her. And Jamie."

"I ken this has been hard on all of ye." Eilidh put as much sympathy in her tone as she could muster with her heart hurting for them. Watching a bairn fail to thrive was slow torture.

"Worse for the wee lass," Caitrin said and stood. "I'll be outside when ye are ready."

Once Caitrin left, Eilidh turned to wee Orla and touched her. Little had changed since she'd seen her before supper. The lass was too quiet, too still, as well as being too small for her age. "Ye are tired of feeling this way, I ken it," Eilidh crooned to her. "But ye will get better. I promise ye. I will see to it."

She let her healing sense seek out all the places that were *wrong* somehow. By the time Eilidh finished, she had a long list. "Ye poor wee bairn," she said. She wasn't certain where to start making Orla well. Or if she should heal the damage before she knew what had caused it. With a sigh, she stepped back from the crib and went to the door.

True to her word, Caitrin waited outside. Her face lit when Eilidh stepped into view, then fell again at Eilidh's lack of expression.

"Did ye learn anything new?"

"Aye, I did. And I have many questions that I need answered before I do much more."

"Would ye speak with my daughter now?"

"Of course. I'll stay with Orla until ye find her."

Caitrin chuckled at that. "Like as not, she's just down the hallway. I'll be there with her in a moment."

In a very few minutes, she opened the door to admit Caitrin

and Orla's mother. Kellina appeared calmer than when she approached Eilidh at the high table. Still, Eilidh had been impressed by the question she had asked when they first met in the great hall at supper. She had not demanded to know what Eilidh could do. She had asked what she could do to help Eilidh make her daughter well. She would tolerate much from Orla's mother because of that one simple question.

Caitrin gestured them both to seats. "I'll send for refreshments. If I understood ye, Eilidh, this could take a while."

Eilidh nodded her thanks and began asking Kellina for the information she needed. She was close to Eilidh's age, but perhaps closer in years to her older sister Lianna.

Caitrin returned after a few minutes and related that she had summoned the healer. Once she arrived, Caitrin introduced them and apologized for her earlier lapse.

"I must apologize, too," Eilidh added, "for failing to greet ye, a fellow healer, as I should have. Please forgive me."

"I understand," the healer told her, accepting her and Caitrin's words. She went on to add to what Kellina told Eilidh.

A few minutes later, a serving lass brought cider, honey cake and cheese, and they resumed the questions. Through it all, Orla slept peacefully. Eilidh kept one eye on her to see how well she responded to the calming she'd laid on the lass.

Caitrin called a halt. "'Tis very late, and Eilidh had a difficult journey to reach us," she said when Kellina protested. "Ye must be exhausted," she added, looking at Eilidh.

Eilidh stifled a yawn and nodded. "I will think on what I've learned from all of ye," she said by way of agreement, stood and stretched.

"I'll escort ye to yer chamber," the healer offered.

Eilidh shook her head. "Thank ye, but I ken where it is. Ye all must rest, too."

"We take turns," Kellina said. "Staying with Orla. I feared she would—" She choked to a halt, swallowed, then added, "I didna want her to be alone if…"

Eilidh immediately understood what she failed to say. "Yer daughter is ill, but not in immediate danger. Ye may go to yer rest," Eilidh told her. "Or sleep here, but *dinna fash*."

Caitrin stood. "Come. Yer chamber is on the way to mine. I will walk with ye."

Eilidh had spent about as much time with other people as she could tolerate, but in a few minutes, she would be alone in her chamber, so she nodded. One did not deny the laird, she knew. And Caitrin was doing her best to be hospitable under difficult circumstances.

"I'd like that," Eilidh told her. She should ask Caitrin if she'd made a decision about the man who attacked her.

They left together, leaving Kellina and the healer with Orla.

Caitrin's expression changed to one of concern once they were out of the chamber. "How bad is it? Truly. Ye must tell me, so I can prepare my daughter. She lost her husband. Losing Orla will—"

"She willna lose her. Not if I can help her, and I think I can. I will."

"But ye dinna ken—"

"I will learn more tomorrow." They reached her chamber door. Eilidh paused outside it. "Ye mustna fash."

Caitrin gave her a grateful smile and went on her way before Eilidh managed to bring up the question she'd meant to ask. Perhaps Caitrin had done her a favor by avoiding the conversation about the attack. It would wait until tomorrow. Tonight was for Orla.

Eilidh opened the door to a cheerful fire in the hearth. The tub had been removed. Flooded with memories of Bhaltair standing over her as she fought the bath sheets to cover herself, she groaned. She shouldn't be thinking about him right now. She needed to think about Orla. And to recall everything her mother had ever taught her about bairns who didn't thrive. She grabbed a plaid to help keep her warm, turned her back on the bed and settled in front of the fire. After another deep breath, she closed her eyes and began sifting through memories.

BHALTAIR REMAINED in the great hall. He'd sprawled in a dark corner, sipping an ale, watching the Fletcher keep settle down for the night. The servants had finished clearing away and cleaning up after supper. A few Fletcher men sat near the hearth sharing a last drink and talking quietly. They'd invited him to join them, but he had politely refused. He didn't want company.

His men—some of them, anyway—were bedded down in the barracks near the smithy. He should join them, but he had no interest in sleep. Not yet. Eilidh was upstairs with the Fletcher laird and the ill bairn. They needed her.

He'd discovered he needed her, too. She'd feared him most of her life. She was six years younger than him, so he had no illusions about intimidating her. He'd always been taller than even the tall Lathan siblings, but he'd quickly grown big, as training put slabs of muscle on his frame. Before long, he had exceeded other Lathan warriors in size. He knew he was imposing. Intimidating. His sheer size sometimes frightened children. He'd even seen a flash of fear in adults who encountered him unexpectedly in the Aerie. Adults who'd known him most of his life, and who had no reason to fear him. He'd cultivated an impassive demeanor to counter his appearance, but it didn't always accomplish what he wanted it to.

Her brothers trusted him. Lianna, two years older than Eilidh, had an ease with him that he'd always been grateful for. Perhaps because her heart belonged to another man. Nothing approaching ease had ever existed with Eilidh. With her siblings and friends in the Aerie, she was capable of animation, even of laughter. But around him, she became a shadow, silent and striving for invisibility, it seemed to him. If their gazes happened to meet, she quickly looked away, as if burned.

Drummond, well known to be protective of his younger siblings, especially his sisters, had told him years ago that she was intimidated by him. Even afraid of him. To keep from causing her discomfort, he'd taken Drummond's words to heart and avoided her. She was part of the family he cared for and guarded with his life. Still, he'd always been a little stung that the youngest of them could not bear to be around him.

But before she was attacked, the first day on the way here, he realized he'd been wrong about her, at least lately. She'd matured enough to become more confident around him, to try to converse with him. He'd begun to hope that on this trip, she might get to know who he was away from his responsibilities to Lathan, and for her to see him differently.

Then yesterday happened. She'd been frightened and exposed to him in a way no woman welcomed, save with her husband—or lover. And today, he'd compounded that indignity by stumbling in on her bath. It was as though the fates meant to tease him with the realization that she had grown into a beautiful woman, and then keep her from him.

He took a sip, trying to convince himself to let go of the useless, burning hunger he'd developed for her since touching her in forbidden places and holding her body against his. From now on, he must regard her only as a healer. He would.

To force himself into thinking of her that way, with as much detachment as he could summon, he turned his musings to wondering what she'd found out about the bairn. He didn't know if it was a lad or a lass, or what she might be called upon to do to save it. And he certainly had no knowledge that would let him understand how she did what she did.

Still, her mother had treated his training injuries and battle wounds often enough that he had a sense of how their special kind of healing felt, and of the sometimes-agonizing effect the healing had on the healer. He also knew how losing a patient—especially a bairn—devastated Aileana. He didn't want Eilidh or this bairn's family to suffer such a loss.

The men by the hearth stood to go just as Jamie Lathan descended the stairs to the great hall. He nodded to the men, but headed in Bhaltair's direction. "I saw ye over here before I went upstairs and hoped to find ye still in the hall. Ye have saved me a cold walk to the barracks."

Bhaltair set his drink aside and stood, but Jamie waved him back down. "What do ye need?" He picked up his drink and waited, giving Jamie time to settle into whatever had brought him here.

Jamie sat in the chair next to his. "Caitrin tells me Eilidh has some idea what is affecting Orla—our granddaughter, but isna yet certain. I dinna ken if Toran said anything about wanting ye to make a quick return to the Aerie—"

Bhaltair shook his head. "Nay, he didna. He was most concerned with giving ye whatever assistance Eilidh—or any of us—could offer."

"Good." Jamie nodded, then repeated, "Good."

Something was clearly on his mind. Bhaltair continued to sip his drink, giving Jamie time to organize his thoughts.

"That man we brought, the one who tried to rob Eilidh—"

"I ken who he is," Bhaltair snapped, frowning. Thinking about what that man had done made his ire rise and tightened his muscles. "Sorry. Go on..."

"I didna want to say anything where Eilidh would overhear, and upset her. 'Tis possible he is one of a band of lost men who roam these hills. We've had some trouble with them before now. Naught like an attack on a lass. Reiving from the herds, stealing from the outlying crofts, that sort of thing. I've tracked them. They move around. I doubt they spend two nights in the same place." He shrugged and ran a hand through his hair.

"Lately, we've heard some men have joined them from the Lowlands."

"What do they want? Land of their own?"

"And cattle and sheep and crofts, all taken from Fletcher, mind ye."

"What will ye do with our prisoner?"

"That's up to the laird. I'd let him spend enough time locked up to reflect on the folly of his actions and reconsider his future."

"Damn it, Jamie, that's not good enough," Bhaltair said, keeping his voice low, and tossed of the rest of his drink. "He wouldha raped her."

"But he didna." Jamie held out open hands, then interlaced his fingers. "Eilidh fought him, and scared him off. Ye arrived to protect her, and our guards hunted him down."

Bhaltair shook his head, determined to make Jamie understand Eilidh's peril. "He must be punished. Sitting warm and well-fed in whatever passes for Fletcher's dungeon isna sufficient."

A crease appeared between Jamie's brows. "What would ye have Fletcher do?"

"What would ye do if instead of Eilidh, he'd had Caitrin under him and tore her clothes?"

"In the moment, I'd have killed him."

"Aye, well, the moment hasna passed."

"But it has. Still, Caitrin has nay had the opportunity to render the laird's justice. I doubt she's even talked to Eilidh yet about what she believes should be done."

"Eilidh is a healer with a soft heart. She already noted the man's poor condition." Bhaltair shook his head. "I doubt she'd recommend anything too severe. But I dinna think she kens how close she came..."

"Aye, she does," Jamie insisted. "Any woman would. And she screamed, but not right away. I think she did that only after she realized she couldna escape him." He frowned and glanced aside.

Bhaltair wondered what had crossed his mind that he had held back. His part in the events that led up to her attack, or an older memory of what MacGregor did to Caitrin? "Or she held him off until she realized we were done with the wolves and could come to her aid."

"Perhaps. She's a wise lass. Either way, he did her no permanent harm."

"Ye dinna ken that. And ye didna see her after it was over. It affected her." Bhaltair could still feel the shivers that racked Eilidh's body as he held her against his chest and fought to control his own fury and fear for her.

"Eilidh is strong."

"And has a soft heart," Bhaltair repeated. "I dinna think she's going to be past that attack for much longer than ye realize."

"So, what would ye have me do?"

Bhaltair wanted to growl in frustration. "He's Fletcher's to deal with now. And ye say Caitrin will speak with Eilidh, so I will have nay part in the decision."

"What would ye do if he werena Fletcher's problem?"

"Like ye, I'd have killed him on the spot, had I found him still on her." He huffed out a breath, hating to admit that Jamie had a point. Eilidh was not physically harmed, save for a few bruises that would fade. "I'd probably do exactly what ye are doing." Jamie started to nod, but Bhaltair continued before he got too far in thinking their discussion was over. "But I might break every bone in his hands first, then keep him locked up while they healed."

Jamie snorted. "Remind me never to get on yer bad side."

"Think about it. Right now, he's better cared for than when living wild on his own."

"Ye dinna ken that."

Bhaltair pursed his lips and frowned. "Nay, I dinna."

Jamie shrugged. "But what to do with our prisoner is not my biggest worry."

Bhaltair found himself intrigued. Something more worrisome than their prisoner? Or ceding part of Fletcher to lost men? He nodded, silently urging Jamie to go on.

"The newcomers, the Lowlanders, are reformers. Protestants."

"I dinna follow."

"They've spread a great deal of unrest in the south. Destroying abbeys, witch hunts, all manner of civil unrest. Can it come here? Aye, of course, if others join them."

"What do ye need from Lathan?"

"I want ye and yer men to ride with mine, find the Lowlanders and the lost men, and send them south before they do more serious harm to Fletcher."

"Likely they are not the only lost men or reformers in the Highlands."

"I ken that. If we succeed in uprooting these, others may follow." He shrugged again, his gaze on the stout door that gave out onto the bailey. "Well, we'll deal with that when the time comes. If it does."

"Are they a danger to the Fletcher keep? To the laird? Or Eilidh?"

"Aye, they could be." Jamie's hand clenched into a fist, then opened.

Bhaltair sensed the effort he made to relax it and sympathized with the need to let go of anger and fear, but Bhaltair wasn't finished with the topic. "Toran has charged me with getting Eilidh home safely. He'll nay be happy about what happened to her on the way here. If we stir up trouble with yer lost men, there may be even more danger on the return to the Aerie."

"I'll send men with ye."

"Men ye may need to secure yer home here."

"Damn it, Bhaltair."

Bhaltair knew he'd pushed back enough. Jamie wasn't telling him everything he knew, and appeared determined to keep something to himself. Bhaltair didn't like walking blind into any fight, even one where friends had your back, but Fletcher was closely allied with Lathan. Toran would expect him to do whatever Jamie needed—as long as it didn't endanger Eilidh. And there was the crux of the issue. He could sit here for as long as it took for Eilidh to do what they came for, or he could help Fletcher. He was no healer, but he was good at fixing other things in his own way.

"We will help Fletcher, of course," Bhaltair said.

"Good," Jamie replied and stood. "I've got some MacKyrie whisky in the solar. Care to join me?"

Finally, something Bhaltair wholeheartedly supported. He stood. "Lead the way."

EILIDH WOKE with the germ of an idea. She wished she could consult with her mother, but nay, in this, she was on her own. Still, in a way, she had. Her memories of her mother's teachings had given her, perhaps, what she needed to save Orla's future. She tossed aside the plaid she'd covered herself with and stood. The fire had gone out, and the room had taken on a decided chill. She'd barely noticed it until her feet hit the icy-cold floor. She dressed quickly and headed down to the great hall. She'd break her fast, then have a conversation with the Fletcher cook before she spoke to Caitrin or her daughter Kellina.

The first person she saw as she started down the stairs was Bhaltair. He sat with the other Lathan guards and Uncle Jamie. Whatever they were discussing must be serious, judging by their intense concentration and the frowns creasing most of their brows.

Had their prisoner escaped? She paused on the stairs, hand at her throat. Nay, surely if that had happened, they wouldn't be in the great hall. They'd be out looking for him. She took a breath, dropped her hand to her side and continued down the stairs. She chose a seat at a table comfortably distant from the men's. She didn't want to appear to eavesdrop if they were planning something of import to Fletcher.

But she sat facing them. Facing Bhaltair. Even seated, he was still taller than the other men. His shoulders were broader and more muscled. The effect of his presence was more than commanding—it was riveting, at least to her. Only Uncle Jamie competed with his presence and appearance of control. He was a big man, but Bhaltair was bigger. Still, Uncle Jamie had twenty years more experience than Bhaltair as a warrior and leader. She was pleased they were working so well together.

"Ye canna be serious."

Bhaltair's objection carried over the general hum of conversation in the great hall. Perhaps they were not working together as well as she thought. Uncle Jamie nodded and his voice rose as well.

"Ye could be Fletcher's master of arms now, instead of Lathan's sometime in the future. We need ye."

Eilidh looked away, stomach sinking at Uncle Jamie's words. He would take Bhaltair from Lathan? How would her father react to that news? She couldn't help herself. She looked back. Bhaltair frowned, but she couldn't hear his reply.

A serving lass brought her a trencher and a cup of cider, distracting her. By the time she looked back at the men, they were laughing at something one of the other guards had said. Eilidh gave up watching them and turned to her food. She had worries of her own to deal with. For all she knew, Bhaltair had told Jamie to forget the idea. The fact that the Lathan guards with them at the table were not upset gave her some confidence in that assumption. And she would get Cole to tell her, later, when she checked the wolf wound on his leg, what had been said. She hadn't taken the first bite of her food before Kellina approached. "May I join ye?"

There went her plan to consult with the cook before talking to Kellina and her mother. "Of course."

"I dinna wish to bother ye," the lass said as she took a seat, "or keep ye from breaking yer fast. But I need to ken. Have ye thought of anything?"

"Aye, I have. But I'm not ready to explain it yet. I must speak to a few more people and get a few questions answered. Then I'll see Orla again. I hope ye dinna mind, but I want to be certain before I speak to ye and yer mother about what I think is the problem. And what to do about it."

Kellina sat back. "Truly? There's naught ye can tell me?"

Eilidh shook her head, concerned that her refusal to provide the information Kellina sought was angering her. "I'm sorry, but nay. I'm not ready yet."

Instead of heating with frustration, her face fell. "I've had to be patient for so long, 'tis hard to wait."

Sympathy filled Eilidh and squeezed her heart. "I ken it, and I'm grateful for yer patience. If I'm right, it must last ye only a wee bit longer." Eilidh studied the other woman, searching for any indication of how she would react.

Kellina seemed ready to continue to push for more information, but she looked away, and, her demeanor changed. "Since ye dinna wish to tell me about my daughter, perhaps ye will share something about the men who came with ye. Are they betrothed? Or married?"

Eilidh supposed Kellina had been widowed long enough to begin to regain her interest in other men. If she understood what the laird had told her, Orla's father had been killed more than a year ago. The wee lass would never remember him. But Kellina had asked what she could do to help Eilidh help her daughter. She deserved to be happy, and to find another love in her life.

Eilidh's gaze skimmed the Lathan guards. She smiled. "Nay, none of them are."

"Are they all good men?"

"Aye, or they wouldna be here. They wouldna be part of the group sent to keep me safe."

"What about that big one? The one talking to my da. Ye and he are not together, are ye?"

Eilidh froze. She should have anticipated the question. Bhaltair garnered admiration no matter where he was or what he was doing. Especially female admiration. Big, blond, heavily muscled, and handsome, he also held an important post in Clan Lathan. If she thought about it, and sometimes she did, she wondered why he hadn't been claimed by some other lass. But he remained stubbornly, stoically single. His responsibilities to the clan were his first and only concern. "Nay, we are not." She hated saying it, but it was the truth. "That's Bhaltair, Lathan's chief guard. He has nay time for, or interest in, any lass. He's a warrior, first and foremost."

"He sounds like he'd be a challenge," Kellina said, resting her chin on her hand and her elbow on the tabletop as she studied the man who'd caught her eye. "Fortunately, I enjoy challenges."

Eilidh's heart sank. "The other lads are friendlier." It was a stupid thing to say, but her friend Cole sat three seats down from Bhaltair and Uncle Jamie. Cole was certainly friendlier than Bhaltair, and he deserved to find happiness, too, even if it meant he remained at Fletcher. What if he became Fletcher's arms master instead of Bhaltair? But Kellina's gaze remained fixed on Bhaltair and Eilidh had no idea how to divert her from the one man Eilidh couldn't look away from. Bhaltair commanded her attention, too. The other lads could not compete with him. They would pale in comparison for Kellina, as well.

"Friendly is good when nothing else is available. But that big guard looks much more interesting."

Of course, he did. No one knew better than she how Bhaltair could claim a woman's notice. Since she had no answer to Kellina's comment, she turned back to her food. While Kellina studied Bhaltair, she, mercifully, stopped talking and let Eilidh sample her meal, but her appetite had fled. Eilidh pushed her trencher away, excused herself, and headed for the kitchen. No matter how much sympathy she might have for the grief Kellina had suffered over her lost love and her ill bairn, and how it might affect her, Eilidh couldn't sit there and watch another woman eyeing the one man she wanted for herself.

7

Bhaltair watched Eilidh leave the great hall. Her walk, her grace, her determination as she headed for the kitchen, all held him captive—and curious. What did she hope to find there? His conversation with Jamie and the other Lathan guards had ended in favor of eating their meal, and he had finished his, so he stood.

"I'll speak with ye again later," he told Jamie and made his way between tables, following the path Eilidh had taken. As he reached the table where she'd been sitting, another lass stood, turned and stumbled into his arms. He caught her before she fell, one hand around her shoulder and the other gripping her arm.

"Ach! I'm so clumsy. Please forgive me," she said in a rush of breath.

But she made no move to step away from him.

"*Dinna fash*," he told her. Certain she was firmly on her own two feet, he released her and stepped back. "Excuse me."

"Wait!" She put a hand on his arm, stopping his retreat before it began. "I'm Kellina. The laird's daughter. And ye are?"

Now that he fully looked at her, he recognized her. "A visitor. Bhaltair Lathan."

"Lathan? Ye came with the healer?"

"Ye were sitting with her, aye? So, I assume ye ken that."

She colored, but didn't release him. "I must admit, I did. I saw ye and had to ask." She tilted her head and studied him. "But ye also noticed me. Why not take a walk with me? I'd love to learn more about ye."

"Some other time, perhaps," he said, striving for a polite tone he didn't feel, and stepping out of her grip. He'd been accosted by lasses since before he could grow a beard. Something told him this one would be difficult to dissuade, but she was keeping him from the lass he wanted. "If ye will excuse me, I have somewhere I am needed." If Kellina continued to delay him and he was wrong about where Eilidh had gone, he'd never find her.

She looked up from beneath her lashes and nibbled at her full lower lip.

She pouted prettily, he'd give her that.

"If ye must," she said, a crease forming between arched brows. "I look forward to speaking with ye soon."

"Of course," he said to be polite as she touched his hand.

Her frown communicated something more than disappointment, but he didn't want to spend the time thinking about it—or invite more conversation by questioning it. He wanted Eilidh, and he couldn't get Jamie's offer out of his mind. Leave Lathan? Had Jamie put Kellina there, hoping to add her to the bargain? Nay, he was cunning, but he wouldn't do something so unscrupulous, and certainly not with his own daughter.

When she finally nodded and released him, he turned away, half expecting her to take his arm again. She didn't. He breathed a sigh of relief and headed for the kitchen.

He soon found Eilidh speaking to the Fletcher cook in the busy kitchen. He waited at the door for her to notice him, but she seemed intent on something the cook was telling her. The conversation lasted only a few minutes before the cook moved away and Eilidh looked up and saw him.

"Bhaltair! Is everything all right?"

Was it? He dared not mention Jamie's offer, not until he'd thought about it a great deal more. "Aye, lass. I saw ye leave yer meal unfinished. Are ye well?" Of course she was. She was beautiful, flushed from the heat of the kitchen. But now that he had her attention, he didn't know what else to say to explain his presence.

"I am. I was just going to go out and inspect the kitchen garden. Care to walk with me?"

How ironic that the invitation from Eilidh he was happy to accept sounded much like the one he'd just turned down from Kellina. "Aye."

She moved to him and took his arm.

Her touch made heat rise in Bhaltair that warmed him deep in his chest. Kellina's touch had done nothing except make him suspicious. It reinforced a notion he'd recently become enamored with, that something might develop between him and Eilidh. Someday.

He put a hand over Eilidh's and escorted her through the kitchen and outside into the walled garden. Her skin was as soft as he recalled, her fingers long and slim, burning through his shirt to scorch his arm. They walked the stone paths that gave access to the various plants growing there. Eilidh pointed out some and explained how they were used. He didn't put a lot of effort to remembering what she told him about them. He was too taken by the seldom-heard sound of her voice. She was rarely this effusive, and never before around him. But clearly she enjoyed talking about herbs. He'd happily spend hours listening to her talk about them or anything else, but she led him to the far side of the garden and kept going.

Set in the far wall, a gate opened into a small orchard. Eilidh explained that Cook told her some varieties of apples had been picked, but a few trees still bore fruit.

"They have pears, too," Eilidh exclaimed, pointing with her free hand. "And plums."

He didn't see any fruit on those trees, but Eilidh was familiar enough to recognize the trees without them. Farther on, bees buzzed around hives, and the ground gave way down to partially harvested fields of grains. Eilidh stopped and studied the view. "Only the latest to ripen are left in the field, but they are grown so close together, I dinna ken how I will get a clean sample to try with Orla," she complained, her brow drawn down.

"I dinna ken what ye mean," Bhaltair admitted.

It dawned on him that she might have sensed much about him while he held her hand. Disconcerted, he forced his attention to their conversation. Eilidh was worried.

She turned to look up at him.

He could look at her eyes until there was no light left to see them, but she expected him to listen to her, so he tipped his head in invitation for her to explain.

"I suspect something Orla is being fed doesna agree with her. The only way to be certain which food harms her is to feed her one fruit, one vegetable, one meat, or one grain at a time. I can sense how her body reacts to each the same way I sense what needs to be healed. But those grains are so close to each other, barley there," she said and pointed, "wheat there and there, oats," she added and dropped her arm, "that the wind blows their chaff onto each other. I will have to carefully clean them, but even then, I canna be sure. Samples I take now may be no better than what Cook stored away from the earlier harvest."

"Did the cook have any way to help ye get what ye need?"

"He agreed to give me samples of the ingredients in the clan's meals, though I had to argue for some of the spices. They're very costly. Mostly, I think he feared I would try to steal his recipes. Still, I convinced him to help. But that," she said and nodded toward the ripened fields, "he canna control."

"I ken little of farming, but I imagine those fields have been planted and plowed many times over the years, mixing the grains into the soil. That canna help."

"Nay." Eilidh let go of his arm and crossed hers over her breasts. "I will have to be very careful. And I dinna ken if my idea will work."

"It willna if ye dinna try," he told her, sensing her distress. He wanted to put an arm around her shoulders, to console her. She seemed so disappointed. But the Eilidh he knew would not stay down for long. "Ye will figure out something," he said.

"Thank ye, Bhaltair." She looked up and gave him a small smile. "I appreciate the encouragement. Ye are a good man."

A good man? Not even close. And not with the thoughts and desires surging through him at her words. They were well away from the Fletcher keep. Shielded by the orchard behind them and the kitchen garden wall beyond that. As alone as they had ever been. What would she do if he touched her face? If he kissed her?

"Eilidh—"

"Bhaltair—"

They spoke over each other, but she'd uncrossed her arms and one hand reached for him, but did not quite touch. His fingers, he was surprised to see, lay just short of stroking her face or tangling in her hair. He dropped his hand, not daring to hope she would accept him. When he failed to touch her, a shadow of a frown creased her brow, and she dropped her hand as well.

"I suppose we should go back," Eilidh said, not looking at him.

"Do ye want to collect some samples while we're here?" He'd do anything to extend this private time with her.

"I do, but I dinna want to keep ye from—"

"I've nowhere else to be but to help ye," he said, a little too quickly. Damn it, take a breath.

She smiled again and started forward. "Then let's try."

He walked with her into the first field and stuffed anything she gave him into his sporran.

In the next two fields, she kept the samples she chose separated, one kind tucked in a fold of the shawl she wore around her shoulders, the other in one of her hands. "That should do it. Let's take these back."

Nay. They might never have private time like this again. "Eilidh, I..." What could he say? That years ago, he'd been politely warned away by her eldest brother, but after he saw her breasts twice in the last two days, he couldn't get her out of his thoughts? That was daft. He'd be better off cutting his own throat now than to wait for her brothers to hear of it—especially Drummond. "I'm happy to help ye any time ye need me," he temporized. Damn, that sounded like he saw her only as his duty, and that was not the message he wanted to send.

"Thank ye," she replied.

Her tone told him she knew there was more he wanted to say. Or perhaps there was more she wanted to say. She looked up at him and their gaze held for a long moment. Gathering his courage, he lifted a hand and traced a finger along her shoulder and up her throat, fighting the urge to cup her face and kiss her. "Holding ye while ye slept was the best thing that's ever happened to me."

"Thank ye for caring for me. I... being held was the best thing for me, as well. Ye were so kind to me." She reached up and wrapped the fingers of her free hand around his. "I dinna ken what this means, but I want ye to ken that I welcome it."

His heart beat a staccato against his ribs. "I, too, Eilidh. I dinna ken if this is wise, or possible, but I think we should give it a chance."

Her face bloomed with the color of summer roses across her cheeks. It made her more beautiful, more desirable. But did it mean she agreed with him? Or was she simply grateful for his care when she was hurting? The urge to kiss her, to put his doubts to rest, nearly overwhelmed him. But this was Eilidh, and this connection between them was too new for him to push her faster than she was willing to go. All too easily, she could go back to being the shadow who avoided him. His concern must have shown on his face.

"We will take as much time as we need to figure out what it means," she said.

Bhaltair locked his knees to stay upright. She wasn't going to hide from him, or turn him away. Not yet.

"I will need yer help. I find I enjoy it."

He laughed at that, breaking the tension that had grown between them, which he divined was her purpose. "I'm at yer service." Taking another chance, he drew her hand to his lips and kissed her knuckles, then released her hand. "But for now, ye have much to do to help the wee bairn. Perhaps we should take these samples inside so ye can begin."

Eilidh took a deep breath and softly blew it out, as if fighting to regain equilibrium his touch had disturbed. "We should," she said and gave him a sweet smile that he tucked away in his memory. "By now, the cook should have samples prepared for me, as well. We can collect them on the way."

EILIDH WANTED TO SING, to dance, to throw her arms around Bhaltair and kiss him soundly. She would if she dared. He'd shown he would welcome her advance. But she was no fool. Anything she started, he would finish. And he'd seen enough of her over the last few days to make it hard for either of them to stay in control.

She had felt the sensations and emotions coursing through him every time he touched her skin. Her talent told her much more about what he felt than he likely expected or would want her to know. To her eye, he'd controlled himself well. He'd kept his touch light, tentative, his breathing steady. But her senses told her his heart beat fast, his blood coursed hotly through his body as he fought to temper his desire for her and hide his arousal.

She felt flushed with power, yet somewhere in a rational corner of her mind, cautious. She must not make too much of this overture of his. They had spoken of taking their time, and they must. Any other woman would not know what she did about how much he desired her in this moment. His desire could fade. She must allow him the privacy of his feelings until he was ready to make them known. And until they had progressed far enough that he understood what the healing talent he was familiar with also showed her.

He was right. She had work to do. A wee bairn was suffering. And so was the bairn's family as they watched her fail to thrive.

And what would happen when the Lathans did go home? This new closeness could still evaporate once they returned to the Aerie. They'd spent years there together—and yet apart. Would Bhaltair pursue her, or would his interest fade once they were back to the life they both knew? Was his interest piqued because they were away from the Aerie—and from her parents? Nay, that did not seem like something he would do. What she had felt from him was real, if only in this moment. Walking alone beside him in a new place, she felt secure and confident that they could learn more about each other—perhaps enough to one day be together.

"I can almost hear ye thinking," he said, startling her.

"Aye? What am I thinking about?" Surely he didn't know the direction her thoughts had taken.

"Yer worries," he said without looking at her.

Or did he?

"The lass," he added. "How ye will discover what is harming her."

He was wrong, but she couldn't tell him that. "Ye ken me better than I ever thought ye might," she told him instead.

"And yet, not well at all. But I now have reason to hope that will change."

It already had. He'd seen her with her clothes torn. He'd seen her in her bath. There wasn't much else that he hadn't seen. And she had seen his desire.

"Ye ken the secret of my healing ability. 'Tis not much left."

He looked her up and down and grinned. Ach, she knew better than to tease a man. But she was seeing sides of this man she never knew existed. He'd always been so stoic, so withdrawn. The touch of playfulness he was showing her was a gift, indeed. Added to how he'd cared for her after the attack, if she hadn't been smitten before, she would be now. And she was.

She smacked his arm for his effrontery, then quirked her lips into a sardonic grin. His arm was as hard as a stone wall. Her hand stung from her casual blow.

They proceeded, smiling, past the hives and orchard into the walled kitchen garden. There, she paused, so Bhaltair did, too.

He looked around at the plants filling the space. "Do ye need to collect anything here?"

She shook her head. "I hope what Cook gives me will include much of this. And I can always gather more from here if I need it. 'Tis easily accessible."

Cook gave her a dozen small cloth packets. "These are for ye to start with. I'll have more for ye later," he promised. "Ye will ken what they are when ye open them. Or ask me if ye dinna."

"Thank ye, I will," Eilidh promised and they went on their way to the Fletcher healer's herbal.

"I would make tinctures from these," she told the healer when she'd explained what they'd brought, "but I dinna want to expose the lass to the alcohol. So, tisanes it will be. If I learn nothing from that, I'll try the actual food."

"I should go, and let ye work," Bhaltair said.

"Not while ye still have grains I need," Eilidh told him with a glance down at his sporran. She looked up at him through her lashes and saw color bloom on his cheeks and nose at the direction of her gaze. He opened the sporran and dumped out the contents on the worktable. "'Tis a good thing there was nothing else in there," she told him as she gathered the scattered grains into a neat pile.

"There seldom is," he said with a shrug. But it comes in handy for collecting things now and again. I learned that with yer sister and her seeds."

"Ah, the seeds making the horses sick. I heard all about that." Eilidh would have enjoyed helping Lianna solve that puzzle, but more so, the chance to be away from the Aerie with Bhaltair. Who knew what their relationship would be by now if she had made that trip with them?

"That sounds like a story I should hear," the healer said, interrupting the gazes between them that were growing more intense by the moment.

Eilidh turned to her. "I'll be happy to tell ye, but Bhaltair was there for most of it. Ye should hear it from him." And that would keep him nearby, where she wanted him.

He settled agreeably on a sturdy stool and related the story of the MacDhai horses and all that happened there, while the healer put water on to boil, and Eilidh prepared the samples in different containers. She let them steep until they cooled. She planned to feed them one by one to Orla, and monitor how her body reacted to each before trying the next one.

They finished preparing the tisanes about the time Bhaltair finished telling his story.

"So the Dule tree seeds sickened the horses. I've not seen that happen here."

"The poison would have killed them, but Lianna was able to save them. In the end, the treatment was quite simple. A lot of water and dandelion tea and greens."

"Which cleanse the system. Sensible."

"And effective," Bhaltair agreed. "But it turned the stables into a swamp the whole clan had to help clean."

"Oh nay!" The healer cackled. Eilidh laughed along with her.

"Ye wouldna think it so funny if ye had to shovel out the mess," Bhaltair griped.

EILIDH'S LAUGHTER was music to Bhaltair's ears. This day was a treasure he would keep in his heart forever. She'd been so enthusiastic, explaining the herb garden to him. He'd never heard her string so many words together. She'd gone from composed and thoughtful on the way back from their declarations beyond the orchard, to thankful when the cook gave her the packets he'd promised, to hopeful once she and the healer set to work. Since she rarely showed much emotion, the day had been a revelation. He'd always been aware of her tranquil and mysterious side, but the more he saw of the many sides to her, the more entranced with her he became.

It made him think that she might feel the same way about him. His usual demeanor was quiet and reserved. He was a thinker, analytical. Both were qualities that served a chief guard well, since planning for how an enemy might attack was as important as when and where. Eilidh's father, as the Lathan laird, depended on him to advise him of any vulnerabilities he found or expected. And he entrusted Bhaltair with his children, from his heir to his youngest daughter.

Bhaltair took that trust very seriously. But it didn't mean he had to be so reserved, not around Eilidh. She'd taught him a valuable lesson this day. He watched her chat with the healer while they made up a tray of tisanes, safe and confident in her element, with someone who loved being a healer like she did. And with him, someone she trusted. And cared for, if he understood correctly what had passed between them in the garden.

It made his heart hurt to think that he'd spent so many years around her, not seeing the real Eilidh. Not recognizing the lass within her who could show him so many things he'd overlooked.

"Bhaltair?"

He lifted a hand, realizing that she had been trying to get his attention for more than one call of his name.

"Sorry, I was thinking."

"Did ye think of anything that would help wee Orla?"

"Nay, sorry. Something else entirely." He looked at the tray filled with cups of what looked like tea and offered, "Let me carry that for ye. If I canna be the brains to help the lass, I can be the brawn."

"Ye can, indeed," the healer quipped with a measured glance at his shoulders, and grinned. Then she sobered. "Thank ye. Yer help will be most appreciated."

Eilidh smiled at the healer's quip and led the way from the herbal up to Orla's chamber. Bhaltair did his best not to drop the tray of tisanes they'd worked so hard to create, but it was hard when all he could see on the stairs was Eilidh's sweet bottom swaying as she climbed a few steps above him.

8

Kellina was in the chamber with Orla when Eilidh arrived with the Fletcher healer. Bhaltair trailed behind her carrying a tray of cups of the tisanes, each carefully labeled, milk, a bit of cheese, butter and honey.

Kellina looked up as the door opened and frowned as Eilidh and the healer entered. "Ye have medicines?" She looked back to her daughter, hope and worry making her eyes brighten and her forehead crease. She stood, one hand on Orla, glanced around again, and this time spotted Bhaltair. Immediately, her whole demeanor shifted. She straightened and her eyes widened as she swept him with her gaze. Then she smiled.

Eilidh did her best not to notice. She didn't understand how Kellina could hold anything in her heart beyond her concern for her child. If Eilidh was in the same position, she would not be thinking about a man, not even one as attractive as Bhaltair.

For now, she wanted Kellina out of the chamber. The healer spoke to her while Eilidh and Bhaltair placed the tisanes nearby and waited for their discussion to end. Instead, it became heated very quickly.

"I will not leave my daughter," Kellina exclaimed, her voice rising above the low murmur that the healer had used with her.

"The Lathan healer canna do her work with others in the chamber," the Fletcher healer told her.

Or reminded her. Eilidh was certain Kellina knew that. She'd been kept out the evening Eilidh arrived, when she first examined Orla.

"She can and she will," Kellina insisted. "I've heard the tales all my life of how her mother saved my da in the middle of a crowd of onlookers. She simply wants me out of her way." She sent Eilidh a glare that would have stopped her heart, had it been made of ice instead of fire.

"That isna true," Eilidh said, deeming it was time for her to intervene and save the Fletcher healer from Kellina's wrath. "Working with a bairn is... delicate... and takes a great deal of concentration. Having someone nearby who doesna ken my methods, who might interrupt me or distract me at a crucial point and cause me to miss something... well, do ye want to put yer daughter through that?"

"I will sit here very quietly and watch."

Orla began fussing at the raised voices. To Eilidh's shock, Bhaltair moved to the crib and picked up the wee lass, cradling her in his massive arms and crooning softly to her. In moments, she settled, looking up at him with adoration. Was there no female on the planet that man could not charm? Eilidh's bones melted at the sight of the huge warrior holding the sick bairn to his chest, stroking her soft cheek with one careful finger.

Kellina appeared equally entranced, her eyes wide and her color high.

"Perhaps ye would be more comfortable in the great hall, having something to drink with me," Bhaltair suggested as he moved to Eilidh and handed Orla to her.

Orla fussed, her eyes tracking the big man. He touched her wee hand and she curled her fingers around one of his fingers, so he took her back from Eilidh, and placed her gently into her bed. Eilidh looked up at him with what, she was certain, must be the same expression of adoration that Orla wore.

Bhaltair winked at her.

Eilidh could have kissed him. She knew he was not interested in Kellina. If Orla's mother had any modicum of her mother Caitrin's talent, she would know he offered her only polite courtesy and nothing else. Eilidh felt certain he would no more want to spend time with Kellina than clean out the MacDhai stalls after Lianna saved the horses. He offered to distract Kellina to help her.

And to help the bairn. Eilidh was seeing a side of him she never knew existed, reinforcing how she felt after the way he cared for her. He glanced at Kellina and back to the bairn reaching for him. She never realized he was so crafty. He was trying to draw Kellina's gaze there, as well. To make her think about what was best for her child.

Too bad Kellina's gaze stayed locked on his shoulders instead.

Eilidh held herself still, though she wanted to shake her head in disbelief. This was the daughter of her father's dearest friend? His cousin. Hers too. Kellina was her cousin as well. She knew the stories of Uncle Jamie and how he'd stood by her da, how he'd traveled for the Lathan clan, taking her da's treaty to the Highland clans, and how he'd saved his wife, who became the Fletcher laird. That their daughter could care more for the size of Bhaltair's muscles than the health of her daughter—she couldn't credit it. Yet she was seeing it with her own eyes.

Or was she? Suddenly, Kellina recollected herself and shifted her gaze to her daughter. "Since I can be of nay help, I will go." She turned to Bhaltair, defiance in the direct look she gave him. "Ye needna escort me. I ken my way around my own home."

Bhaltair inclined his head to acknowledge her, and she left.

"Well." The Fletcher healer frowned at the door. "I've never seen the lass behave so badly. She must be worried sick."

Eilidh was beginning to have her doubts, but she set them aside. Perhaps Kellina had detected Bhaltair's lack of interest in her and refused to be manipulated. Eilidh gave her credit for having enough pride to rebuff him. "Let's begin. The sooner we have an answer, the sooner this lass will feel better."

"I will leave ye to it," Bhaltair offered. "Ye dinna need me now, and I can fetch food and drink for ye to have once ye are done. If ye need me, leave the door open a wee, and I will look in."

"Thank ye, Bhaltair," Eilidh told him. "The healer and I will be well. I will send her to ye when we are nearly done with the tisanes."

Bhaltair nodded and left them to begin their work.

"Where do ye want to start?" The healer looked over the contents of the tray.

"What is the most commonly used food for the weans? Potato? Milk?"

"Milk, I'd say."

"Then we'll start with a few drops of milk."

The healer lifted Orla into a sitting position and put pillows at her back so she could remain upright and swallow.

Eilidh put her hands over Orla's chest and belly, taking her measure. The lass watched, wide-eyed but not responding to their presence, her mother's earlier outburst, or Bhaltair's absence. That worried Eilidh as much as her physical condition. Whatever plagued her appeared to be affecting her mind, as well. Eilidh nodded to the healer, who dribbled some milk into the child's mouth. Eilidh sensed the bit of nourishment make its way to the lass's stomach. It would take time to go from there into her lower abdomen. Given how sluggish Orla seemed to be, Eilidh couldn't predict how long that would take, but she realized they would not get through many of the tisanes today.

She kept her focus on what happened in Orla's body, but was dimly aware the Fletcher healer had taken a seat near the hearth.

By the time the milk had coursed through Orla's body, hours

had passed and there had been no reaction. No damage. Eilidh straightened, only then realizing that the healer had put a chair behind her knees and she'd been sitting while staying connected to Orla. She turned to the healer. "Thank ye. I didna realize…"

"'Twasna me. Bhaltair looked in and moved the chair for ye. A good man, he is."

"Aye, he is." Eilidh's body warmed at the thought of his kindness. "Did Kellina look in?"

"Nay. Likely she's off sulking. The lass has always had a short temper. I hoped to spare ye, but I failed."

"I've seen worse. *Dinna fash*. And thank ye for yer efforts."

"Do ye want to try another?" She gestured at the tray. "'Tis near on time for supper. Perhaps ye need to eat?"

"This is going to take much more time than I originally thought. I've never done the like before, and it wears on me more than I expected." She shrugged. It had been a long and emotional day, but the healer did not need to hear about the time she'd spent with Bhaltair out in the gardens, or her body's response to seeing him cradling the ill bairn. "I'm learning as we go. So, aye, a meal would help." She stood. "Who will take care of the lass?"

"Her mother or I. I'll feed her. Or would ye rather I didna…"

"Nay, let the bairn eat or hunger will add to her misery. Perhaps a few hours after she eats, I'll learn something from that."

Hours had passed, and the clan had gathered for the evening meal, yet Eilidh had not sent the Fletcher healer to Bhaltair to bring her sustenance. Were they still at it? He frowned at the stairs leading up from the great hall. Should he go check on them again?

"They're fine," Niall told him. "Ye are worse than a hen with chicks. I've never seen ye this antsy over a lass. Are ye sure ye are not sweet on her?"

"Mind yerself," Bhaltair warned him quietly. "We're here because of what she's doing up there. The sooner she's done, the sooner we go home."

"And out of the reach of a certain laird's daughter. Ach, they both are lairds' daughters. Ye have two—"

Bhaltair grabbed Niall's shirt front and pulled it tight across his chest. "Ye will *haud yer wheesht* if ye ken what's good for ye. We dinna need yer blether to cause trouble with Fletcher."

Niall nodded, eyes all but crossing as he stared at Bhaltair.

Bhaltair released him and stood in time to hear him mutter, "I thought ye could take a jest. I can tell I was wrong."

"Ye are talking again."

Niall's mouth shut with a click of crashing teeth.

Bhaltair hid a grimace and left Niall gawking at his back. He stalked toward the stairs in time to see Eilidh and the Fletcher healer appear out of the upper hallway and begin to descend the steps. His annoying companion forgotten, he took a breath and the tension drained out of him at the sight of her. She looked tired. Frustrated. Things had not gone well? How was that possible? Lathan healers could fix anything short of death, or so he'd observed and always believed. Aileana had patched him up often enough.

He moved toward the stairs to meet the healers as they reached the main floor. "Eilidh?" She shook her head, clearly understanding his unspoken question.

"'Tis going to take much more time than I'd hoped."

"Do ye still believe it will give ye the answer ye seek?" He took her arm, and on his other side, the Fletcher healer's, and led them to chairs at a nearby table.

"I still hope so."

Bhaltair beckoned a serving lass. "Take care of the healers," he told her. "Whatever ye have ready, bring it. And cider."

"Aye, sir," the lass replied and hurried off to do his bidding.

"Thank ye, Bhaltair," the Fletcher healer said.

He took a seat opposite them. "The burden is on ye, Eilidh, but for anything else ye need, can others help the Fletcher healer? Can Kellina?"

"Others could, I suppose," Eilidh said.

"Not the mother," the healer added. "She hasna the patience 'twill require."

"Jamie intends to put some of the Lathan guards to use, tracking down yer attacker's associates. But the rest can assist ye as ye need. We all ken how to be patient."

Bhaltair knew, more than most. Looking at Eilidh, being this close to her, this much in her confidence, was new and made him want her more. But he would wait.

Eilidh didn't react. She must be exhausted. He considered for a moment going after food and drink for her himself, but saw the serving lass headed their way, arms laden with a well-provisioned tray. As she placed the contents before the two women, Bhaltair watched Eilidh's eyes. She stared into space, paying no attention to what was going on around her.

"Eilidh," he said, softly at first, then repeated her name louder.

That got her attention and she met his gaze. "Eat. Drink. Ye ken what ye need."

She nodded and took a long drink of cider, broke a piece of bread, and put a chunk in her mouth. But her gaze still seemed a hundred miles away.

"Chew, Eilidh. Come on, lass."

The Fletcher healer eyed her with concern. "Eilidh?"

She complied. After a few more bites of bread and cheese, she seemed to wake up, and ate with more intent, as if she'd finally recognized her healing-induced hunger.

Bhaltair told one serving lass to bring a pitcher of cider,

another to bring honey cakes or anything sweet the cook had on hand. Eilidh needed the energy that would supply.

After finishing the contents of the first tray and the sweets the servant brought, aided only in small part by the Fletcher healer, she slowed, then stopped. "I'm better," she announced. "Now I will sleep. When I wake, I'll try the next sample with Orla."

"Will ye tonight?" The healer seemed concerned.

"Who is planning to stay with the lass tonight?"

"I am. Ye willna wake the lass if she is sleeping, will ye?"

"Nay. She needs sleep, but if she's restive, I'll try another sample. I can manage one on my own, but ye may remain in the chamber and sleep. I ken what to expect now, so I will be able to rest some, as well." She stifled a yawn and sent an apologetic smile to Bhaltair. "Can ye escort me to my chamber? I dinna wish to stumble on the stairs."

"Of course." He stood and held out a hand. "Come, let's get ye upstairs. Healer, thank ye for helping Eilidh."

"I'm proud to do it. I wish I could do more."

"We will," Eilidh said around another yawn. "Later."

Jamie entered the hall and came over to them. "Do ye have some time, Bhaltair? I need to discuss something with ye."

Bhaltair frowned. What enticement had the Fletchers come up with now? "Let me help Eilidh upstairs. Will ye be in yer solar?"

"Aye. Eilidh, did ye learn anything?"

"Nay, not yet."

Bhaltair shook his head at Jamie, telling him without words that this was not the time to interrogate her, and led her away. She entered her chamber and sat on the bed. "I canna stay awake to talk with ye," she said, apologizing.

He lifted her feet onto the bed and covered her with a woolen blanket. "Sleep well."

"Will ye be near?"

"After I find out what Jamie wants, I'll be outside yer door."

She didn't answer, and her slow, deep breathing told him she'd succumbed to exhaustion and her meal. He left her, closed the door softly and headed back downstairs to the laird's solar. It was actually Caitrin's but Jamie used it, too. Would they both be there?

He entered to find Jamie settled at one of the hearthside chairs, rather than at the desk. Caitrin was not with him. Jamie gestured for Bhaltair to join him and poured two fingers of whisky.

"MacKyrie?"

"Aye, what else?" Jamie took a sip.

Bhaltair did the same, letting the spirit roll around in his mouth, savoring its complexity and its heat before he swallowed. "There's naught else like MacKyrie makes," he said in appreciation. "But ye didna ask me here to drink yer whisky."

"Nay. Our prisoner has escaped."

Bhaltair choked in mid-swallow and coughed, fighting for air to soften the whisky burning its way down his chest. "Escaped? How?" The urge to dash up the stairs and check on Eilidh nearly drove him to his feet. She was alone up there, her door unlocked. But first, he needed to hear what Jamie had to tell him.

"He had help—one of the lasses assigned to take food to him. The guard left for a comfort break while she was there. She opened the door and walked him out of Fletcher's gate as pretty as ye please." He sighed in disgust and tossed off the rest of the whisky in his glass.

Relief melted the tension tightening every muscle Bhaltair had spent years honing. The man was gone from the Fletcher keep. Eilidh was safe—for now. "Ye want me to find him?"

"I want ye to find him and all his friends. He might have been alone when he encountered our camp—and Eilidh off by herself —but he doesna live alone. Or make mischief alone. He might be from a nearby clan, or be a Lowlander Protestant spreading heresy into the Highlands. He said some things to the guards that makes me think it possible. Or he could have used those phrases to lie about who or what he really is."

"Other than where we camped, we canna ken where he and his friends might be."

"I hope they decided to move on and bother someone else, but I dinna believe it. At any rate, 'tis too dark to track him now. 'Tis a problem for tomorrow. I will send Fletchers out, too, but I ken ye want to find this man and have him punished."

"I do. I'll have my men ready to go in the morning."

Jamie poured more whisky into their glasses. "That'll do. Where are ye sleeping?"

"With my men last night. Tonight, outside Eilidh's door. She's in a healing sleep. I dinna want her disturbed."

Jamie nodded. "Take care of that lass. She's worth more than we can count. I'd like her to stay here, too, ye ken." He pursed his lips, but said nothing more.

Jamie had grand—and unrealistic—ambitions, if he thought it possible to convince Eilidh to remain at Fletcher. Aye, she was worth more than any of them could count. Jamie had no idea how much she was worth to Bhaltair. And taking care of her was exactly what he wanted to do—for the rest of his life, no matter where they were.

EILIDH WOKE. She wasn't sure what time it was. The window was covered and no light leaked in around the edges. The hearth fire had burned down to a comforting glow and still kept the chamber warm enough for her to throw aside the covers and put her feet on the chilled floor. Chilled, but not cold enough to burn.

She moved to the window, pulled aside the covering and peered out, shivering as cold air enveloped her. The sky had the pearly glow of the pre-dawn hour. She dropped the cover, moved to the hearth and stood rubbing her arms while she warmed up.

Treating Orla would demand much of her time this day, but there would also be much time spent waiting for something to happen. Time Eilidh could put to good use. But how?

She missed her twin, Tavish. He always came up with something to get both of them into trouble, but that she would enjoy doing. Sometimes, he even managed to get them out of trouble again. Like the time they let all the horses out of their stalls to run free in the Aerie's bailey. It had been the first sunny day after a long cold, rainy spell and their tutor had refused to let them delay the day's lessons. Their punishment had been to help round up the horses and see them safely back to their stalls, then clean up all the horse droppings they'd left behind. So, while they didn't enjoy cleaning up after the horses, at least they were outside, where they wanted to be.

That time, their father had threatened to tan their hides for endangering the horses—and the people in their way. Their mother took them aside and made them apologize to the stable master, then confined them to their chambers for another day to let them think about what they'd done—and what could have gone wrong.

While Eilidh enjoyed the solitude, Tavish, more social, had chafed against his detention, and spent the time coming up with more outrageous things for them to do. Eilidh drew the line at many of those as being too dangerous or too potentially hurtful to others.

Eventually, they grew past such antics. But right now, having Tavish help her devise something to keep Kellina away from Bhaltair, without hurting her, would cheer her. Kellina had been through too much the last months, losing her husband, then seeing her bairn grow progressively sicker. She had a right to act out, and Eilidh should be happy for her that she was beginning to take interest in life again. In other men. Just not in Bhaltair.

Finally warm enough to move, Eilidh dressed and pulled on her boots. She heard voices out in the hallway, so hesitated at the door. Should she open it? She leaned her ear to the door and recognized Bhaltair's deep tones, and a woman's higher, lighter voice. A serving lass? Perhaps she'd brought something to break Eilidh's fast.

She stepped back and opened the door, expecting to find Bhaltair and a lass assigned to help her. "Good morning," she said, then stopped. Kellina stood close to Bhaltair. Too close for Eilidh's liking, nor, from the look on his face, Bhaltair's.

Bhaltair took advantage of her interruption to step away from Orla's mother. Kellina turned to Eilidh with a smile that failed to reach her eyes. "Ah, healer. I didna ken ye slept here." She turned back to Bhaltair. "With ye?"

"Nay," Eilidh answered for him. "I sleep quite alone."

"Odd that I found him outside yer door."

"I am her chief guard." Bhaltair's tone was calm, flat, with no trace of friendliness or patience in his voice or expression.

"Thank ye for keeping me safe, Bhaltair," Eilidh told him, worried that he might frighten Kellina. "If ye would escort me down for the morning meal, I would appreciate it."

"Of course, Healer Eilidh," he said, seeming to recollect himself, and giving her a title she'd never heard him use in reference to anyone save her mother. Even if he said it only to remind Kellina whom she was dealing with, it made Eilidh proud. There were many ways to protect someone. Bhaltair appeared to be expert at most of them.

"If ye will excuse us, Kellina. I will be up to see to Orla after I break my fast. I'll speak to ye later." She moved past the woman and took the arm Bhaltair offered. Halfway down the stairs, she glanced up, but Kellina was nowhere to be seen.

"I'm sorry she bothered ye," Bhaltair said as they continued down the stairs.

"Me? It was ye she was intent upon. She didn't like me appearing in the doorway as I did."

"Still, ye will care for her daughter," he said as they reached the bottom of the stairs. He led her to a seat near the hearth and away from the draft coming in the keep's door every time someone went out or came in.

His acknowledgement of her dedication to her patient warmed her. "Of course. 'Tis why we came, and it wouldna matter if I didna like the woman. That should never affect how I treat my patient. Besides, Orla is Uncle Jamie's granddaughter."

"And the Fletcher laird's."

"And Caitrin's, aye." With a smile, she accepted the trencher a serving lass brought her. Bhaltair settled across from her and soon tucked in to his own meal.

"What were ye really doing outside my door before sunup?" Eilidh held her breath, hoping she wasn't being too forward. She would never want Bhaltair to associate her behavior with Kellina's.

"Sleeping," he replied succinctly.

"So ye told Kellina the truth."

"Aye. Ye ken her mother is a soothsayer. I dinna ken if she has the gift—"

"But why take the chance. I understand. I wasna aware ye kenned about the Fletcher talent."

"Yer mother warned me," Bhaltair replied evenly, as if learning of another unusual ability surprised him not at all.

Eilidh shrugged off the revelation. "I do thank ye for keeping me safe through the night. I mean that."

"'Tis why I'm here. But I have news about that, as well." He hesitated.

Eilidh's hackles went up. Bhaltair was solemn, measured in his approach except when in the midst of a battle, and never hesitated, not that she'd observed. "What is it?"

"I'm taking some men out of the keep this morning. The man who attacked ye escaped last evening. Walked out with the help of one of the serving lasses. Jamie wants him found. And his associates."

"Of course. We do, too, ye and I, but we've nay idea where—"

"Perhaps, but I ken the place to start. We're going back to where we camped. If there are tracks, we'll find them. While I am gone, ye must not leave the Fletcher keep for any reason."

A cold shiver crawled up Eilidh's back. "Ye think he's still nearby?"

"I dinna ken, but I willna have ye take any chances. Ye will stay where ye are safe. In here."

Eilidh fought down the childish urge to stomp her foot. Or better yet, to stomp Bhaltair's foot. She didn't like being told what to do, or being treated as though she could not take care of herself. But she'd tangled with her attacker once and did not want to do it again. And she didn't want to add to Bhaltair's problems. His words were meant to keep her safe when he could not be here to do it. So, she nodded. Her appetite had fled, but she continued eating. Her body would demand the fuel for the work she must do with Orla.

9

Bhaltair fought the urge to glance back over his shoulder at the open Fletcher gate. Would they close it, now that the man who'd attacked Eilidh had fled? And now that half of the Lathan guard and more of Fletcher's own had left the keep to search for him? They hadn't gone far before he heard the shouted command to close and secure it, and he relaxed. Eilidh would be safe behind Fletcher's stout walls while she cared for the bairn Orla, and, he hoped, soon found a way to cure her. She was a lovely wee lass. 'Twas a shame she was so ill. He'd enjoyed holding her, but more, he'd enjoyed the look on Eilidh's face as he did.

Niall exchanged a glance with him. "About time they did that," he remarked loud enough for their Fletcher escorts to hear. "If they kept them closed, the bastard wouldna have got out in the first place."

Bhaltair cut him a quelling look, but didn't comment. Sideways glances were coming from all the Fletcher guards, but they refrained from rising to Niall's bait. They knew he was right. So did Bhaltair, but to make an issue of the comment now was to invite argument, and that would not help them find their fugitive.

Instead, he kicked his horse into a faster gait. He knew where they were going. The Fletchers didn't. So they could follow Lathan's lead, at least for this much of their mission. And without the wagon that had slowed them on the way here, they would reach their campsite within a few hours, rather than traveling most of the day. What came after they reached the burnside and either found or didn't find tracks that led to their quarry remained to be seen. If it were Lathan land, Bhaltair would have traveled every inch of it and known every cave, every hidden glen, every hole in a tree where a man might hide. He hoped they found enough to suggest a hiding place to the Fletchers. Jamie had sent his best men. They should know this land very well.

The hours and the miles passed quickly, but not so quickly that Bhaltair didn't wonder which of the Fletcher men Jamie would hope to betroth Eilidh to if he convinced her to stay. Bhaltair thought the chance of that happening was nonexistent, but perhaps Jamie didn't understand the relationship between Eilidh and Aileana. Eilidh was her heir as much as Drummond was Toran's.

They kept watch as they went, hoping to encounter the man or men they sought before they traveled too far, but saw no one. They followed a burn near their destination. Before long, Bhaltair recognized the site of their campground and called a halt.

"This is the place," he informed the Fletcher guards. "We'll fan out from here. Pair yer lads with one of mine, and keep sharp. They may be huddled in a cave somewhere, but they could be spread out among all these trees."

"My men can work together more efficiently..."

"Yer men havena spent any time searching this area. Mine did, and have a good sense of the lay of the land hereabouts. So ye will search in pairs, one Fletcher with one Lathan. Ye and I will coordinate from here."

The Fletcher lead nodded, but his frown told Bhaltair he

wasn't convinced. "Ye men," Bhaltair said, raising his voice to be heard by all, "water yer mounts in the burn, then pair up."

In less time than he expected, one pair reported back that they'd found tracks. Bhaltair and the Fletcher lead guard went with him to investigate, and Bhaltair backtracked to the burn. The tracks were fresher than those made by his men when they camped here. He went back up the hill where the others waited by the tracks. "Follow them."

They left the horses with one of the men and continued on foot up the hillside, each man searching for any tracks that split off from the main set while they followed the leaders. The trees thinned and the ground got rockier as they went. Before the ground gave way completely to stone, the lead scout called a halt.

Bhaltair joined him and squatted next to the last set of footprints headed away from the burn before they disappeared onto rocks. They'd spent part of the day getting here from Fletcher, more getting past where his men had searched after the attack, and now, the trail they found had gone cold. "Damn," he muttered under his breath, but the Fletcher guard with him heard.

"The ground is rocky from here into the mountains," the man said. "We might find a trace here and there of a broken branch or a track in a patch of mud, but it'll be slow going. It'll be too dark to see in another hour. We should make camp and set out again in the morning."

Bhaltair hated to stop, but the Fletcher's advice was sensible. They'd accomplish nothing stumbling around in the dark except possibly to obscure any track they might come across. "Do it." Bhaltair stood and planted his fists on his hips, gazing up into the rocky hills. The tree cover got thinner the higher he looked. "If they're up there, they'll spot our camp fire. We'll have to do without one tonight."

"Aye. I hope ye brought plenty of plaids."

Bhaltair snorted. "Always."

EILIDH MET Caitrin outside Kellina and Orla's chamber. "How are ye doing?" the Fletcher laird asked.

Eilidh dropped her gaze, then straightened and met Caitrin's eyes. "'Twill take more time than I hoped to eliminate the foods the lass can eat and find the ones harming her. I wish I had a better answer for ye, but I believe this is the best way to be sure she is never harmed again."

"Then by all means, take the time ye need. Anything else ye need, simply ask and it will be provided."

Eilidh nodded and entered the chamber. Kellina held her daughter, looking so peaceful as the bairn slept in her arms that Eilidh hated to disturb them. It was the most simple and honest expression she'd yet seen Kellina wear. A mother's love for an ill child shone in her eyes, and the furrow on her brow expressed her worries.

She looked up as Eilidh entered the room and her expression turned fearful.

"Are ye going to hurt her?" The anxiety in Kellina's voice sounded real.

"Nay, of course not. I'm doing everything I can to make sure she's never hurt again."

Kellina's expression smoothed, as though she recalled that Eilidh was the one person who could save her daughter.

"Give her to Eilidh," Caitrin said, coming from behind Eilidh to regard her daughter and granddaughter. "Ye go get some sleep. Ye look knackered."

"I am. I wish I could sleep as well as she does."

"We all do," Caitrin said and gave her daughter a gentle smile.

Eilidh didn't know whether Caitrin referred to wishing Kellina slept as well, improving her mood, or that anyone would wish they could sleep as well as Orla. She stepped forward, took the lass from her mother, and placed her sitting up in her crib.

She nodded to Caitrin, who shepherded Kellina out of the room. When it was quiet and Orla seemed content to doze leaning against the pillows, Eilidh centered herself with a deep breath and touched Orla's face. She seemed the same as yesterday, so Eilidh chose another tisane and had her drink it. She didn't like the flavor of this one and spat or dribbled out much of it, but Eilidh sensed that enough had made it into her to give her the results she needed. She pulled up a chair and settled in to wait.

Hours later, the results were the same. No reaction. She tried another, one that Orla liked and swallowed happily. It also did no harm, but Orla was getting hungry. And so was she. It was time to call a halt for a while.

She went to the door, hoping to find Kellina or the Fletcher healer, who had been in earlier to change the bairn's swaddling, but the hallway was empty. Orla was fussing, so she didn't dare leave her alone. Resigned, she picked up the lass and carried her downstairs so the lass could eat a real meal. With Orla on her lap, Eilidh fed her bits of vegetables from a cooling bowl of stew, some potato from the stew, and a bit of bread and butter. It was enough to satisfy her and she soon dozed off again. Eilidh finished the stew, then carried Orla back to her crib, sat and waited.

Hours later, she woke from a light doze. Something had happened. She didn't know which of the things she fed the lass were harming her, but this reaction was enough to narrow her search.

Kellina returned just before the evening meal. "How is she?"

"I'm getting closer to an answer, but not there yet. Did ye sleep?"

"Aye. I'll take her now."

Eilidh filled her in on what she'd done with her daughter that day, then took her leave. She went back to her chamber to refresh herself, then back down to the great hall to eat. Delicious scents filled the air and her belly rumbled in response. Uncle Jamie saw her and beckoned her to his table. After filling him in on her progress, she attacked her meal. He left her in peace to enjoy it. When she finished and pushed back from the table with a sigh, Jamie chuckled. "Have ye ever used yer talent this way before?"

"Nay, never. I find it less intense, but so lengthy that the result is much the same. I need food, then sleep."

"I willna keep ye. Go to yer rest."

Only when she was in bed did she recall that she'd failed to ask after the guards he'd sent searching for her attacker. Bhaltair was one of them. She supposed if Jamie had heard anything, he would have told her. But she couldn't help wishing Bhaltair was back inside the Fletcher keep, safe, with her.

THE NIGHT PASSED UNEVENTFULLY, the guard changing every two hours. Bhaltair took his turn near dawn, wanting to be ready to continue the search at first light. He needn't have bothered. Trouble came to them.

He heard rustling before he saw any movement. They were coming down the hillside, but they weren't quiet. They moved from scraggly tree to bush, using whatever cover they found, but their woodcraft was poor. Were these the Lowlanders Jamie mentioned? They would be unused to moving quietly in the steep Highland mountains.

Bhaltair quickly roused the men, warning them with a finger over his lips to be silent. If the raiders thought the camp still asleep in the pre-dawn hour, he didn't want to disabuse them of the idea, not until it was too late for them to escape the combined Lathan and Fletcher force hunting them. Carefully, men drew weapons from sheaths and scabbards. Bhaltair motioned for a few to continue to feign sleep, while the others melted into the scattered brush and small trees around their camp. The raiders would come in after the sleeping men, and the ones in the trees would surround them and take them prisoner.

The first arrow missed its target's heart, but lodged in his arm. His yelp warned the rest of the men on the ground, who scrambled for cover, one pulling him along with them before more arrows fell on them. Bhaltair swore. His men were hidden, but so were the raiders. He signaled for his men to split into two groups and flank their attackers. He stayed with the injured man, cut the arrow shaft and wrapped the arm while watching for any indication of what the attackers planned to do next.

In moments, he heard the unmistakable sound of hand-to-hand fighting. "Go to the horses," he told the injured man. Ride for Fletcher. Tell Jamie we'll be coming with more injured. He'll ken what to do."

The man nodded and slipped away.

Bhaltair hoped the raiders hadn't scouted the horses before they began their noisy descent. That could have been a ruse to distract them, except that the fighting he heard was taking place where he'd heard the men come down from the hills. As soon as he heard a rider take off back the way they'd come, he headed for the fighting.

His men were outnumbered. One was down, injured, but he got back up before Bhaltair reached him. The others fought on, some against two opponents. Bhaltair waded in with fists and fury, breaking bones. He wanted them alive and talking. He didn't pull his dirk until one man came at him with a blade. Bhaltair swung, sending the man's blade flying and leaving a long slice on his fighting arm. The man backed off, but Bhaltair kept an eye on him as he engaged the next opponent. The first man found his blade and headed for Niall's back. Bhaltair picked up his own opponent and threw him. He knocked the first man down, and they stayed down. Niall glanced over his shoulder at the fallen men, then up at Bhaltair and grinned. "Thanks."

Bhaltair headed for the next two-on-one and quickly settled

the score there, as well. He looked for another opponent, but they were all either down or his men were finishing up with them. So he studied faces. The man who'd attacked Eilidh was not here. Was he part of this group, or had they been wrong to assume he had associates? Perhaps he had been what Eilidh supposed: a lone man down on his luck and taking the opportunity to better his circumstances—at a woman's expense.

He didn't believe it.

"Where is he?" He walked among the captives, grabbing a fistful of hair to pull their heads up and stare into their faces. The only thing he found was wide eyes, fear, or anger. Their quarry was not among them. "Where is the one called Pritchard? Ye ken that name, aye? Ye ken that man. He's one of ye."

A few of the captives looked at each other and shrugged. But one man met Bhaltair's gaze. Unflinching, he stared as if he knew something, but he didn't speak.

"Ye," Bhaltair challenged him as he stomped toward the man. "What do ye ken?"

"I met a man by that name a few days ago on the road south. He's long gone by now."

"How many days ago?"

The man closed his eyes and tilted his head as if giving Bhaltair's question some serious consideration.

"Answer me. How long ago?"

"Three days, I'd say."

"Ye are lying." The man they sought had escaped only two days ago.

"Maybe another man with the same name as the one ye seek?"

The fury rising in Bhaltair's throat chilled to cold contemplation. This man knew something. "How many more of ye are there?"

The man frowned at Bhaltair's sudden change of subject. "We are all there are."

"I think not." Someone had shot one of his men. "Where is yer archer?"

"Here." A man stepped out of the trees, bow cocked, arrow aimed at the middle of Eilidh's friend Cole's chest.

Bhaltair twisted away from the man he was questioning, and charged to the side to put himself between Cole and the arrow that would kill him. "Put that down. Ye've nowhere to go that we willna find ye. Make it easy on yerself."

The archer eyed Cole over his shoulder, but turned his attention to Bhaltair. "Easy fails to interest me. Ye, however, do. Ye are willing to die to save yer man for the few seconds it would take me to nock another arrow. I could have killed any of ye but I chose to enjoy the battle from the trees." He lifted his chin. "Ye are quite a fighter. So, tell me, how well do ye fight with an arrow in yer leg?" His aim dropped and he loosed the arrow. Before it struck Bhaltair's thigh, he'd notched another. "Or yer arm?" The next arrow sank into the muscle of Bhaltair's opposite arm.

Bhaltair fought the scream of agony that filled his throat. It escaped as a hiss through clenched teeth as he advanced on the man.

The archer was slower to ready the next arrow, and when he loosed it, it went wide of the mark and lodged in someone behind him. Bhaltair didn't look around when the man cried out. He kept his gaze on his tormentor. The archer's eyes widened with each step as Bhaltair closed the distance between them. Bhaltair didn't give him time to nock another. He swung with his good arm and fist. The archer dropped like a stone. Bhaltair picked up his bow and broke it over his wounded leg.

"God's teeth, Bhaltair. I've never seen anything like that," one of the Fletchers exclaimed as several others ran to their wounded man. The arrow had cut a swath through the outside edge of his upper arm, nearly a miss. His clansmen were binding the wound to stop the bleeding. He would live.

"Pray ye never do again," Bhaltair answered. He gestured to

Cole. "Cut these shafts off and bind them before they do more damage. I need to ride. Him, too," he said with a nod to the wounded Fletcher.

"We're going back?"

"I am. If the Fletcher can ride, send him now. He'll reach Fletcher faster alone than I will and can send help if the first man didn't make it. Ye lot will continue the search for Pritchard."

"What do ye want us to do with them?"

"Release them. All but him," he added, nodding toward the archer. "He goes back with me. And that one," he said and pointed to the man who seemed to know something. "Make him talk. He kenned the name. I think he kens the man, and where he is." He pointed up the hill. "Maybe still up there."

"We'll find him," Cole promised.

"See that ye do. Bring both of them back to Fletcher. And bind the archer, hands behind his back. I dinna care if he pisses himself or worse. Tie him to a horse."

"I should come with ye," Cole insisted. "Ye took the arrow meant for me. Ye may need help."

"Ye should do what ye're told," Bhaltair growled. His wounds were throbbing and he had an hours-long ride ahead of him, with a prisoner he couldn't outfight and dared not trust. He was in no mood to be contradicted—or coddled.

10

Eilidh knew she should be exhausted, but she couldn't sleep. Bhaltair was still out there, somewhere. And she'd woken up before dawn with a bad feeling that hadn't lessened as the morning progressed. She continued to work with Orla, giving her tisanes made from the ingredients in last evening's meal in pairs, hoping to speed up the process. So far, she hadn't reacted to anything.

Tired, frustrated, and hungry herself, Eilidh called a halt at midday, letting the healer step in for her and keep an eye on the bairn. If she showed signs of distress, the healer would send someone to Eilidh. In the meantime, she would try to eat and rest.

While she finished an early midday meal, Bhaltair stayed on her mind. In her imagination. Did she have some of her twin Tavish's foretelling talent. Was Bhaltair in danger?

That was daft. He had men from both clans with him, and he was the most feared warrior she kenned. Surely they all would return soon, with or without their quarry. She hoped that man had fled the area. She didn't want to think about what Bhaltair might do to him if he caught him.

She needed to stretch her legs and forget her worries. She'd take a walk around the bailey. Maybe there would be some people to meet to take her mind off Bhaltair—and Orla and her mother. She'd been too busy since she arrived to make friends with any of the Fletchers besides Caitrin, but Eilidh would not impose on her. The laird had many important things to do.

She wandered the bailey and exchanged greetings with the Fletchers she passed. Finding them all too busy to stop and talk, she made her way to the stable and petted each horse that came to its stall door to greet her. They cheered her. When one of the stable lads also greeted her, that cheered her even more. Perhaps not all of the Fletchers wanted to avoid her.

"What's yer name, lad?"

"Brian, Lady Eilidh."

"Ah, ye ken who I am."

"Everyone does."

"No one seems to want to speak to me."

"They dinna wish to disturb ye. They ken ye are working very hard to save wee Orla, so they leave ye in peace."

"I think I've had enough peace. Tell me, do ye have cats in the stable? Are there any kittens?"

The lad grinned. "Aye. All the lasses want to play with the kittens."

"I'm a lass, too."

He got a stricken look on his face. "I didna say ye were not."

"Nay, ye didna. *Dinna fash.*"

He relaxed and smiled at her. "The kittens are in the back stall. We keep an eye on them, but the horses are really good. They dinna step on them or anything."

"Wise horses ye have here."

"Aye, we just got some from MacDhai. Best in Scotland."

"So I've heard," Eilidh replied, entirely without irony. The lad couldn't know her connection to the MacDhai laird, her older sister's husband.

"Here they be," the lad said. "The lasses like to sit on that bale, there, to keep their skirts clean. Well, sort of. If ye have a bit of meat the kittens will come right to ye. They're near to weaned."

Eilidh's face fell. "I didna think of that."

"Wait a moment. I'll fetch some." The lad ran across the aisle to what served as a tack room, and came back with a chicken leg. "Ye tear off a wee bit. Dinna give them the bone or the gristle, just a wee bit of meat."

"I promise," Eilidh told him and took her bribe into the stall. As the lad predicted, the kittens came running, and soon she had a lap full of them, all trying to climb her to get to the meat. She fed each tiny pieces, then tossed the bone and gristle back to the lad. Undeterred, the kittens continued to search her, licking her fingers and making her laugh. "I needed this," she said to herself, but the lad, still there, heard her.

"I like to come in here myself," he admitted shyly. "They're fun to watch."

On cue, two of the kittens abandoned her to chase each other around the stall. A third pounced on a fourth and pandemonium broke loose. Eilidh laughed through it all.

"'Tis good to laugh, aye?"

Eilidh glanced up in surprise to find Caitrin leaning against the open stall door. "Aye. 'Tis medicine for a tired healer."

"Or for anyone."

"What brings ye out here?" Eilidh noted that the stable lad had stepped away. She and Caitrin were alone.

"A rider just came in with an arrow wound. Says they were ambushed before first light, but he expected the fight to go in our favor. Bhaltair sent him back to be cared for, and to tell Jamie what had happened. Jamie will be taking out more men."

"But ye need me to care for the wounded man."

"I'm sorry, but aye. Playtime is over."

Eilidh cuddled the last kitten in her lap, a wee tri-color that had curled up and gone to sleep once her littermates abandoned

Eilidh to play on the floor. Then she set down the kitten, stood, and followed Caitrin back into the keep.

DESPITE THE BINDINGS keeping the arrows in his leg and arm from shifting too much, Bhaltair was losing blood. He knew it, and worse, his prisoner knew it, too. The horses were tied together, and Bhaltair used a lash to encourage his prisoner's horse to stay a length in front of his. He didn't want the man out of his sight, behind him, or close enough to reach him. But the archer kept looking back at him.

"Ye know if ye pass out, I'll leave ye dead and ride away with two of yer horses," the man boasted.

Bhaltair knew he was starting to sway. His vision was clouding over and he had to blink hard to clear it. He had to stay in the saddle to get them back to Fletcher. Bhaltair kept forcing himself to breathe, to clear his vision, and to convince his captive that he wasn't ready to fall yet. Pain was his friend. It kept him awake, if not entirely alert to his surroundings.

They'd been riding for hours. He couldn't stand the pace they'd set when they left Fletcher yesterday, but they had to be in Fletcher territory by now. Had the man arrived whom Bhaltair sent ahead with the arrow in his arm? Had he been another victim of this archer? Or were there more? It didn't matter. He and the archer should be met by Jamie and his men before they reached the Fletcher keep. Bhaltair hoped so. He was beginning to think he might not make it that far.

He didn't bother to answer the archer's boast. He kept his gaze on the way ahead and tried to ignore the throbbing agony in his leg and arm. He was strong enough to bear it for a few more hours—as long as he didn't bleed out. Once he got back to Eilidh, she would take care of him. He'd be healed in no time.

But the archer would have a lot to answer for. "What are ye and yer men doing in those hills?"

"My men? What makes ye think they're my men?"

"I ken a leader when I see one. Those men watched ye with a great deal of interest. They ken ye, and they follow yer lead. So, what are ye doing up there?"

"What anyone does. Surviving. Living."

"Stealing from helpless lasses?"

"Ah, the name ye mentioned. Did he steal from yer wife? Yer daughter? Or did he do more than that?"

Fury made a red haze fill Bhaltair's vision. And made him lightheaded. He needed to stay calm or he would bleed faster. "He didna get the chance. He ran, like the coward he is."

"Yet ye caught him, but *ach*, how sad, he got away."

"By seducing another lass into helping him. She lost her position because of it."

"Too bad. So ye are searching for him again. Why? Wouldn't it be simpler to forget him? He's already gone."

"So ye say. And how did ye ken we caught him? Or that he got away. I never mentioned that." Bhaltair felt a rush of satisfaction. The archer could make a mistake. And he'd just made a big one. "He is one of yer men, aye?"

"What if he is? Do ye truly expect me to give him up?"

"We captured the rest of yer men and released them. Perhaps that is worth giving up one man in trade."

"Ah, but since ye already let my men go, I have no need to trade for them. Still, ye have me as well, though I doubt ye are willing to release me. What else can I bargain with?"

"I'm sure ye ken many things of interest." Bhaltair winced as his mount's gait altered on a downhill slope.

"Ye give me too much credit."

"Perhaps. But when I get ye where we're going, ye willna be able to lie."

His captive frowned at that. "What do you mean?"

Did he sound nervous? His accent, never strong, had slipped and he sounded more like someone from the south, or farther, on the borders with England. "Ye will find out when we arrive."

"There are many ways to make a man talk. None guarantee that he will speak the truth." The archer gave a noncommittal shrug. "If ye plan to torture me, I can assure ye, I will say anything ye wish to hear to make it stop, whether 'tis the truth or nay."

Bhaltair snorted. "I ken the value of torture. Ye waste yer breath trying to make me doubt yer word. I will ken the truth when ye speak it."

"How will ye do that?"

"For a man who claims he will say anything I wish to hear, ye seem disconcerted."

"What ye speak of hints at unholy methods. I have heard that ye Highlanders have such among ye as can wield spells."

Ye Highlanders? So, he was from the south. "Spells?"

"The power of compulsion, among others."

"Who among us might those be? I've never met anyone, but they could be useful."

"Witches doing the Devil's work." The archer spat. "Torture is cleaner."

Bhaltair frowned, but smoothed his expression as the archer looked around at him. "So ye prefer pain? As much as ye like to inflict it, that doesna surprise me." But Bhaltair was surprised. The man had just admitted he was not a Highlander, and that Highland tales had made an impression in the Lowlands likely to bring trouble. What else was coming their way?

"Eilidh, they're back! Bhaltair needs ye!" Caitrin's voice echoed down the hall to Orla's room. Eilidh had just finished seeing if the latest set of tisanes had produced any changes. They had not.

She'd hoped to get some supper and rest again, but it sounded like that would have to wait.

Bhaltair was back? A rush of relief made her giddy until she realized Caitrin's voice had held real urgency. Who was hurt? Not Bhaltair! He'd gone out with several men, and the man who's arrow wound she'd healed earlier had said the fight was still going on when he left. But that was hours ago. Another man had arrived a few hours ago with only a flesh wound. The Fletcher healer had insisted on caring for him, certain he did not need Eilidh's special care.

"How many are hurt?" Eilidh wiped her hands on a clean rag and met Caitrin at the door.

"Only Bhaltair," Caitrin replied, grabbed her arm and started marching her toward the stairs.

But Eilidh's knees went weak and she reached out to the wall for support, halting them. "Bhaltair?"

"He's in Jamie's solar. Arrow in one arm, one leg. He's lost a lot of blood. Thank goodness his man got here earlier and had Jamie ride out with more men. They met him on the way—with a prisoner—and hurried him back or he might not have made it."

Eilidh's stomach roiled. "He's dying?" Anger spiked, too. Pritchard was not worth Bhaltair's life.

"Not if ye can save him, lass. Come! He needs ye."

Dear God. "Aye, take me to him."

She followed Caitrin down the stairs as quickly as she dared, and ran across the great hall to the laird's solar. They'd put Bhaltair on the table there, and the Fletcher healer was fussing with the wrappings around arrow shafts. "Stop!"

Her command came out as a croak, but the healer froze and turned to Eilidh, wide-eyed. "We need to remove the tips carefully, without doing more damage. I can. While I do that, make him drink. Watered ale or cider. And find me a bottle of whisky."

"Now is not the time for ye to drink, lass," the healer chided.

"'Tis for his wounds, not me," Eilidh replied, exasperated. "Someone, hurry."

"I'll get what ye need," Caitrin said and left the room.

Eilidh lay her hands over the wound in the meat of Bhaltair's thigh. It wasn't close to the groin or it would have cut the big vessel there, and he would not have lived to return. But it was the more dangerous of the two wounds. There were other big blood vessels in the leg, and if the arrow had pierced the biggest, she might not be able to heal the wound fast enough to save him. Blood would spurt with each beat of his heart. How he had survived the ride back mystified her. Blood still welled where it had soaked the makeshift bandage and run down the leg of his trews onto his boots. She suspected his mount was covered in it as well.

Nay, she couldn't think that way. She would save him. This was Bhaltair. The strongest man she knew. He would fight to live, and she would fight along with him with everything in her. She moved to his arm. As she suspected, the arrow had lodged in muscle, like the leg wound, but would be a much easier task to heal.

Caitrin came back with a mug and a pitcher. "Cider. For him and for ye. I ken ye dinna have time to eat yet. This will help. Jamie keeps MacKyrie whisky in here. I'll find it."

"Perfect," Eilidh said and drank down two cups full. "Now him," she said to the Fletcher healer. "Dribble some into his mouth. Dinna choke him. Just encourage him to swallow. He might rouse enough to raise his head and drink more."

While the healer did that, Eilidh went back to studying the damage the arrow had done to Bhaltair's leg, dimly aware of Caitrin searching and finally murmuring, "Aha." Eilidh turned to the healer. "I need yer sharpest blade. If ye dinna have one, ask cook for a boning blade. Something thin and sharp."

"I ken just the thing." The healer left.

Caitrin took over and managed to get enough liquid into Bhaltair to make him splutter awake. "Wha' the hell?"

Eilidh moved quickly to where he could see her. "Ye are wounded."

"Eilidh." He reached toward her with his good arm. "Ach, ken that. Hurts like hell."

"I'm going to fix it, but ye need to drink as much of this cider as ye can."

He nodded and she helped him raise up on his good arm's elbow. Caitrin handed him the cup and he downed it, then another and another. "Enough?" He lay back down.

"For now. I'm going to put ye in a healing sleep—"

"Nay. Yer mother does that. I'd rather ken what ye are doing."

"Ye'd rather not. Trust me," she said, and with a look, asked Caitrin to back up out of the way. She touched Bhaltair's forehead and told him to sleep.

"That was fast," Caitrin remarked.

"It always is."

The healer returned with a selection of blades. "This one is mine, that one is Cook's, as is that one."

Eilidh nodded. "Thank ye." She picked up all three and examined them, then chose one, poured whisky into a clean cup and plunged the blade into the spirit.

"What are ye doin'?"

"It will help keep the wound from going putrid."

She made quick work of cutting away the bandage and the leg of his trews around the wound. The blade was sharp. "I need ye both to be still and quiet. Close the door and lock it. Sit where I canna see ye. I'll ask for help if I need it. Ready?"

Eilidh dunked the blade in the whisky again, applied it to Bhaltair's leg and cut a slit on either side of the arrow's shaft. "This is why I want ye asleep, ye daft man." She kept one hand on his flesh, feeling for the tissue the blade parted, sealing off blood vessels as she went. Her leg throbbed in sympathy, but she ignored it. She made slow and careful work of cutting until she reached the arrow's tip and freed it. The major blood vessels were intact, but that part of Bhaltair's leg looked like a flayed-open trout.

"Now to put it all back together," she muttered. "Can someone hand me the whisky bottle?" It was out of her reach and she didn't want to let go of Bhaltair. Someone, she didn't know who, put it in her free hand. She nodded and poured whisky into the wound.

Whoever handed her the bottle hissed in sympathy, telling her it must have been the Fletcher healer.

"Or this, either, Bhaltair. Ye'd be shouting loud enough, they'd hear ye in the Aerie."

As it was, her leg suddenly felt like it was on fire. Damn. "I need to sit." She felt a chair slide close and touch behind her knees. Gratefully, she sank down onto it, never losing contact with her patient.

Healing the wound, knitting together the severed tissue, blood vessels, nerves and other structures, went slowly. It was fully dark outside by the time she finished. Over the metallic scent of blood and smoky whisky, she smelled whatever Cook had prepared for supper. She let go of Bhaltair's leg and leaned back with a sigh. "I'm done with this part."

"How is he?" Caitrin came to her, but didn't touch her.

Eilidh gave her a grateful smile. She didn't need any more stimulation right now. "He'll sleep until I wake him, or until morning. I want to eat something, then I'll take care of his arm. It will heal much faster, and then I can rest."

"Will he be able to move to a bed?"

Eilidh knew she was tired when she failed to react to that. "Nay, he'll stay where he is. When he wakes, he'll need food and drink, and a bath and clean clothes. I'll stay with him. I can sleep on a pallet on the floor."

"I'll have the lads bring in a cot."

"Ye willna need the solar?"

"Nay, Jamie took more men out to help the ones left behind."

Eilidh nodded. "Thank ye. Now, supper?"

Food and healing Bhaltair's arm took the rest of the evening. The fire was stoked and a cot covered in quilts waited for her. Caitrin brought more blankets for Bhaltair, too. Once Caitrin and the healer left, the solar became still and quiet. She had time to wonder if Uncle Jamie and the other men would return soon, or if they had, and she had been too tired to notice. She was in no shape to deal with life-threatening wounds. Not without sleep.

Still, she took a minute to stand by Bhaltair and just look at him. Even in sleep, he was formidable. Muscular. Heartbreakingly handsome. She wanted to curl up against him, but he took up most of the tabletop. And if someone came in—nay, she dared not try. She turned to her cot and lay down.

Before she could doze off, raised voices reached her from the great hall. What was going on?

11

The solar door opened and Caitrin rushed in. "I'm so sorry, Eilidh. Jamie is back with more wounded men. Apparently there was a battle this morning. Bhaltair was not the only one hurt, just the worst injured. Can ye see to them?"

Eilidh rolled to sitting and rubbed her face with both hands. "Aye, of course. Is the healer awake?"

"I've sent for her. She'll handle the minor wounds, which should be most of them. I ken ye are at yer limits."

"Nay, I am not." She stood. "Let's go."

On her way past him, she put a hand on Bhaltair's arm, stopped and frowned. "He's warm."

"Too many blankets?"

"Nay, he's too warm for that." She probed the wound on his arm, then moved around him to his leg. "Damn, this isna good."

"What do ye need?"

"Something for fever. More for him to drink. I dinna want to wake him, because the newly healed tissue is fragile, and he willna be still, but I will do what I must to fight a fever."

"I'll get what ye need from the healer and Cook."

"Thank ye. While ye do that, I'll see to the men in the great hall."

Eilidh worked through the night, the healer nearby caring for the lesser wounded. In between healing and checking on her patients in the great hall, she slipped into the solar and checked on the man who concerned her the most. She'd let Bhaltair sleep, but by sunup, she would wake him and start treating the fever. The leg was infected, though she didn't know how. She'd cleaned the wound, and poured whisky in it. It should not have festered. But it was the worst of the two wounds he'd taken, and the arrow had remained in it for hours, jostled the entire time by riding. Perhaps the arrowhead had been dirty, or deliberately dipped in something, to cause a wound to fester. She didn't know, and that worried her. She didn't want to cut it open again, but she might have to.

Uncle Jamie came in during one of her visits. "How is he?"

"He should be well, but he's got a fever. I'm puzzled, but I will find the cause and fix it."

"I ken ye will, lass. When will he wake?"

She glanced toward the window. Pearly gray light leaked in around the coverings. "Soon. If not on his own, I'll wake him."

"Good. I want his impressions of the archer before I interrogate him."

Eilidh nodded. They'd gone after her attacker and found something worse. What was going on in the mountains around Fletcher?

BHALTAIR CAME TO. One moment he wasn't aware, and the next, he was. He could hear and see and feel. Mostly what he felt was hot. And thirsty.

"Here, drink this."

The soft, feminine voice drew his attention and he looked toward it. Eilidh! She leaned toward him with a cup. He lifted his head, but didn't think he could drink like that, so he raised up on one elbow. His head spun, but she held the cup to his lips and tipped it. He swallowed greedily, grateful for the cool wetness that revived his parched mouth and throat.

Then the taste registered. Willow bark tea. Bitter. Nasty. And used to treat fevers. His wounds had festered. He glanced down at his arm but saw only the faint redness of a scar. His leg was under the covers. He tugged them aside and saw it healed, too. He pushed the cup away, spilling some of what remained of his shirt.

"What happened?"

"Drink, and I'll tell ye." She met his gaze steadily, a slight crease between her brows.

He knew that look. She would not quit. So he drank, grimacing the whole time, and finished the cup.

She set it aside. "Lie back and rest. Yer wounds are better. The leg festered a wee. I'm watching it. It should not have done so, but it did. If need be, I'll open it and clean it out again."

Bhaltair dropped back with a groan. "Poison?"

"I dinna think so. Not in the conventional sense. I think the arrow tips were dipped in excrement. Animal or human, I dinna ken. Despite cleaning the wound and pouring whisky into it—"

"Ye did what?"

"Ye were asleep. Ye never felt it. And it should have kept this from happening. But there must have been a wee fragment left. 'Tis an insidious, diabolical way to ensure that even a flesh wound will likely kill the intended target. But in this case, the archer didna count on me."

"Is he in the dungeon?"

Eilidh shrugged. "Ye'll have to ask Uncle Jamie. I've been too busy to inquire."

"Who else?"

"Hurt? Several of yer search party had minor wounds. The Fletcher healer took them. I had ye to tend to, and a few others with greater damage from yer fight yesterday morning. They'll be fine in a few days. They told me what happened to ye."

"How do ye do this, Eilidh? How do ye care for so many?"

"Ye should be used to it. As many times as my mother has had to patch up ye and yer men, what I do should be no mystery to ye."

"It isna. And yet, 'tis. I'm glad to be in yer care." He rolled to his side and regarded her. "Will I break anything if I sit up?"

She frowned, then held out a hand. "Nay. Let me help ye."

"I can do it."

"Ye have lost a lot of blood."

He silenced her protests by simply sitting up and taking her face in his hands. "I will be fine. Ye have the care of me."

"And ye need more to drink—not willow bark tea," she said when he scowled. "Not yet. I have cider and watered ale. Which do ye prefer?"

"Ye always say cider is better for regaining strength."

She stepped out of his grasp and found another cup, filled it and handed it to him. Ah, cold, sweet and free of willow bark bitterness. He finished it and held out the cup for more. He was feeling revived enough to take note of Eilidh. She looked frazzled. Exhausted. Pale and tired. Dark circles shadowed the skin under her eyes. She had healed him and taken his pain, then done the same for others. Yet she found the will to wait on him and to give him an encouraging smile when he drank down the second cup of cider. If ever he'd thought he was the stronger of the two of them, he'd been wrong.

"That's enough for now," she told him when he held out the cup. "Or yer belly will protest."

"It already does. 'Tis empty."

"Let the cider settle for a few minutes. I'll fetch ye some stew."

"Nay, stay with me." He grabbed her hand before she stepped away. "Someone else can fetch and carry. Ye need rest. Sit with me."

She settled on the tabletop beside him. He put an arm around her shoulders.

She leaned against him, careful not to overbalance him, but seeking his warmth. His strength. "I feared for ye. There was so much blood."

"I'm tough to kill."

"I'm glad. I wonder what the archer thought as ye advanced on him with two of his arrows in ye."

"I plan to ask him that question. Among others. I dinna ken what that band is doing in the hills, but Fletcher will be at risk as long as they are there. And as long as men like the archer associate with them."

Eilidh frowned. "He's a monster."

"He'd like his victims to think so."

"Ye dinna?"

"I dinna ken yet. Cruelty, especially needless cruelty, is a sickness, but it also weakens those around him. Many would be dismayed by his actions. If he is the leader of that band, he rules by fear, and fear doesna inspire loyalty."

"Let Caitrin be there when ye question him. She will see through his lies."

"I ken it. I've heard the tales."

"They're true," Eilidh said and with a sigh, leaned her head on his shoulder. "She can help."

As if summoned, Caitrin entered the solar, followed closely by Jamie. Bhaltair was glad to see them. They'd have answers to some of his questions.

"Still with us, I see," Caitrin remarked, approached and took his free hand. "I'm glad of it."

"Nay half so glad as I am," Bhaltair replied with a grin, then he sobered. "What have ye learned?"

Caitrin turned to her husband. "Jamie?"

"Little so far. The archer and a few others are locked up. I've left him to contemplate his sins while we waited for ye to wake up. The men still out searching havena reported in yet. I brought in the rest of the wounded last night. Is she asleep?"

Bhaltair glanced down at Eilidh. She felt boneless, leaning against him. His arm around her shoulders kept her propped up. "Aye."

"Thank goodness," Caitrin said. "She's exhausted every reserve of strength she possessed."

"I'll carry her up to bed," Jamie offered.

Bhaltair shook his head. "She'll want to be here. Put her on the cot and let her sleep. Tell the healer. I dinna ken how often they want me drinking willow bark tea. Nasty stuff. But if it keeps me alive and able to act, I'll drink a hogshead dry."

"I'll tell her," Caitrin said. "Jamie, can ye move Eilidh without waking her?"

"She isna a bairn. I dinna ken, but I'll give it a try."

"I'll help," Bhaltair offered, but in truth, he wasn't certain he could stand and stay on his feet, much less help carry the lass.

"Nay need," Jamie said and lifted her easily with an arm under her thighs and the other behind her back. He moved to the cot and draped her on it, then covered her. "I think she's down for a while."

"I hope so," Caitrin said in agreement.

"Then ye can help me," Bhaltair said with a meaningful look in Jamie's direction. Eilidh had been forcing him to drink. It was time to take care of that.

"Under the table. I'll go fetch the healer," Caitrin said.

"And some stew," Bhaltair said, "if ye please."

"Of course." She left them.

The healer arrived after a convenient period of time, slapped a hand on Bhaltair's forehead and pronounced him better. A serving girl followed with a tray bearing a bowl of stew, a hunk of bread and watered ale, then took away the chamber pot.

"Eat all ye can," the healer advised. "Yer lass will want to ken ye are stronger when she wakes up."

His lass? Distracted, he tore off a chunk of bread and dunked it in the stew. Rich, meaty aromas drifted up, making his mouth water. But he had sense enough to take it slowly. His lass would be upset if he made himself sick.

He glanced around at the sleeping beauty on the cot behind him. Eilidh barely moved, even to breathe. She was spent.

"What do ye remember about the archer?"

Jamie's question startled him and he twisted back around to face him. "How do ye mean?"

"How did he behave?"

"He shot me."

"How? Was he methodical? Emotionless? Or did he enjoy it? How did he relate to the other men, and they to him?"

"I didna have time to notice. I was getting skewered." He thought for a moment while he took another bite of stew. "Actually, I do remember this. He seemed quite sure of himself. Of his accuracy with the bow. He never meant to kill me. Not then anyway. He enjoyed torturing me and I got a flash of anger from him when I didna immediately fall from the first arrow. And fear when I advanced on him, before I attacked him, despite being wounded. He wasna used to having his quarry defy him."

"That's more than I kenned about him so far. He'll be afraid of ye. When ye walk in with yer wounds healed, ye will see the proof."

"He'll think I'm a witch. Or that someone else here is one." He twisted to study Eilidh's sleeping form again. "He said a few things on the way here. I'm not certain letting him see me is a good idea."

"He's a monster, so fair's fair. I expect bluster and lies, but Caitrin will see through those."

"Do ye want her anywhere near him?"

"Aye. I want him off balance. I want him to ken we understand what he is."

12

Hours later, Eilidh woke to find Bhaltair sitting in a chair between the hearth and her cot, his gaze on her. "Ye are watching me sleep," she said, not certain if that comforted her or made her nervous.

"I am. Ye are worth watching."

"I must look like I spent the night in a Highland storm," she protested, shoving her hair out of her face and sitting up.

"Ye need food, and more sleep, and more care than I can give ye, but I can watch over ye."

"I could say the same about ye." She pushed to her feet and went to him. Before he could move, she put a hand to his forehead. "Cooler, but still a wee high."

"The fever is gone. I'm warm from the hearth. And seeing ye. For a while, on the way here, I wasna certain I would get the chance ever again."

"Bhaltair..." She choked on his name, his despair and fear making her belly hollow out. But she was still groggy enough not to want to be able to analyze how many ways he meant it, except that he feared he would die before he reached her. The thought nearly took her legs out from under her.

"I have eaten all the stew the healer brought me. I feel well enough that ye dinna have to stay with me. Go have a bath and another sleep."

"So should ye," she told him. He still smelled of the blood soaking his trews and boots. He must be uncomfortable.

"Aye, I should, but I wouldna leave yer side."

Her heart clenched. Was that devotion? Or merely Bhaltair taking care of his duty to her da? "I thought that was my job," she told him.

He looked up and captured her gaze, his eyes the clear blue of an icy loch in winter. She'd always suspected they were the same as his heart, cold. But she'd found out just how wrong she'd been.

"Why canna we both care for the other?"

Eilidh straightened, a rush of heat in her blood making her sway. "What are ye trying to say?"

Bhaltair lifted a hand to her waist. "That I nearly died. I had time while it was happening to regret a few things, including that we've given each other hungry looks long enough."

"We have?" She thought she was the only one guilty of that. Had he been looking at her the same way? How had she missed it? They'd talked of taking time—as much time as they needed, not hungry looks.

But she hadn't missed his attention on her. She knew he watched her. She just always thought he was looking out for her. Guarding her. Doing his job. Not that he cared for her in this way.

"Ye still fear me," he said, breaking the silence. "Even now."

"I... used to, aye. I thought I hid it, but I guess I didna."

"And now?" His hand moved up her back and pulled her closer.

She let herself take the step he demanded. "I dinna think so."

"But ye are not certain of me, even after all the years ye have kenned me. After this? Healing me? Touching me with yer senses?"

"I want to be."

"Let me show ye." He pulled her onto his lap and held her in the circle of his powerful arms. "Ye have slept in my embrace twice now. 'Tis time for me to give ye more than simple comfort."

"More?" She must still be groggy. Her brain felt like *porritch*. She couldn't seem to put a coherent sentence together, yet she liked where she was. She wanted to stay. So she lifted a hand to his cheek. "What do ye have in mind?" She needn't ask the question. Her touch told him how his body responded to her.

"This," he said, bent his head and kissed her. His lips touched hers softly at first. As her chest rose on a breath and they parted, he kissed her more firmly. For a man as big and hard as he was, his lips were full and soft against hers, hot and gently demanding. He moved them over hers, encouraging her to respond. She couldn't stop herself. His kiss woke something in her that she had kept tightly leashed, but with his touch and the desire she sensed in his blood, she could no longer control herself. She kissed him back, then nipped at his lip. He tasted of cider and stew. And himself, that heady musk that she could not resist.

He groaned and pulled her more tightly against him, his big hand splayed on her back, then he traced the seam of her parted lips with his tongue. She touched the tip of hers to his lips, then met his tongue and opened to his exploration. Her talent gave her a sense of what he was feeling, making her breasts swell and a strange clawing sense of need twist the lower half of her body. Neither of them had energy to spare, yet this touching, this exploration, seemed to revive them both. Bolts of lightning kept flashing from everywhere he touched her to the apex of her thighs, making her squirm in his lap. The flames in his blood leapt higher with every move she made.

"Ach, Eilidh, dinna do that, or I willna be able to stop until I've loved all of ye."

Eilidh heard the desperation in his voice and liked it. It made her feel strong and powerful. She could make the man she wanted, a man as big and strong and fearsome as Bhaltair beg for her. Want to seduce her. To have her.

Before she returned to the Aerie and he stayed at Fletcher? That thought chilled the passion coursing through her. She lifted her head.

What was she thinking? They were in the laird's solar. Anyone might open the door and come in at any time. She put a hand on his chest. "I'm not ready for that, nor are ye. And this is not the place or time."

He rested his forehead against hers for a moment, then straightened up. "Ye are right. I'm sorry. I shouldna—"

"Did I complain? Did I run screaming from the chamber?" She slipped off his lap and stood, smiling, to soften her rebuke. Even though she couldn't yet be sure of him, he'd been through so much, she couldn't chastise him. "Dinna apologize." She held up a hand when he opened his mouth to speak. "Please. We both need a bath and more food and rest." Ach, why did she have to mention a bath? Immediately she saw he was recalling her in hers. "Stop it. I'll tell the steward to ready a bath for ye in yer chamber—or are ye sleeping in the barracks with yer men when ye are not sleeping outside my door?" How did she not know that?

"Aye, I have been, until this."

"In the barracks, then. Ye can get cleaned up and have another meal. I'll do the same." She started toward the door. "I need to check on Orla, too." She turned back and raked him with her gaze. He stood, not bothering to hide the evidence of his desire for her. She closed her eyes and took a breath. "We'll continue this... later." Then she fled, as fast as her feet would carry her. Her dreams of having Bhaltair, of making him hers, might be coming true, but despite having longed for him and dreamed about him for years, she wasn't ready. She didn't fear him anymore, not in the way she had as a younger lass, afraid of a large, intimidating man. But she had sense enough to know they had to go slowly. That must not change. And they both were smart enough to realize it. They'd both thrown down a gauntlet. It remained to be seen who would be the first to pick up one of them.

BHALTAIR WALKED BACK into the great hall for the evening meal feeling restored and hungry. A hot bath, several hours sleep, and clean clothes seemed to make all the difference. As long as his fever didn't return, he could concentrate on regaining the strength in his arm and leg, and on dealing with the archer, and with the rest of the problems Eilidh's attacker had caused.

And Eilidh.

How would he face her? He'd been much too forward. Much too eager for the first time touching her. Kissing her. How would she react when she saw him?

He stopped inside the doorway and looked around, finding several of his men, a few still sporting bandages, at one table. Jamie and the Fletcher laird were at the head table with their daughter Kellina, but he didn't see Eilidh. He hoped she was still resting, but knowing her, he doubted it. She'd mentioned checking on the bairn Orla before she left him in the solar. He'd bet she'd gotten involved with her and had not gotten any rest at all.

He was tempted to go up there and drag her out by her hair, make her eat, and carry her back upstairs to bed. He quelled the urge and headed for his men.

"What news?" He sat down and looked around the table. They all paused their conversations or eating and gave him their attention. "Have ye heard anything while I was healing?"

"Nay," Niall said, shaking his head. "I think they're waiting for ye."

"Jamie told me as much," Bhaltair said. "He thinks I'll scare the archer into talking when I show up without any wounds." He should enjoy seeing his tormentor suffer, but the prospect worried him, too. "Have they found the man who attacked Eilidh?"

"Nay. I'd lay coin that he's either fled the area, or yer friend the archer killed him and got rid of the body."

Bhaltair thought about that while a serving lass put a trencher, cup and pitcher of cider in front of him. "The laird says ye are to drink all of that," she told him with a wink. He ignored her and she backed off. He wasn't interested in dallying with the servants when the woman he wanted was up those stairs. He couldn't help keeping an eye on the steps, hoping Eilidh would walk down them soon.

He listened to the ebb and flow of conversation at nearby tables while he ate, but there was nothing of interest being said anywhere. No news that affected Eilidh, his men, or the Fletchers. Eventually, he made a show of upending the pitcher of cider, pouring the last drops into his cup and emptying it where Caitrin could see him. She grinned and he grinned back.

When the hall started clearing, Jamie stood and came over to join him and his men. "When do ye want to speak to the archer?"

"Where's Eilidh?" Bhaltair said at the same time.

Jamie laughed. "I see where yer priorities lie. She's sleeping, or should be."

"Or with the bairn?"

"She was earlier, but Caitrin threw her out. I dinna expect to see her until tomorrow."

"Good. I want to sleep a few more hours. Let's wake that bastard after midnight. If he's tired and groggy, he might let something slip he wouldna otherwise say."

Jamie nodded. "That makes sense. I agree. He's said nothing since we brought him here except to ask for food or ale."

"Have they been given to him this evening?"

"I dinna believe so."

"Dinna do it. Let him wonder what happened. Let him try to sleep hungry. He'll be more off-balance."

"I'll tell Cook." Jamie stood. "Come down here at midnight and we'll go."

Bhaltair nodded and Jamie left.

"Ye need more rest than a few hours here and there as well," Niall objected.

"I'll rest when we ken what we are dealing with." He stood, then shrugged. "I'm going upstairs to check on Eilidh. I'll rest until midnight in the chamber the steward gave me. Ye lot go about yer business."

They wished him good hunting. They were good lads, well trained and even when wounded, ready for anything. He hoped they wouldn't have to take on a horde of Lowlanders. If the man in the Fletcher cell was the leader of the gang, they might not have to. He planned to find out the truth tonight.

The door to Orla's chamber was closed. He listened for a moment, but heard nothing. He knocked softly, then opened it. The bairn lay in her crib. The Fletcher healer sat beside her, singing softly. Bhaltair nodded and closed the door. If Eilidh wasn't here, she must be in her chamber.

He went to the door and repeated what he'd done at Orla's. He heard nothing, so he knocked softly and opened the door. Eilidh stood in a night rail and shawl, at the window, looking out over the bailey toward the barracks.

"Looking for me?"

She whirled, a hand over her heart. "Bhaltair! I didna hear ye."

"I wouldna expect ye to. Ye did a good job putting me back together. I can still move silently." He came into the room and closed the door behind him. "How are ye?"

"I should be asking the questions," Eilidh told him and reached out a hand.

He went to her and took her hand in his. She closed her eyes for a moment, telling him that she was "reading" him, opened them and nodded.

"Ye are doing well. The fever is gone. The wound is healed and strengthening. Another day or two and both yer arm and yer leg will be back to normal."

"And ye? Are ye back to normal? Have ye slept, or have ye stared out that window looking for me since Caitrin ejected ye from Orla's chamber?"

"I slept a wee, and hoped ye did, too."

He nodded. What was he doing here? She was not upset at having him in her chamber. So, what did he hope to accomplish? To take up where they left off? He lifted a hand and smoothed her hair back from her face. She'd braided it for sleep, but tendrils had escaped and curled over her ear.

She leaned her cheek into his palm. "I'm glad ye are here, but we canna—"

"And we willna. Not yet. This is too new, this... change... between us. This understanding."

"Aye. I want to give it time to grow. To strengthen, if that is what it will do. Our future to Clan Lathan is too important." She paused and her gaze held his captive. "We canna mistake this."

"I dinna think we have. We can take our time. But Eilidh, ye ken I want ye. Ye must never doubt that. Or that I will take care of ye. 'Tisna just my job, my role in Lathan, or what yer da ordered me to do. 'Tis what I live to do. To see ye safe and well. To be with ye." Did she know what Jamie had offered him? If so, his words should have reassured her. He didn't realize it until he said them, but his decision was made. He would not stay at Fletcher. Not without her. And she would not leave the Aerie.

"I feel the same. I want ye safe and well. But that isna love. 'Tisna enough for a lifetime. Not yet. And this attraction, this infatuation, isna either. It must grow—or not—as it will."

"Or as we make it grow." He kissed her, softly at first, as he had in the solar, but wanting more and taking more as she kissed him back. Her hands traced up his chest and shoulders to encircle his neck and her fingers combed through the hair at his nape. Her touch sent tingles racing down his spine making him shudder with need. She pressed closer to him, her breasts separated from his chest by two thin layers of cloth—hers and his. He longed to see them. To feel them. His hand slipped down her back to cup her bottom and pull her tight against the erection that was straining his trews. "I dinna ken how long I can wait. Ye are making my need for ye grow."

"Bhaltair." She said his name on a low breath. A plea. For mercy? Or for more? He reached up and cupped her cheek again, trailing kisses from her other ear down her neck. His hand followed on the other side. He trailed heated fingers down her chest and cupped one breast. It was as full and heavy as he recalled. He bent and licked the nipple through her gown, and suckled, teasing it to a hard peak with lips and teeth.

Eilidh arched against him and moaned his name.

He caught her gown and pulled it up until he met the bare flesh of her hip, then slipped his hand between her thighs. She widened her stance, giving him access. She was wet, and she cried out as he found her nub and stroked it. "Ach, Bhaltair, I canna stand."

In answer, he picked her up and laid her on the bed, then trailed kisses down her throat to her breasts, all the while stroking her. She was so responsive, he couldn't wait to have her. He entered her with one finger, then two, and she clamped down hard. His cock responded, twitching, hardening, threatening to split his trews. He longed to ease them down out of the way and hold himself while he pleasured her, but he'd rather caress her.

Lightning struck when she reached for him and trailed her hand down his belly. He fought for control against the unexpected firestorm of desire, but when she cried out and shuddered her release, he lost his battle and rode her release along with her.

EILIDH WAS LOST. Her battle to deny her feelings was over. She had let Bhaltair touch her as no man had ever done. And he had taken her someplace she had only heard other women talking about, rhapsodizing over the early years of their marriage, when their husband could drive them to a place where nothing existed but the two of them and shooting stars.

Eilidh knew Bhaltair had just given her a small sample of what he anticipated for the two of them to learn as they explored each other. As they gave themselves to each other.

She might not survive it.

But she didn't want such intimacy with any other man. She never would. She had loved him for years, and now? Now she was certain she would never love another man but him for as long as she lived.

What could she do? What should she do?

She opened her eyes.

He gazed at her, a frown creasing the skin between his dark blond brows. "Are ye well, Eilidh, love?"

Eilidh-love? He'd never called her that before. Perhaps he'd come to the same conclusion she had. They'd just taken a big step, one they could not turn back from.

"I am," she replied and stretched her arms over her head, enjoying the release of a full-body stretch. Then she recalled that her gown was above her hips. She reached down to cover herself. Bhaltair helped her, and covered her with a quilt.

"Ye will sleep now, more sweetly than ever, I think."

He smiled and she was transfixed. She'd never seen him smile like that. A genuine, happy smile that crinkled the corners of his eyes and lifted his lips. His pleasure lit his eyes. Nowhere did she see a hint of tension or dismay. He seemed pleased with her, himself, and the rest of the world. Satisfied. Aye, he'd taken them to the next step—or well beyond it—and seemed happy with the result.

Was she? Oh, aye. She took his hand away from the bulge he tried to shield from her, so he let her look. "'Twill be an adjustment..." she said, doubting it would even be possible. He was huge, but not as big as he would be in the heat of passion.

"I will make ye ready before I enter ye, Eilidh, *dinna fash*. I willna hurt ye any more than absolutely necessary."

"Of course." She knew what happened. And that the pain didn't last long. And if a woman had the right partner, from then on, she would have bliss. Still... it would be an adjustment.

"Sleep well, Eilidh love," he murmured, bent and kissed her, stood and straightened his clothes. "I'll be in the next chamber. The one the steward meant for me to have," he added with a grin, no doubt thinking again about coming in here in the middle of her bath. "Call out if ye need me."

She smiled and nodded, suddenly on the verge of sleep. So, this was what utter relaxation felt like. She looked forward to what else Bhaltair would teach her.

Bhaltair left, but the sleep she felt about to claim her instead eluded her. She thought back over the experience and recalled how her talent let her sense the desire coursing through him, and how it amplified her own arousal. When she'd touched him, she'd been consumed by a fire that raced along her veins and set her blood to boiling. Was that need all hers, or what he felt, too? Was that why she had let him go so far?

13

Bhaltair closed the door to Eilidh's chamber and paused in the hallway with his back against it, overwhelmed with what had just happened. After years of avoiding each other, of denying the attraction that lately simmered between them, they had finally given in and given each other pleasure. Eilidh was so responsive, more than any lass he'd ever had, he knew there would be no others for him. When the day came that he claimed her, they would burn so brightly, no one else would ever be enough for either of them again.

That worried him.

He had always believed that Eilidh was not for him. That she would marry outside the clan to strengthen an alliance, and would bring her husband to join Lathan. But finding out that she no longer feared him, and that she had wanted him for years... he shook his head and pushed away from her door. Jamie had better forget matching her with a Fletcher.

Could they make it work? Or was Jamie's desire to keep her at Fletcher the least of the possible barriers between them. Would her father allow it? Or would loving her, and having to see her wed to another man her father chose, drive him from the only home he'd known, and the position of responsibility that he'd earned? Back to Fletcher? There was too much at stake to rush into this. Too much for both of them, perhaps, but more for him.

Still, he'd dealt with risk all his life. He would handle this.

Resolved, he entered the next chamber and fell across the bed without bothering to undress. He'd sleep for a few hours, then deal with the archer. But every time he closed his eyes, he saw Eilidh, her night rail thin enough to see through, pushed up above her waist. Her scent still clung to him and he still recalled the weight of her breast, the slick heat between her thighs. With a groan, he unlaced his trews and took himself in hand. If just thinking about her got him this hard, what would he do the next time they were alone? And they would be. His climax hit as he imagined taking her for the first time, teaching her what her body enjoyed, and what he liked.

Panting, he got up and cleaned himself at a basin of water someone had left for him, retied his trews and pulled a quilt over him, then another. He only had a few hours to sleep. Perhaps now, he would.

Just after midnight, he woke and got out of bed. Jamie would be waiting for him in the great hall. He rubbed his face with his hands, and groaned as the friction released Eilidh's scent. The remaining water in the ewer was ice cold, but that suited him perfectly. He dipped his hands and scrubbed them over his face, grabbed a bit of linen folded beside it and dried off. He couldn't think about her while he interrogated their prisoner.

In the great hall, Jamie sat by the banked hearth. Warmth still radiated from it. Bhaltair joined him. "How long have ye been here?"

"Only a few minutes. If ye hadna come soon, I wouldha stirred the fire, but we'll leave it banked. We willna be here for long."

"The laird?"

"Still asleep. Though she could help us, I didna have the heart to wake her."

Bhaltair nodded. "How do ye want to handle this?"

"I should ask ye that question, since ye took his arrows."

"And Eilidh took the pain he inflicted on me. I'd happily break his arms and every joint in his fingers so he could never pull another bow."

"The threat of that might elicit some answers. But if he refuses?"

"How badly do ye want to ken what his band were doing on Fletcher land?"

"Ye ken the answer to that. Thieves and brigands are bad enough, but led by a man who uses torture for his own amusement? What kind of men join with a leader like that?"

"If he is the leader."

"Ye said they deferred to him. None objected."

"He could have killed them as easily as he wounded me."

Jamie pursed the corner of his mouth and nodded. "Ye have a point." He stood. "Let's hear what he will tell us."

They made their way down to the cell where the archer was held. The man must have come awake as soon as their footsteps sounded on the treads, because he was standing near the pallet he slept on when they turned the corner, Jamie in front, Bhaltair behind.

"Ah, visitors," the archer said. "To what do I owe the pleasure of yer company?" His eyes widened when he looked past Jamie and saw who stood at his back.

"You!"

Bhaltair stepped forward and spread his arms and legs. "Yer aim is nay as good as ye thought."

"Yer arm. Yer leg. Ye should be dead by now," he snarled.

He sounded more in command of himself—and his speech—now that shock of Bhaltair's appearance had passed.

"Or near enough as makes nay difference," the man added when Bhaltair failed to react.

Instead, he asked, "What did ye put on yer points?"

The archer paled. "How did ye ken?"

"Answer the question," Jamie barked.

The prisoner cut a glance at Jamie, then back to Bhaltair. "Shite. Cow shite, human, wolf, whatever I had to hand. Why are ye—" he gave up speaking and simply gestured.

"Who are ye?" Bhaltair ignored his demand and answered with one of his own. "And what are ye doing in those hills?"

The archer crossed his arms and stared with narrowed eyes. Color had returned to his skin.

"If I have to come in there, I'll start breaking bones. Ye said ye preferred torture. I can make certain ye will never draw a bow again."

The archer paled again, but kept his mouth shut.

Bhaltair spared a glance at Jamie.

"He'll do it," Jamie said, his voice projecting calm certainty. "He didna like having those arrows dug out. Best ye tell us why ye are here."

Silence greeted Jamie's advice.

The archer had more grit than Jamie expected from a sadist. "Perhaps ye'll enjoy the snap of yer finger bones as much as ye enjoyed putting arrows in me," Bhaltair said as he took the key from the far wall and inserted it in the cell door's lock. He took his time, moving slowly but smoothly, giving the archer long moments to think, or to fear. Either would suit Bhaltair's purposes.

"If ye harm me, ye'll never learn a thing," he warned. "Ye'll never be able to trust a word I say." He didn't move, but simply watched Bhaltair turn the key in the lock. The *snick* of the lock disengaging cracked the silence and made him jump.

It nearly made Bhaltair jump, as well. He gave Jamie a side-eye glance, then turned his attention back to their prisoner. The man stood a head shorter and several stone lighter than Bhaltair, but he didn't budge. He couldn't possibly prevent Bhaltair from tearing him limb from limb. He had ballocks, or perhaps he didn't believe Bhaltair and Jamie would follow through on their threat.

Bhaltair was glad they hadn't threatened to kill the man. He would survive a broken finger or two, if that's what it took to convince him to talk. Given the way the man's gaze darted from side to side, looking anywhere but at his two jailers, Bhaltair didn't think it would take much more than that.

With a shrug, he opened the door and stepped into the cell.

Suddenly, the archer charged and rammed Bhaltair's midsection with his head and shoulder, dodged past him and out the door, bowling Jamie over as he passed.

"Damn it, dinna let him get away," Bhaltair snarled as he pushed to his feet.

Jamie was doing the same, but it was obvious that he was hurt. "Gates are closed. Go after him. I'll be fine."

Bhaltair nodded and launched himself up the steps, cursing. This was not how the interrogation was supposed to go.

EILIDH WOKE IN THE DARK. Something had disturbed her sleep, but what? A noise in the hall? The fire in her hearth had burned down to glowing coals that gave off enough light for her to see her chamber was empty. Bhaltair had not come back. She sat up and listened, but heard nothing more.

Curiosity drove her from the bed. She padded across the cold floor and listened at the door. Hearing nothing, she opened it a crack, then closed and locked it. She didn't know why she woke up, but it didn't matter. She would go back to sleep. On a whim, she went to the window, uncovered it, and looked out at the stars.

Their position told her dawn was still far off. From the corner of her eye, she noticed movement in the bailey and glanced down. Bhaltair crossed toward the stable. He seemed intent and she didn't want to wake the rest of the keep by calling out to him, so she grabbed a woolen blanket from the bed, wrapped it around herself and waited in the window to see what was going on.

He was looking for something, that much was plain. His head turned constantly as he moved, taking in everything around him, then he disappeared into the stable.

She was about to cover the window and go back to bed when she saw a man leave the smithy carrying a sword. He had dirks tucked in his belt on both sides, the metal catching what little light there was to be had at this hour of the night. He stayed in the shadows, moving quickly from building to building, searching along the outer wall. He disappeared behind the next one and it dawned on her he was searching for a postern gate. Had their prisoner escaped? Bhaltair might assume he'd go for a horse, which would explain why he disappeared into the stable. He couldn't know the man had armed himself and was looking for another way out.

She dropped the blanket and pulled her dress over her head, slipped her feet into boots and threw her cloak around her shoulders. In her haste, she tugged on the door, forgetting she'd locked it. She got it open and ran down the stairs in time to meet Uncle Jamie coming in.

Something was wrong. Her senses went on immediate alert. "What happened?" She touched him and was immediately swamped with his pain. "Sit," she told him.

He shook his head. "Got to help Bhaltair search for the archer. He got away from us."

"I think I saw him from my chamber. Bhaltair went into the stables. Another man took weapons from the smithy and was moving along the walls."

"Looking for the postern, for a way out." Jamie pushed up and grimaced.

"Ye have a broken rib, Uncle Jamie. Stay still for a minute and let me fix it or ye willna do Bhaltair any good."

He nodded and she went to work. In moments, his pain inhabited her, but his rib was mended well enough for him to do what he must. He had some bruising and a sprained wrist. She took care of those, then stepped back.

"Ye'll do, so long as ye dinna get into a fight. The man was headed toward the wall behind the kitchen garden. He may be gone by now."

"If he is, we'll find him. If the watch on the wall near the gate didn't see him, I'll alert Bhaltair and wake the guards."

"Ye get the Fletchers. I'll find Bhaltair."

"Ye need food and rest after healing me."

"Not that much, and not yet. I'll be fine going to the stable."

"Be careful, lass. The archer may not have made it out of the keep yet."

"I will." She headed out the door while Jamie went up the stairs, moving much more easily than when she first saw him. She ran across the bailey to the stable and paused in the doorway. "Bhaltair?" She heard a horse shift and whicker, but he didn't answer. He must still be in there. She called his name again. Getting no answer, she left the stable and headed toward the barracks to rouse his men. Perhaps he'd already thought of that, and she'd find him there.

Ahead, she heard the sounds of a scuffle, blows landing and men cursing. One of the voices was Bhaltair's. She ran toward them in time for the archer to go down, one of the dirk's he'd carried buried in his side. Bhaltair was cursing him, bleeding from a cut on his arm that looked deep.

"Bhaltair!"

"Eilidh, what are ye doing out here?"

"I came to find ye. Uncle Jamie is rousing the guards."

"No need. But I need ye to save him," he said and gestured toward the man on the ground. "We didna get any answers from him yet. There's much he didn't tell us."

"Yer arm—"

"Will wait." He was putting pressure on it with his other hand, so he was probably right. And Uncle Jamie could bind it when he got here.

She dropped to her knees and reached into the wound with her healing senses. The dirk had gone deep, and left alone, he would surely die. But she could save him. She reached in with her senses while she slowly pulled out the dirk, closing the wound as she went and fighting the pain that pierced her own side. She realized only as she neared finishing with him that he'd been awake the whole time.

"Dinna touch me! Ye are a witch!" He spat at her as she withdrew the dirk from the last finger's width of the blade's tip.

"Would ye rather I let ye die? I am not a witch. I am a healer."

"No healer can do what ye just did."

"Actually, several can."

"Ye admit ye belong to a coven?"

"Nay, to a family."

"Eilidh." The tone of Bhaltair's voice reminded her to be cautious.

Jamie showed up with three men and took charge of the man on the ground.

She stood. "Let me see yer arm," she said and took Bhaltair's arm in her hands. "I'd rather clean this before I close it," she told him.

"There isna time. Fix it. Ye can open it later if ye need to."

She nodded and closed his wound.

He nodded his thanks and wiped the blood from his arm, revealing a thin pink line of new tissue. Unfortunately, their prisoner had watched Eilidh heal him, and looked on with disgust.

"That is what she did to me?"

"Aye. It was that or let ye die. Ye still owe us answers."

"I owe you naught."

"Take him back to his cell," Jamie ordered the men. "Search him and make sure he didn't steal any more weapons and conceal them on his person. Strip him to his skin if ye must."

The men hustled the archer away as Jamie bent to retrieve the sword and dirks from the ground. "He's resourceful."

"He's a problem," Bhaltair answered. "One I mean to solve."

"Now?" Jamie frowned and glanced at Bhaltair's arm.

"Why not? He's shaken. When will there be a better time? Only now, ye might want to wake the laird."

BHALTAIR COULD HEAR Caitrin berating Jamie for their daft stunt as they came down the stairs. He shared a grin with Eilidh, then schooled his features and watched the Fletchers approach the great hall's hearth where they waited.

"They got ye into this as well?" Caitrin frowned at Eilidh.

"I got myself into it. I heard something, I suppose, and woke up. I saw Bhaltair entering the stables, then another man with weapons searching along the walls."

"Looking for the postern," Bhaltair supplied, "or another way out. That's where I found him. We fought. He had weapons. I took a dirk from him and stabbed him to keep him from separating my head from my shoulders with the sword he'd stolen. He's not just good with a bow. Eilidh healed him so we can get answers. He thinks she's a witch. That's what's happened up to now."

"Except for the part where we went to question him and he attacked and got by us. Broke my rib. Eilidh fixed it," Jamie added when Caitrin sucked in a breath.

"Well, ye have been busy." Caitrin gave each of them, including Eilidh, a penetrating stare.

"We're not done yet. He seemed quite rattled by Eilidh healing him. We want ye there to sense his lies when we question him again."

"Or try to, ye mean?"

Jamie shrugged one shoulder and glanced toward Bhaltair, who stepped into the breach.

"He's fast, and a furious fighter. This time, we'll have guards with us, to keep ye safe. And Eilidh in case something happens."

"Or if ye have to do what ye threatened earlier," Jamie said grimly.

"Oh? What was that?" Caitrin didn't look pleased.

"Break his fingers and arms so he'll never draw a bow again. That seemed to upset him."

"Ye'll do no such thing." Caitrin's tone was flat.

"I didna plan to, but he didna ken that."

"No wonder he fought his way out. I wouldha fought ye, too."

Bhaltair glanced at Eilidh. She looked displeased as well. Damn it, she was seeing him as the bloodthirsty warrior again. Maybe having her present during the interrogation was not such a good idea. "Perhaps Eilidh shouldna join us."

She looked up in surprise. "Why not? Ye may need me."

"Can ye let us do what we must and not interfere?"

Bhaltair was surprised Jamie asked that question, but it was front of his mind as well.

She squared her shoulders, frowned and nodded. "Aye."

Privately, Bhaltair hoped that the women's reactions to his threats would convince the archer that the peril was real, and he would capitulate and talk. He hated reinforcing Eilidh's fear of him, but in this instance, her obvious discomfort might do some good.

"I dinna want him to ken ye have any sort of talent," Jamie told Caitrin. "So ye will simply clench one fist if ye sense he lies, aye? On yer side away from him, so he doesna become aware ye are signaling me?"

"Aye, that makes sense."

Eilidh nodded. "Ye need me there, too."

Jamie glanced at Caitrin, who nodded.

They were committed.

14

Eilidh walked with Caitrin down the stairs leading to the cells where they'd put the archer. Despite the hidden talents she and Caitrin brought to this interrogation, she was nervous. Almost sick to her stomach. Her pace had slowed more and more the closer they got to their destination, causing her and Caitrin to drop well behind Uncle Jamie and Bhaltair. She still wrestled with what she'd heard upstairs. Bhaltair had been ready to break the man's bones to make him talk. To cripple him for life if he wouldn't answer their questions. He said he only threatened it, and said he would not have done it, but she was certain if the situation demanded it, he would. He would count it as a lesser evil than killing the man, which he had almost done in the bailey.

And he was no different than any other man trained as a warrior and faced with an enemy, fighting for his life and the lives of those he loved. But his emotions were so strong—and so tightly leashed—that she feared the day he lost control. Did she really think she could pacify him when his anger got out of his control? Even her Voice might not be enough to protect her. How would she know she was strong enough until the worst happened and she had to wrestle with his emotions—and her own—and win? Was he worth spending a lifetime fighting for him, or worse, with him?

She wasn't sure how she would get past what she'd learned. Even though she wanted him, knowing what he was capable of, could she ever truly love him? She wished Uncle Jamie had never brought it up. She wished she didn't know. But she did. And now, she must accept it—and Bhaltair—or reject him because of it.

"Are ye well?" Caitrin's question startled her into almost missing a step. Caitrin grabbed her hand to steady her.

"Aye."

Caitrin held up their joined hands. "I ken ye are lying."

Eilidh glanced at their hands. "And I ken ye are anxious. Neither one of us likes this."

"Nor do our men. Look at the tension in their shoulders. They're worried they'll have to torture the poor man, worried he'll escape again, worried we'll be harmed, worried they'll learn nothing. And more I canna think of, I'm sure. They dinna want this to go badly, either. If they can make him talk, that will save everyone a lot of grief. That man included. He fears ye—or what he thinks ye are. That will help."

Caitrin was right. Eilidh took a breath and nodded. Bhaltair was counting on her presence to save him from something he did not want to do, despite his threat. "I'll be ready," she said and Caitrin nodded. She had sensed the truth of Eilidh's statement or she would not have done so.

At the bottom of the stairs, a short hallway led to the cells. Four Fletcher guards waited outside the cell holding the archer. Jamie conferred with them in a low voice. Two moved farther down the hall, but close enough to intervene if needed. The other two moved past the women and took up posts at the bottom of the stairs. If the archer got out of his cell, he would not get past six trained warriors.

Eilidh hoped he realized that and decided to cooperate.

"Ye brought the witch down here?" The archers voice held nothing but contempt. No fear, no remorse for the trouble he'd caused. He took one look at her and reacted with anger and disgust.

Eilidh's head drew back. She couldn't help the instinctive movement. She'd never met anyone truly disgusted by her ability. Fear she understood. Despair. Even gratitude. But not this. Once she got her own reaction under control, she worried that her presence would not help as much as Bhaltair hoped.

"*Haud yer wheesht*," Jamie warned. "There are nay witches here."

"Then explain to me how she did that," he said, pointing at Bhaltair's arm. "Or this," he added, pulling up his shirt to reveal the new scar on his side.

"I have methods ye obviously dinna ken," Eilidh answered softly. "They saved yer life. I would think ye'd be grateful, not making wild accusations."

"Accusations? They're facts."

"Very well. Let's assume she is a witch," Jamie said with a snort. "If ye insist. She healed ye. What do ye think she can do if she means to harm ye?"

The archer paled at that. "Dinna let her near me."

"We willna. If ye answer our questions. Who are ye?"

"My name isna important."

"I want it. Who are ye?"

The archer's gaze moved from Jamie to Eilidh to Bhaltair.

She could almost hear the thoughts that must be running through his mind. Take his chances with her? Or with the big warrior? Or just answer the question? She almost felt sorry for him, but this man had fired arrows into Bhaltair's arm and leg and smirked the whole time. She couldn't abide a sadist. She'd heard too many stories from her parents about the man who led the Lowlander army that had besieged the Aerie, and hints of what Caitrin had gone through at MacGregor's hands. She would not let anyone be made a victim of the same sort of madness again.

She was about to intervene when he spoke.

"Thomas LeClair."

"French?"

"On my father's side. English on the other."

Jamie shook his head, disgust twisting his lips. "What are ye doing here?"

"You brought me here."

"Let me rephrase the question. What were ye doing in those hills with yer men?"

Silence reigned for long moments while LeClair considered. Eilidh watched his eyes. They tracked, as they had before, from Jamie to her to Bhaltair and back. He seemed not to notice Caitrin.

"Do ye recall what my friend here offered to do to make ye talk?" Jamie crossed his arms.

Le Clair's eyes widened, tracked to Bhaltair and studied him.

Bhaltair glared at the man. Eilidh couldn't tell if he was trying to intimidate him or was angry that his threat was again hanging over them all. Bhaltair dropped his gaze to LeClair's hands. So, intimidation. And from the way LeClair paled, the threat was working.

He clenched his fists and took a step back, but he still didn't speak.

Bhaltair shifted his weight. "In the hills, ye heard me ask about a man named Pritchard. What do ye ken about him?"

The archer smirked but still didn't speak.

"Yer silence leaves me nay choice," Bhaltair told him. Without looking around at Eilidh, he opened the cell door and stepped inside, then closed it behind him. "Ye thought to give me an agonized death. I willna do the same to ye. I will let ye live, but ye will suffer. One wee bone at a time. Then bigger ones." He took another step toward the archer. "Until ye tell us what we want to ken."

"I ken the man," LeClair said.

"Where is he?"

"Gone, as the other man told ye."

"I dinna believe ye. Why was he in the area? Why were ye?"

LeClair paled and glanced aside at Eilidh. She lifted her chin, daring him with her posture to even think the other man could have succeeded in what he tried to do to her. She told herself she was strong, and she had stronger friends.

"Well?" Bhaltair barked the question, showing impatience Eilidh suspected he didn't feel, but used as a tactic to pressure LeClair.

"Hunting witches." The man said it so softly, Eilidh wasn't sure she'd heard him correctly. Ice filled her veins and made a shiver of fear dance down her spine.

"So ye can treat innocent women the way ye treated me? As yer playthings? For target practice?" Bhaltair roared those questions, and Eilidh wanted to cover her ears. His words echoed from the stone walls around them, and likely up the stairs. It was a good thing they did this in the middle of the night or half the keep's remaining guards would be on their way down here.

Instead, she stood her ground and glared at LeClair. She didn't need to look at Caitrin to guess she was doing the same.

"Innocent? After what I saw her do? She is a witch."

"I am a healer."

"Many witches hide behind that title. Ye are a real witch. I have seen no others who can do what ye did."

"Did ye kill the others even though they couldna do what ye thought a witch could do?"

He snorted, but thought better of it as Bhaltair took another step closer. He wiped all expression from his face and dropped his gaze.

"Jamie, take the women upstairs. He has earned the pain I

threatened." Bhaltair's voice was low and graveled, his fists clenched and his muscles bunched.

He was vibrating with suppressed fury, and ready to break every bone in LeClair's body. Bhaltair would kill him—slowly. And Eilidh could not let him carry that stain on his soul for her.

"Bhaltair." She said his name softly, calmly. He turned his head toward her, but she could tell he kept LeClair in the corner of his eye.

"Go, Eilidh. Ye, too, Caitrin. This man will tell me what I want to ken, or he will die in agony. Slowly. He and his friends would do the same to ye. They dinna deserve yer sympathy."

"But they have done nothing to me. Ye dinna need to do this."

"Jamie, by God, take the women upstairs."

Jamie reached for Caitrin's hand, but she shrugged him off. "I stand with Eilidh."

Eilidh opened the door and moved into the cell, heart in her throat. She didn't want to touch this man. But she had to. Bhaltair would try to prevent her from getting near him, but he didn't know what she could do.

She reached him first and touched his bare hand. "Bhaltair, stand aside," she said in her low but powerful Voice, the talent she'd inherited from her mother that let her compel others. The one talent that they kept deeply hidden. He fought the command, but moved as she directed to the side of the cell. She couldn't imagine what the Fletchers thought she had done to budge him, but now was not the time to worry about what she might reveal. She could make them forget.

"LeClair," she said as she neared him and picked her point of contact. Not his hand. Too familiar. A tear in his sleeve would serve as well. He backed away from her, eyes wide, until he hit the wall behind him, trapped. She grabbed his arm, his skin hot against her palm, and leaned toward him as if she was going to share some secret. Instead, for the second time in that many minutes, she used the hidden power her mother had given her at birth. "Tell Bhaltair and Jamie what they want to know. Answer every question, fully and truthfully. Dinna hide anything, or anyone, or any location, or any plan. Tell them all ye ken. As soon as I release ye and leave this cell, ye will forget I was ever in it."

LeClair's eyes had glazed over. He stared at her, eyes wide. Because she had approached him? Or because he understood what she had just done? That idea made more ice slide down her spine. She wanted out of here—now. She released him, went to Bhaltair, touched his hand and told him he could move about as he wished.

He nodded and she left the cell. Caitlin watched her, frowning. Jamie was frowning, too, but there was a hint of recognition in his eyes. Had her mother ever used her Voice on Jamie? "He's yers to question," Eilidh told him. "He'll answer both of ye now."

She went to the stairs, then turned back. "Caitrin, we can go. The men willna need us."

Caitrin traded a quizzical look with Jamie. He nodded and tipped his head toward the stairs. Without a word, she joined Eilidh and they left the men to learn everything the archer knew.

BHALTAIR FELT like he'd been hit over the head. He'd stepped aside and let Eilidh go near their captive. Had he lost his mind? He didn't recall agreeing to that, but he'd allowed it, and he'd heard every word she'd said to the man.

Whatever she'd done worked. LeClair answered every question he and Jamie put to him. They now knew who was in Fletcher's hills and why—and where. Come sunup, Fletcher would send more men to meet up with the men they'd left out there conducting the search for Pritchard, and round up the troublemakers.

When they were finished, they locked the cell and left LeClair to consider what and whom he had betrayed. In the laird's solar,

Jamie got out the bottle of MacKyrie whisky and poured two generous cups full. "We've earned this."

Bhaltair didn't argue. Maybe the whisky would clear his mind. He remembered as though through a fog Eilidh coming into the cell and asking him to move aside. He knew the man could have killed her with his bare hands. Likely, she knew it, too. So why did he obey her command and allow her close enough to touch their prisoner?

"I ken that look," Jamie said after a few deep pulls on the whisky.

"What look?" Bhaltair set aside his empty cup. Jamie offered the bottle, but Bhaltair waved it away.

"Ye have just met the talent the Lathan healers keep hidden."

"If they keep it hidden, how do ye ken it?"

"Because Aileana used it on Toran. He told me about it once when he was deep in his cups."

"What talent?"

"With their voice, they can command action—or inaction. Ye never wouldha needed to start breaking LeClair's bones to get him to talk. Ye had a secret weapon at yer back the whole time, and didna ken it. If LeClair kenned what she did to him, he would be building the witch-fire and screaming condemnations to the heavens. If he remembers what she did, ye will have to kill him to protect her."

"Is that likely?"

"Toran seemed to be able to resist Aileana, at least to some extent. And eventually recall. Ye, too? If LeClair does, his days are numbered."

"I'll take that whisky now." Bhaltair tossed off another pour, set the cup aside and stood.

"It appears Eilidh has much to explain. If only I had her talent, to make her talk."

"She'll tell ye when she's ready. If she's as much like her mother as I think she is, she'll share everything about herself with her husband. It will be up to ye to protect her and keep her safe.

Bhaltair sank back into his seat. "Ye ken..."

"How ye look at each other? Aye. 'Twillna be easy to win her. She's devoted to Lathan and to the future that has been hers almost from birth, but I think ye already have her heart."

"And she has mine, if she will take it. She feared me for most of her life. I'm not certain she's gotten past it. But I *am* certain ye had best not try to pair her with a Fletcher."

"Do ye think me such a fool? Nay. And now, with what I told ye, ye have reason to fear her, as well. Tell her so. Once she gets over being angry with me, it will reassure her."

EILIDH HAD BEEN TOO wound up to sleep, so the rest of the night passed slowly as she tossed and turned, expecting Bhaltair to barge in her door at any moment, demanding explanations that she wasn't sure she should give.

Now that she'd had time to think, away from him and from the tension in the dungeon, she regretted her actions. Not so much about what she'd done, but how she'd done it. She should have been more circumspect, shielding her handiwork from Caitrin and Jamie at least. Even from Bhaltair.

And God help her if LeClair was like her father, and the compulsion she laid on him to forget her presence ever wore off. He would never give up. If he ever found her again, she would find herself tied to a stake, flames licking at her hem. She shuddered and moved to the window once she was dressed, wishing it would show her sunshine to wash away the remains of remorse filling her. But the sky was cloudy, the day gray and misty.

She wrapped a shawl around her shoulders and turned to her door. It was time to face the day. And Bhaltair, and the Fletchers. No doubt they had questions.

Caitrin met her when she entered the great hall. "Good morning. Jamie and Bhaltair have taken more guards and gone to round up the rest of LeClair's men—again—and the one who attacked ye."

Well, that took care of having to face all three of them at once. "So, he did answer their questions," she said as they walked to an empty table.

"Aye." They sat down and Caitrin signaled to a serving lass, then said, "What did ye do to make him talk?"

Eilidh could lie and say she'd simply assured him Bhaltair would do what he threatened, but lying to a clan's laird didn't seem the wisest course to choose. Or to a friend, which Caitrin was trying to be. She decided to temporize. "What has Jamie told ye about how my parents met?" Perhaps Caitrin already knew and was testing her, to find out if she'd admit to having the same ability.

"Jamie has told me the tale of the invasion, the siege, and the madman leading the army."

"Is that all?"

"Ye are trying to avoid answering my question."

Eilidh frowned, then nodded.

"Very well," she said as their breakfast arrived. "If there's aught I need to ken, ye will tell me."

They ate in silence, but Eilidh's mind was in a whirl. In the same situation, what would Aileana tell Caitrin? She couldn't come up with an answer, so she said nothing. Instead, she thought about Bhaltair. Normally, that would be a more pleasant pastime, but if he had any remnant of sensation that she had manipulated him, he would be furious, and Bhaltair's fury directed at her was something she never wanted to experience.

Uncle Jamie had seemed to know what she'd done. Had he seen her mother use her Voice? Or had her father told his best friend about his wife's strange ability? And had he kept the secret all these years, even from Caitrin?

She had no way to find out without betraying the very secret she was trying to keep. At least not until Uncle Jamie returned. In the meantime, she'd neglected wee Orla. It was past time to continue trying to help the bairn. When she finished her meal, she cleared her throat and announced, "If ye dinna mind, I'll go see to Orla now."

Caitrin gave her a distracted smile and nodded. "Aye. Of course. I hope today is the day ye find the problem."

"I, too," Eilidh assured her and headed for the stairs. Kellina was holding her child when Eilidh arrived in the room "How is she?" She approached them, giving Kellina time to answer or react to her presence.

"Fussy," the young mother said. "I just sent the healer away to rest. She's been here all night. I just got Orla to settle down. Must ye wake her?"

"Nay. I can return when she is awake. Ye said she was fussy. What did she eat last eve?"

"The same as everyone else."

Eilidh thought back. Had she noticed what she'd eaten? "Did anyone give her anything else?"

"I didna. Healer and I were the only ones with her except Mother stopped by a few times."

"Very well. I'll return—"

Orla shifted in her mother's arms and whimpered, then started a low, chuffing cry.

"That didna last long," Kellina said and sighed. "She's awake."

"Put her in her cot," Eilidh requested. "I'll see what I can do."

Eilidh touched Orla as soon as her mother put her down. Poor wee lass, her belly churned, keeping her uncomfortable. Eilidh did what she could quickly do to calm the storm. She'd do more once Kellina left the chamber. Yet she didn't appear to be in a hurry to go. She stood on the other side of the crib, watching.

Eilidh lifted her hand and sighed. "She'll sleep better for a wee. Have ye eaten yet?"

"Nay, I wasna hungry when I got up." Her stomach chose that moment to growl and she gave Eilidh a sheepish grin. "I am now."

"Go on and take care of yerself. I'll watch the wean."

"Thank ye." Kellina wasted no time leaving.

Eilidh shook her head. The woman seemed to change like the wind, one moment a caring mother, the next, eager to escape. Perhaps because Orla had been ill for so long, Kellina was afraid to care too much.

15

By mid-afternoon, Bhaltair, Jamie, and the guards with them reached the area where the hideout LeClair named was supposed to be located. They had ridden hard, but Bhaltair knew the longer they took to arrive, the better the chances that the men would have fled.

He picked up several crisscrossing trails right away, but with no clear indication which they should follow.

"Spread out," he ordered. "Find our men. If ye find LeClair's, report back here. Dinna think to take them on by yerself. That will only get ye dead."

The men nodded and headed out. The Lathans were well practiced in this radial search, and Jamie had taught it to the Fletchers, as well. As soon as one radiant yielded results, he'd recall the men from the opposite search and reinforce those moving at angles to the productive direction.

By dark, they'd located the guards left behind to search, mounted and heading their way. They had four of the bandits in custody. Bhaltair was disappointed that Pritchard, who'd attacked Eilidh, was not among them.

Bhaltair pulled aside Ailbert, the man leading them. "How many more are still out there, do ye think?"

"They willna tell us. We've been all over these hills. If there's a cave we havena searched, 'tis too small for a man to enter. No matter how many there were, I think the rest fled when ye caught the archer and we released them."

"And no one kens where Pritchard got off to?"

"Naught who will admit to it. We got the last man this morning and were headed back to Fletcher when ye found us. Cole and I were debating whether to risk making camp for the night or riding on in when ye showed up."

"We'll make camp," Bhaltair decided quickly. "That drew them to us the last time. Perhaps 'twill work again. Only now, there are more of us. Spread out the men under the trees. Tie our friends lying around the fire, facing away from the light. If any more of their friends show up, they'll mistake them for ye lot."

Ailbert nodded. "That should confuse them."

"And keep our men alive, if they've another archer with them."

"Bad for them," Ailbert said, gesturing to the captives.

"They'll shout themselves hoarse at the first arrow shot, but give us time to take out their friends."

"What's to stop them from shouting a warning?"

Bhaltair grinned. "Our archer."

"Ye brought one?"

"Nay, but they dinna have to ken that. Just impress upon them that if their men dinna kill them, we will."

"Aye."

Ailbert went off to organize the camp. Bhaltair pulled Jamie aside from watching over the prisoners. "Have ye heard anything that will help us?"

"Nay, damn it. They're as close-mouthed a bunch as they were the first time we caught them. Too bad we didna keep them. 'Twould have saved us this trouble."

"They're bent on drowning or burning innocent women. I dinna have any sympathy for them. I want Pritchard. One of them must ken something."

"I'll see what I can do."

Bhaltair nodded and walked into the trees, inspecting the guards' postings. He exchanged a few words and confirmed who had first, second, and third watches through the night. He hadn't slept much last night, and the bandits had attacked before dawn the last time. Counting on them to be creatures of habit, he opted to bed down and take the last watch. Jamie would take first.

Someone woke him hours later. "All quiet," the guard told him. Bhaltair nodded and got up, cursing the early morning chill. Sunrise was still hours away, and autumn was turning the early mornings frosty. He made his rounds, checking that the watch had turned over smoothly and that the watch standers were alert. He found Jamie asleep near one of the younger Fletcher guards. Bhaltair approved. He'd keep the lad steady if they were attacked.

He made his way back to his pallet and rolled it up, ready to go once the sun came up. He was still crouched when he heard footsteps moving through the woods. More than one person, more than two, and not well-versed in moving silently.

He stayed down, listening, counting steps until he separated them into individuals—four, perhaps five at most. Three together and one ranging to the side, which implied another had split off on the opposite side. He hoped they didn't trip over one of his sleeping men.

Not that he was worried. His men were trained well enough to wake at the first hint of danger. Jamie's men, too, no doubt.

One of the outliers was headed right for him. He let the man get past him, stood and took him down with a hand over his mouth and a dirk to his throat. "Not a sound," he breathed. "Not a twitch, or I'll kill ye and go after yer friends."

The man froze and stayed that way. Bhaltair let him live. He wanted to question him, but not until his four friends were taken down. Before long, an owl's hoot, the prearranged signal, gave the all-clear. Bhaltair hauled his prisoner to his feet and marched him to the fire. In moments, he was joined by four others with their prisoners.

"Tie them up," Bhaltair ordered. "We'll wait for daylight to move them." He studied each man, but was again disappointed. The one man he wanted was not among them.

Eilidh needed to remake some of the tinctures. They'd been sitting too long, and she wanted fresh ingredients before she'd feed them to Orla. She headed to the kitchen to see what Cook had on hand.

"What do ye need, Lady Lathan?"

She held up three small pouches. "I need to gather some fresh grains for Orla. May I see what ye have been using?"

"I was going to the orchard for more apples, if ye care to walk with me."

"I will, thank ye. I'll gather what I need from the fields while ye do that."

She followed much the same path with Cook that she'd walked with Bhaltair. She could almost picture him at her side rather than the older cook. The walk with him had been on a sunny day, rather than under low clouds. The contrast made her miss him more. She hoped he and Uncle Jamie were successful and would be back soon.

She listened with half an ear as Cook talked about how he hoped to begin to expand the gardens and orchard in the spring. Where would they be, she and Bhaltair, by spring? Together at Lathan? If Bhaltair took seriously Uncle Jamie's offer, he would be here, in a position commanding the level of respect he deserved, but one that would not be his at Lathan until Duncan stepped aside. She could be here with Bhaltair, married, and learning to love each other more with every passing day. The idea made for a beguiling daydream of a life different from the one she'd grown up expecting to lead, but it was only a pleasant fantasy. Her future—her loyalty—lay with Lathan. His did, too.

She shook herself out of her imaginings only to realize they'd neared the outer postern gate that led to the grain fields. Men were working to finish harvesting the late wheat at the far end of the field. "Ach, nay, they'll mix the grains."

"Nay, lass. They're from the village, and have brought in the harvest for years. They'll work that field today, nay more, and carry it in to be stored."

She didn't take the time to explain to him how the wind would carry the chaff onto the other grains. She opened the gate and ran to gather her samples before they became covered in dust from the harvesting.

On her way back, the harvest had moved closer to the near side of the field, and closer to where she walked. A few of the men paused in their work to watch her. She nodded, but only glanced their way, and kept going. After a few steps, recognition hit and she nearly stumbled. One of those men reminded her of the man who'd attacked her. Not daring to look back to see if she was right, she hurried to the orchard gate to rejoin the cook, shaken but certain that if the man tried to follow her, the others would call him back to work and she'd hear. She closed the gate behind her, and risked a glance at the field. All the men were still there. With a relieved sigh, she turned into the orchard. The cook was gone. He must have gotten the apples he needed and left. She was alone out here. Well, he hadn't promised to remain with her.

She gulped and hurried through the orchard to the kitchen garden gate. Only once she was inside it did she feel safe. She looked back again, but couldn't see the grain fields for the orchard in the way. Most importantly, she still didn't see anyone following her. She must have been mistaken. Thinking about walking in these gardens with Bhaltair, so close after her attack, had made her imagine more than a future with him. She had formed a vision of her attacker where she least expected to.

Straightening her spine, she chided herself for her lapse, entered the kitchen and waved at cook as she passed by. He'd had no reason to fear leaving her alone in his gardens and fields. She couldn't blame him for her imaginings. Instead, she headed for the herbal to repeat the work she and the healer had done days before. It was time to concentrate on the task that had brought her here.

BHALTAIR WAS glad when the Fletcher keep appeared as they crested the last hill with their prisoners. The sun would be setting soon. The day had remained cloudy and chill. The idea of a hot meal and a warm drink in front of a hearth drew him, but what he really wanted was Eilidh.

Despite what she'd done to move him aside, and despite what Jamie had told him, he did not fear her. She'd done what she did to help, and though she was right and he would have stopped her if he'd known what she planned, he had to respect her bravery. He didn't know how her talent worked—or how fast —or what sort of danger she'd put herself in. That, they were going to discuss, just as soon as he got her alone. She might think she was invulnerable, but if her control relied on her ability to speak, well, he could think of dozens of ways to silence her.

And something he hadn't noticed before now, but she'd touched his hand, and she'd grabbed LeClair's arm at the tear in his sleeve. If she had to lay as much as a finger on skin, she could not control anyone from a distance. Nay, she needed to understand how vulnerable she really was. And that she needed him to keep her safe when she could not do it for herself.

Jamie led them inside the walls to the stable. "They'll have to go where we have LeClair. They can share cells," he ordered. "Lock them up. The rest of ye, get cleaned up."

That comment was greeted with hoots and laughter. After days of riding, Bhaltair expected hot water would be welcome. The barracks had three big tubs the men would share, one after another. He'd see Eilidh first, and worry about being clean enough to appear for supper afterwards.

Bhaltair headed inside. He followed Jamie to the laird's solar, where Caitrin waited. "Welcome back. I heard ye arrive. Good hunting?"

"Not good enough," Bhaltair groused.

"We dinna ken if we got them all, but we've got nine. Ten with LeClair. But not the one Bhaltair wants."

"Maybe ye will find out more about him from one of the new captives."

"They didna give anything away on the trip back here."

"Ah, but ye didna have Eilidh."

Bhaltair's pulse spiked. "Ye ken?"

"I dinna ken what I observed, but something did happen."

"I guess I owe ye an explanation," Eilidh said, entering the solar. She shut the door behind her and took a seat opposite Caitrin. Jamie and Bhaltair sat down with them and waited.

She looked so unsure of herself, Bhaltair wanted to take her hand, but that would only confuse her senses. And his.

"I made him talk," Eilidh said quietly.

"How? How did ye do that?" Caitrin's question seemed to make Eilidh freeze, her gaze locked on Jamie.

It was clear to Bhaltair that she was conflicted about revealing her secret.

"Shall I help ye, lass?" Jamie waited for her to answer.

"I... he had to be willing to speak, even if he meant to lie. If he refused to speak at all, 'twould be harder for me to compel him to answer ye. Or impossible. And I made him forget. Mother has something similar, but not quite the same."

"To compel someone to speak?"

"Or act as she wishes them to, aye."

Concern was written all over Jamie's face. Bhaltair was certain he wondered if Aileana ever forced him to do something and made him forget.

"Mother never used it on anyone but da and her children, and only if we were in immediate peril."

"Toran?" Caitrin's expression was part horror, part amusement. Bhaltair wondered what sort of history the two had between them.

"Aye, 'tis how she found out who he was when the Lowlander captured him."

"And I'd wager how she escaped the Aerie to go into the Lowlander army's camp trying to rescue her half-brother," Jamie murmured. "Toran would never let her go."

She nodded, so he began speaking. "So ye have a second talent, perhaps somehow related to yer healing talent. After all, ye tell the body what to do when ye heal it. But with this touch and spoken command, ye tell the mind what to do, and what to think or to forget. Am I right?"

She nodded again.

"Yer mother has it, of course. I dinna ken if any of yer siblings do. 'Twould be useful for Drummond, certainly."

She reacted with a snort. "Dear God, nay. He's insufferably bossy enough as he is. He doesna need Mother's Voice."

"Is that what ye call it? Voice?" Bhaltair needed to know more. To know what he was up against. She could order him not to love her. Or had she already done the opposite? How would he know?

"Aye. And nay, I canna force anyone to do anything they're set against. But if deep down they want to, or dinna much care, I can guide them."

"So, LeClair—"

"Probably wanted to talk, but wanted more to appear mysterious and in charge. What did he tell ye?"

Bhaltair exchanged a glance with Jamie. "They're witch hunters. From the Lowlands. They're convinced the Highlands harbor all sorts of witches, in league with the devil."

Eilidh paled. "The man who attacked me asked if I was 'one of them.' Is that what he meant?"

Bhaltair felt fury rise in his blood again. No woman would be safe as long as men like these roamed freely in the Highlands. "Probably. He is connected in some way to that group. In their fervor, they might suspect any woman." He wished he'd brought back the know-it-all, too, when he captured the archer. The only one other than the archer that Bhaltair suspected of knowing anything about Pritchard, the know-it-all was among the missing. Leaving him behind went against Bhaltair's gut instinct and had been a mistake. That man might have told them more than the ones they brought back.

"No woman is safe from them," Caitrin said, eyes wide, echoing Bhaltair's thought. "What are we going to do with them?"

"Let the Sheriff escort them back to the Lowlands?" Eilidh didn't look like she believed her question would get an affirmative answer.

"And have them come right back? With more men?" Caitrin shook her head. "We must find a way to convince them they're on a fool's errand. That there are no witches."

"If only they knew..." Eilidh murmured.

Bhaltair shook his head. "That, they never will. I'll kill them all before I'll let them put either of ye in danger."

He would do it, and gladly, to save those he loved. Eilidh's family would be at risk, as well as Caitrin, Ellie MacKyrie, and the newlyweds, Eilidh's twin Tavish and his new bride, Yvaine MacKyrie, and probably many more in the Highlands they knew nothing about.

"Perhaps I am the solution to that problem. If I can deal with them, one at a time, away from the others of their group, I can command them. They'll go home and never return to the Highlands."

"That is a better solution that slitting all of their throats, aye," Caitrin said, with a glance at Bhaltair, who nodded in agreement.

"That is what we'll do. Bring them here, one at a time. But first, we must decide exactly what I will tell them. Do they leave immediately? Do ye want them to wait outside the gate for all the rest, forget they've ever been in this part of the Highlands once they get far enough south? Those are the things I must ken before I meet with them. 'Twould be cruel to send them on a march to nowhere, with no memory at all."

Bhaltair relaxed. They would have a plan, and Eilidh would solve their problem.

16

The plan went ahead as Eilidh outlined. She met with each of their captives individually, touched them and gave them the commands she, Bhaltair and the Fletchers had agreed upon. Touching the skin of men who'd wanted to kill her made her stomach turn, but implanting new ideas in the minds along with the false memories was too important for her to let queasiness force her to quit.

The Fletcher allowed them to leave in pairs or groups of three. It took hours, but before the end of the day, they were sent out with supplies, weapons they would need for survival, and a set of false memories that would explain their absence.

Eilidh taught them to believe they'd come north hunting wolves, having heard the pelts were thicker and turning a desirable silver in the colder months that lasses in the south would covet. The word "wolves" was close enough to the word "witches" that it was easy for their minds to accept. Eilidh wanted them to be unsuccessful hunters in that quest, but Bhaltair insisted the story would be more readily believed if they demonstrated they'd killed a few, then decided to return south before the weather turned raw up north. Fletcher stores were searched and half a dozen half-cured pelts found. The fact that they were not the desirable hue Eilidh planted in their minds would reinforce the idea that the story was false and wolves looked much the same everywhere. There would be no need for more men to come north searching for more. Each group of two or three men left with one pelt rather than one pelt on each horse. That left two pelts for any other uses that might be needed.

Eilidh had grown more confident with each man she "controlled" as the afternoon wore on. Finally, the archer was the only one left. Despite her arguments against doing so, Jamie and Bhaltair decided they wanted to keep him for a while. He might yet give them information that would help them find Eilidh's attacker. She feared the longer he stayed in confinement, the harder it would be for her to overlay those memories with the wolf-hunting story or any other story they concocted for him.

"We should send him with the other men. They will reinforce each other's recollection of the memories I planted. If ye keep him, most likely ye will have to kill him rather than let him go. He'll have been here too long."

"We'll have nothing left," Jamie argued. "No contact with the witch hunters."

"Is that not what we want? To have them gone from here? Gone from the Highlands forever? That's what we've accomplished with the rest of his men. Why not him?"

"She is right," Caitrin said after a long pause, weighing in with her decisive Laird tone of voice. "Ye are not taking her ability into account. We dinna need him, even if we catch Pritchard. She can get any information from him directly. Ye dinna need to hear the two of them conspiring together in our dungeon. Let him go."

The muscle jumping in Bhaltair's jaw told Eilidh that he wasn't convinced, but after a moment, he nodded. Jamie did, too.

It took another hour for her to give him his false memories, then have him talk to her about them, fixing them more firmly in his mind while she held him in thrall. He left with the same supplies as the others, and with two pelts in the pack behind his saddle. As one of the group leaders, either he would have been more successful in the hunt, or he would have kept any pelts taken by men who died on the journey.

Eilidh heartily wished that was the last they would see of any of them. Even her attacker. Though Bhaltair still seemed determined to find him and exact punishment, Eilidh would prefer to forget what happened, finish with Orla and go home.

She was tired. More tired, physically, and heartsore, too, than she could ever recall. What made her think she needed to feel important? To have secrets that made her special. By the time she finished, she wanted nothing to do with this talent. Healing grievous wounds and accepting their pain was easier.

She and Bhaltair took supper with the Fletchers in the solar rather than with the rest of the clan in the great hall. Eilidh was exhausted from the heavy exercise of a talent she rarely had a reason to use, and the rumble of conversation from so many people irritated her and exhausted her even more. She planned to sleep for a sennight once she finished eating. But of course, she couldn't do that. "Orla awaits me," she said when she finished eating and stood.

"Eilidh, ye are spent," Bhaltair insisted. "Why not sleep tonight and see her in the morning. Ye'll be better able to sense what is happening. As ye are, ye might doze off and miss the very reaction ye need to find."

She couldn't fault his logic. She was stretched to her limit. She didn't blame Bhaltair for not wanting her to see the lass until after she rested. She fought down a yawn and headed for the door. Before she could open it, Bhaltair was at her side and pulled open the heavy oak. "Thank ye."

"I'll walk ye to yer chamber. I dinna want ye to fall on the stairs."

"I'm nay so spent as that." She yawned again. "Well, perhaps."

~

BHALTAIR WANTED Eilidh to stop pushing herself so hard. She needed a respite from using her talents, either of them, and a night's rest. She had burned herself out with the witch hunters. Caring for Orla was too much of a burden tonight. The fact that she was too tired to fight with him about it proved to him that he was right. She had eaten mechanically, saying little, her gaze on her trencher, not reacting to the conversation he and the Fletchers were having. Her shoulders were slumped and her skin looked sallow.

He was more worried about her than he'd ever been.

"If yer mother saw ye now, she'd be furious that I let ye work yerself into this state," he told her as he walked her up to her room. She trudged up the stairs, hanging onto the handrail. He was tempted to pick her up and carry her, but everyone left in the great hall would see, and Eilidh would be furious. So, he simply followed her to ensure she didn't stumble and fall down the stairs. He talked to her to keep her awake until she reached her chamber.

"My mother is well acquainted with this state," she told him as they reached the top. Her breathing came harder than he was used to hearing. "And ye didna *let* me do anything. It comes with the use of our talent."

"Not always. I've never seen her work herself into this state, not even after healing Donal MacNabb."

"Nay, not always," Eilidh conceded. "I've never had to use that particular talent for more than a moment or two. Spending hours at it was new—and painful. Today was an unusual day."

"That's good to hear. Ye dinna need to be this spent very often, or ye willna be able to help anyone, least of all yerself."

She stopped in the hallway and turned to face him. "Dinna lecture me, Bhaltair. I am the healer, not ye."

And yet, she was in trouble. And being stubborn about it. "Ye need someone to take care of ye, lass."

"Are ye volunteering for the job?"

He ran a hand through his hair in exasperation. "I am responsible for yer safety. I would do more if ye'd let me. If ye would trust me."

"I do," she said on the heels of an equally exasperated sigh, opened her chamber door and walked in.

Bhaltair stood in the doorway as she crossed the room and fell, fully clothed, onto her bed. He was torn whether to follow her in and at least cover her with a blanket, or close the door and let her sleep. If he went in, he did not know what might happen, except that he would not leave her side. He couldn't predict how she would feel about that when she woke up in the morning. She said she trusted him. Would she continue to do so if she found him asleep inside her chamber?

He bid her good night, knowing full well she was already asleep and would not hear him, and closed the door. He would remain nearby in case she needed him.

EILIDH CAME AWAKE from a dream in which Bhaltair stayed in her chamber and watched her sleep. She opened her eyes. He wasn't there, but he had been, in the laird's solar. It was a memory, not a dream. And not reality.

Disappointed, she sat up and shoved her hair behind her shoulders. Several decisions rose to the forefront of her mind. Whether it was the restorative sleep she'd finally had or a dream she didn't recall that let her sort out what to do, today was the day to heal Orla. The lass had suffered too long. And so had Kellina. But first, Eilidh had one more tisane she wanted the lass to drink. The one she suspected was the cause of the problems, and the one that might be the most difficult to deal with.

She got up and changed out of the dress she'd fallen into bed and slept in, went down stairs to break her fast, then sent Kellina to get something to eat while Eilidh cared for her bairn. After a few hours, the result was clear to her and to the Fletcher healer, who'd joined her. This was the one she'd begun to expect to be the culprit—Orla's body reacted badly to wheat. It was the one Eilidh had hoped not to find, since wheat was used in bread and cakes.

"Orla loves honey cakes and the clan eats bread at every meal," the healer said as she digested the news. "How will we keep them from her?"

Eilidh pursed her lips, then shook her head. "I dinna ken how, only that ye must," she told her, then asked for time with no interruptions to heal the lass's vitals. When she was done, she called the healer back to stay with Orla while she went downstairs for something to tide her over until the midday meal, and to talk with Kellina and Caitrin. The healer had told them what she'd spent the morning doing, so they were eager for her news.

"I will consult with my mother and I may come back in the spring if we can devise a way to prevent the reaction from happening. But for now, Orla is healed. Just keep wheat out of her food. No breads or cakes unless Cook can make them with another grain, once he is certain it is clean of wheat chaff. She's sleeping, but she'll wake before the evening meal is over. She will feel better. She will have more energy and demand more attention." She looked at Kellina when she said that. "I hope ye are prepared to have a healthy daughter."

Kellina nodded, hand over her mouth as she choked back a sob. Tears streaked her face.

"Ye will ken if she eats anything containing wheat," Eilidh continued, trying to give her time to collect herself. "It will hurt her, and the more she eats, the more harm it will do. Ye will see the same signs ye have seen for the last year."

"I understand," Kellina said, wiping her face with both hands.

"I'll make sure everyone knows not to give her treats. I always hoped, but I never thought she could actually be well." She held out a hand, reaching for Eilidh's, but Caitrin intercepted it. "I...we dinna ken how to thank ye," she added with a glance at her mother.

Caitrin squeezed her hand and released it.

"Ye already did." Eilidh smiled and stood, covering a yawn. She was grateful Caitrin had prevented Kellina's touch. Her emotional turmoil might be enough to take the rest of what little strength remained to Eilidh. "Now, I'm going to speak to Cook, then I want to go outside for a while before I sleep."

Eilidh wanted sunshine. She'd been inside the keep for too long, and her walk outside yesterday with Cook had been under forbidding, cloudy skies.

"We'll go with ye," Caitrin offered.

"Nay, ye should go to Orla," Eilidh objected. "I could use some time to myself."

After speaking to the cook about Orla, she inquired whether he needed anything from the gardens or the nearby woods.

He gave her a list of late season herbs and warned her to stay away from the wild areas. "Ye've been out as far as the grain fields. 'Tis safe enough along the edge of the trees during the day, but predators roam those woods later in the day, especially come sundown. Get ye back inside for the midday meal and stay in."

"*Dinna fash*," she told him. "I'll be back within the hour." With his blessing, she went outside and began searching for what he'd asked for.

The sun had come out, peeking through broken clouds and the winds had died down over night. It felt good to be among the sun-dappled leaves of trees and away from the keep, if only for a little while. She couldn't ask for a more pleasant day to be out of the castle.

As she looked for the herbs Cook wanted, her mind stayed quiet. Her work at Fletcher was done. She could rest today, and prepare for the trip home. Here and there, she noticed a sunny spot that would be pleasant for a nap on any other day, but after the extended healing session with Orla, once she fell asleep, she would be down for hours, unable to defend herself or to return to the keep if the weather worsened. Instead, she kept moving and breathing deeply, to give her body a welcome change from sitting inside Orla's chamber.

With Cook's advice in mind, she stayed along the edge of the woods, not venturing too far under the trees. Too late, she remembered Bhaltair would be furious if he knew she was out here alone. Her basket contained little, but she should go back. Or she should have asked one of the Lathan guards to accompany her.

She turned and retraced her steps along the woods back toward the keep. She could see the Fletcher keep's walls, so the guards peering out from them should be able to see her. She hadn't gone far when a man appeared out of the deeper forest into the filtered sunlight of the first rows of trees. Pritchard. The man who'd attacked her. She sucked in a breath and stood very still next to a large pine, hoping he wouldn't see her. But he headed her way, grinning the whole time.

"'Tis ye. I dinna think I'd ever see ye again, yet I saw ye near the grain fields. And now ye have come to me. So ye wish to finish our dance."

"I dinna, and if ye touch me again, my guards will kill ye."

"What guards? I see no one but ye."

"Would ye expect to?" She looked around as though spotting where her men might be concealed.

Cook knew where she had gone. She'd promised to be back in an hour. Surely she'd been out here longer than that, and someone would be looking for her by now. She put as much confidence in her voice as she could muster, speaking louder. "They are nearby." If she convinced him her men were in earshot and would soon be here, perhaps he would run.

"Nay, they are not. And the watchers on the keep's walls are too far away to save ye."

How did he know she was alone?

"Ye have been following me." He'd known where she was since she'd left the keep.

"I have. So, dinna bother to scream," he added with a grin. "If ye do, I'll kill ye here and now. But first, I want answers I think only ye can give me. I stopped a few of my men when they left that keep. What they said about what happened to them inside and why they were released made nay sense. I was right. There is a witch in that keep. Probably more than one. And ye ken who. Or perhaps the witch is ye."

Eilidh fought the fear that chilled her with his accusation. "Ye are wrong. There are nay witches, save in tales told to bairns. Did ye hear such as a wean? Ye shouldha outgrown them by now." *His men*? Not the archer's? If Bhaltair knew, he'd have redoubled the effort to find Pritchard instead of accepting the archer's assurance that he'd left the area. His admission meant she was in greater trouble than she'd feared, but if she could keep him talking, someone might notice she was here, and not alone, and would tell Bhaltair.

"Said like a true witch, trying to hide her evil soul," he snapped.

Her remark had gotten under his skin. That cheered her, but only a little. She was still in trouble, and perhaps had just made it worse. "I am not a witch. There is no such thing. Witches exist only in tales."

"Ye lie. Once I kenned my men had been cursed, I prepared what would be needed. Ye will come with me to be tested. God will decide whether ye are or nay."

"Nay!" Eilidh shouted her denial, hoping the guards on the walls would hear. She took a few steps to the side, toward the open glen. Even if they didn't hear her shout, they had to have seen her as she wandered. Surely they would send help. Perhaps Bhaltair was already on his way.

Pritchard reached for her.

She swung her basket at him, but he laughed and danced out of the way, then pulled his dirk.

"Start walking. That way," he said with a flick of his wrist, making the dirk's blade flash sunlight in her eyes as he used it to point deeper into the woods.

"I willna." On impulse, she took a step toward him rather in the direction he indicated, but he raised the blade. The defensive move gave her a welcome touch of confidence. She couldn't get close enough to him to touch his skin and use her Voice—yet. But if he truly thought she was a witch, he feared her. Though he would only come close if he meant to kill her, if he did, he would give her a fighting chance. Otherwise, he'd stay where he thought he was out of range of her spells. Sadly, out of her reach, as well.

She had to reason her way out of this. She had tried to fight him at the burn. Running seemed like a much better alternative. If she could get away from the trees, out into the glen where the guards could see her—and see Pritchard chasing her—she'd stand a better chance. She tossed the basket at his face and ran toward the keep, but only managed a few steps before he caught her by the arm, dragged her to her knees and held the dirk to her throat. The open edge of the glen was so close! Did no one see her? She tried to grasp the hand that held the blade, but Pritchard pulled it back.

"That was a daft thing to do. Now get on yer feet and walk, or I'll cut yer throat right here."

Eilidh batted at him, behind her, as she stood, but only encountered his rough clothing. She couldn't make contact with his skin, and with him a pace behind her, the point of the dirk pricking her back, she wouldn't be able to. She walked a few paces, then pretended to stumble, hoping he'd reach out to steady her and give her another chance at him, but he let her fall to her hands and knees.

"Get up." His command left no room for argument.

"I am not who ye seek."

"I dinna believe ye. Now, get up or die here."

She had no choice. Until she could get a hand on his skin, she was at his mercy. She stood and walked deeper into the trees.

17

Bhaltair finished his midday meal with the other Lathan guards and sat back, gaze still fixed on the stairs. Eilidh hadn't come down yet. Was she with wee Orla? Maybe. The Fletcher healer, Kellina, and both Jamie and Caitrin sat at a table on the other side of the hall. Like her mother, Eilidh preferred to work alone, so their presence gave him some assurance that she was with the bairn.

But his gut told him something wasn't right.

He stood and left the other men to finish their meals. Making his way across the great hall, he hoped he was mistaken.

Jamie noticed him coming and stood. "Is something wrong?"

Bhaltair schooled his features to a more neutral mask and shook his head. He didn't want to worry the Fletcher or her daughter. "Is Eilidh with Orla?"

Jamie shook his head. "I dinna ken. Kellina? Who is with Orla?"

"The healer. Have ye heard?" She turned her gaze to Bhaltair. "Eilidh healed Orla!" Her smile lit her face, making Bhaltair aware that she was an attractive woman—for some other man. The years of fear and grief were falling from her shoulders. He was glad for her, but he still didn't have the answer he sought.

"Eilidh isna with her?"

"Nay. Should she be?" Kellina frowned and turned a questioning gaze to Caitrin.

"I havena seen her since late this morning, when she told us she had healed Orla."

"I'll go check on her," Bhaltair said. "Even if she fell asleep, she should be awake by now and down here for more food."

Caitrin crossed her arms. "She seemed fine when she left. In fact, she said she was going to go speak to Cook about Orla's food."

If she had said that in an attempt to make him feel better, she had miscalculated. If Eilidh seemed fine, she could have gone anywhere from the kitchens, and it would take even longer to find her than if she was safe in her chamber. He still needed to check there first.

She wasn't in her chamber. After he knocked softly, he opened the door. Her bed was made and she was gone.

He hurried downstairs and gathered his men. "I dinna ken where she is, but 'tis not like her to miss a meal after she's done healing work. Fan out and search the stable and the keep for her. I'm going to talk to Cook. That's the last place we're certain she went."

Cook didn't have much help to offer until he repeated the conversation he'd had with Eilidh. Bhaltair's blood ran cold. "She went into the forest?"

"Aye. Along the edge, after herbs for me. The lass needed to get out of the keep for a while, so I gave her something useful to do. But, I told her not to venture into the trees."

"Damn it, man, which way did she go?"

"Out the usual way, through the orchard and by the grain fields, most likely. She told me what she learned about Orla and we talked about how to keep the bairn well. Then she left."

"How long ago?"

Cook peered toward the open door. "Judging by the light, and the fact that the lasses are bringing back things they're clearing from the midday meal, at least two hours ago. Maybe three." He frowned. "She said she'd only be gone an hour."

Bhaltair wanted to wrap his hands around the man's neck and squeeze until he choked, but he didn't. Such thoughts would not find Eilidh any faster. "I'm going after her. I didna send any of my men in that direction. Send a lad to Jamie and tell him where I've gone—and why."

"Aye. Of course."

Bhaltair clenched his fists and moved—out the door into the kitchen garden, through the gate and the orchard to the postern that led out to the grain fields. There, he slowed. If she met with anyone bent on doing her harm, it would have happened outside that gate. But Bhaltair took a few moments to study the area, the ground, the fruit trees. Nothing appeared disturbed, so he went out through the gate and into scout mode, first looking over the fields for anything that seemed out of place. One field had been harvested. The others were undisturbed. There was nothing there, so he moved slowly forward, and was soon rewarded with the impression of a woman's boot in a patch of soft earth. If he'd hurried, he would have missed it. He continued in the direction it indicated.

When he reached the edge of the woods, he turned along the trees, trusting that Eilidh would have had sense enough not to venture into the forest. Before long, he saw signs of struggle and his heart sank, his worst fear confirmed. Someone had her. The question was who? And where? One of the men they'd released? Had her compulsion worn off so soon? Or not worked at all? The thought chilled him to his ballocks. They'd released ten men, any of whom would eagerly take revenge on her for what she'd done —though it had saved their lives.

Two of his men reached him before he turned to go deeper

into the forest. "The guards on the wall told us they saw her moving along the edge of the woods an hour or more ago. They haven't seen her since."

"Fan out," he told them. "I'm tracking her, but in case I lose the trail in the undergrowth, ye may find it." The men nodded, split away from him, and went off at angles to his left and right. He kept on, and kept finding footprints—two sets on clear ground—that drew him forward.

Someone had her.

He found her basket on the ground, clearly tossed aside, the contents spilled out in a wilted fan of greens and browns. He quickly found two places where she'd fallen. Hand and knee prints on disturbed ground told him the story. She'd tried to get away, or tried to lure her captor close enough to get a hand on his skin and use her Voice to control him. But it was clear she'd failed. Both sets of footprints continued into the trees, hers leading, and bigger, deeper prints following a pace behind. Someone heavier. A man.

Bhaltair imagined the scene. Eilidh being marched at dirk or sword-point ahead of her captor under threat of death if she tried to run, and knowing if she did, she would not escape the fate he promised. He should have talked to her about the limits of her hidden talent like he'd planned. If he had, she would have understood how vulnerable she was, despite her ability, and no matter how exhausted she was in body and mind, she would never have left the keep alone.

Bhaltair clenched his fists and stalked on, studying the ground, but also the undergrowth, looking for broken branches, threads from garments or plaids, anything that told him more about what he would be up against when he found her.

He continued to believe she was being held by one man. Where was he taking her? The more he thought about it, the more he feared it was the one man they hadn't been able to find. The man who'd attacked her near the burn. Pritchard. He'd hunted her until he caught her, intending to finish what he started.

LeClair had lied about the man being gone from the area. Bhaltair owed him for that. They'd let their guard down, thinking the crisis was over, all of the witch-hunters neutralized and sent packing. He should have known better.

Eventually, a new scent teased his nose. Something deeper and more acrid than the usual smells of loam and evergreens.

Smoke!

He broke into a run as soon as he realized what he smelled. The scent grew stronger the deeper into the woods he went. Ahead, he saw light breaking through the tree canopy, and hazy smoke-filled sunshine. When he broke into the clearing, he nearly roared his rage. But this was no time to give vent to the horror filling him.

Eilidh was tied to a small pine, kindling, deadfall branches and dry grasses being layered around her in deadly piles by the man he'd thought of as the know-it-all. He had to save Eilidh or she would die an unthinkable death, in agony, before his very eyes.

"Witch!"

Pritchard stalked her, focused, it seemed on Eilidh's impending torture, ignoring the man still assembling his witch-fire. He circled around her with a burning branch in each hand, taken, Bhaltair assumed, from the small campfire off to one side. He and his companion had been here for days, setting this trap.

"I dinna ken what ye did to the other men, but they were not the same when they left that keep as when they went into it. Ye cursed them. Ye gave their souls to the devil. And for that, ye will die screaming."

There was still time. Thanks to the soft loam of the forest floor, they hadn't heard him arrive. Bhaltair moved carefully around the edge of the clearing, intent on getting behind Pritchard to reach him before he dropped his torches into the pyre around Eilidh. He would not allow anything to happen to her.

Know-it-all had a few feet more to fill with dry grasses before completing the circle. Rather than sharing Pritchard's frenzy, he seemed intent on his task. His gaze remained on the ground, never lifting to watch Pritchard threaten Eilidh. If he didn't approve, why was he helping, and not stopping Pritchard before he carried out his threats? Bhaltair couldn't fathom the reason, but as long as the man kept his gaze lowered, Bhaltair would reach Pritchard before his companion could shout a warning.

"Nay!" Eilidh shouted, her glare fixed on her tormentor. "I saved their lives," she said, her tone turned pleading.

Bhaltair suspected she'd noticed him and was intent on keeping Pritchard's attention on her.

"Ye dinna understand," she continued in the same tone. "They're alive. They're going home. That's all. I talked to them and convinced them to go home."

Pritchard waved one branch in her face.

She winced and turned her head aside, eyes squeezed shut against the heat of the flames.

Bhaltair moved closer on silent feet, intent on his target.

"I should shove one of these down yer throat so ye canna ensorcel me. But if I did, I couldna listen to ye scream as I watch the fire consume ye."

"Nay!" Eilidh cried out. "I have done naught to harm ye. Why—"

The other man's voice cut off her cry. "'Tis ready."

"Say yer prayers, witch, if ye ken how." Pritchard dropped the flame into the circle at the edge of the pyre in front of her and tossed the other branch to her side. Both caught immediately, grass and pine needles crackling and smoking for a moment, then bursting into flame.

Bhaltair didn't wait. He charged in, dirk raised, and brought it down in a killing blow, half severing Pritchard's head from his neck. The man collapsed and fell to one side, a shocked expression frozen on his face. Forever. His companion, still on the far side of the fire, backed away, hands raised, turned and ran for the trees.

Bhaltair jerked his dirk free, jumped through the flames and cut Eilidh's bonds, flinching away from the blaze that threatened both of them. In moments, she was free, but the flames were climbing, and the smoke that made her cough blinded his eyes with tears. The grass was fully involved, and the kindling was adding to the fire. Her skirt was aflame!

He scooped her up and jumped back through the growing flames to safety.

EILIDH WAS IN SHOCK, barely aware as Bhaltair dropped her on the ground and beat out her flaming dress with his bare hands. In moments, the flames in her skirt were out. Eilidh coughed and gulped clean air as she rolled to her side, reaching for him. He wrapped her in his strong arms and murmured her name, again and again as two more men arrived on horseback.

Bhaltair had found her! He'd saved her! She clung to him, grateful he was the one to rescue her, the one to hold her, despite the emotions that boiled in him. He wouldn't release her even to mount the horse his man led to them. She got a glimpse of the blistered and blackened flesh on his hands as he grasped the saddle, and cringed at what it must have cost him to hold it and lift her with him onto the horse. He stiffened but made no sound as he settled her across his lap.

She was dimly aware of more of his men running up. They captured the other man who'd helped Pritchard. She was grateful he hadn't been able to get to her or Bhaltair to finish what Pritchard had started.

Eilidh tried to take stock of their conditions, but Bhaltair's fury amplified her own and her left-over fear, preventing her from sensing more. Her feet likely had been protected by her boots, but her legs felt hot and must be scorched. Nothing hurt yet, but she knew how burns behaved. If they were bad enough, she would feel nothing at all. She couldn't tell, and that frightened her. Bhaltair's arms were blistered, too. She needed to heal him before his burns worsened.

But she kept fading into blackness, too spent, and too emotionally fraught, to summon her healing talent. Staying awake, being aware of her surroundings, took more strength than she possessed. She could only feel Bhaltair's arms encircling her, holding her safe in his embrace as they rode back to the keep, controlling their horse with his burned hands and blistered arms, probably in shock himself.

She had to help him, but she was powerless.

Tears slid down her face. The man she loved was in agony, suffering because of her. Why hadn't she stayed in the keep? Gone to her chamber to sleep instead of insisting on going outside? She knew her limits, and knew she was close to exhausting all her reserves when Caitrin helped her avoid Kellina's hand. Because of her selfishness, she had nothing to give to the man who meant the most in the world to her.

She succumbed and everything went black before they reached the Fletcher gate. When she woke, she cried out. "Bhaltair!" Where was he?

"He's right here," the Fletcher healer told her, approaching but not touching her. The woman gave her a gentle smile and nodded when Eilidh pushed herself up to sitting. "I gave him something to make him sleep until ye could wake and tend to him."

"How long?" Her voice was still little more than a croak from the smoke she'd inhaled.

"'Tis past the supper hour, but I have food and drink for ye."

Dear God, she'd been out for hours, and all that time, Bhaltair had been suffering. "Cider," she moaned. The healer gave her a cup, then poured another and another.

"Ye have some minor burns above yer boots, but they protected yer feet," the healer told her while she drank. "Yer man took the worst of it."

Tears filled Eilidh's eyes, but she blinked them back. She had no time for them. The cider was helping. She felt a little more awake, more refreshed, but only a little.

"Eat something, lass," the healer told her.

Eilidh shook her head and stood, fighting dizziness until her head cleared, then she crossed to the same table where Bhaltair had been placed with the archer's arrows in him. They were in the laird's solar again.

His hands! Eilidh's stomach turned and she feared she'd lose the cider she'd just consumed. She forced herself to control her revulsion at the red and blackened, flaking mess Pritchard's witch fire had made of Bhaltair's strong hands and lower arms. She had to heal him. If she didn't, if she couldn't, he would lose both hands and part of his arms, as well. He was Lathan's chief guard. The clan's most feared and fearsome warrior. What would he be without his hands?

He would never find out. She would not let him face a future where he did not know who and what he was to the Lathan clan, to himself, and to her.

She became aware that her legs hurt. She didn't care. He needed his hands more than she needed her legs. Healing his burns would be agony. She wouldn't have the strength to tend to her own burns when she finished with him. That didn't matter. He needed her. So, she drank more cider and ate a little of the food the healer provided.

The healer watched her consume every bite, nodding and smiling encouragement. "Ye need yer strength for this, lass," she told her. "Ye can do this. I have faith in ye."

"I may not be able to do it all at once. Have ye enough of yer potion to keep him asleep until I can finish?"

"If I dinna, ye can make him sleep."

Of course. Eilidh took that as a sign of how depleted she was. Putting a patient into a healing sleep was one of the first lessons her mother had taught her. One of the most important. And she'd forgotten it in favor of the Fletcher healer's potion.

She pursed her lips and nodded. "I will do all I can. I ask that ye stay nearby. I may need ye. I may not be able to tolerate—"

"I ken it. Ye will do the best ye can, rest, then do more until 'tis done. I will make sure ye have what ye need."

"That blade, the sharp one I used on him the last time."

"I'll get it. Eat and drink some more while I do. Dinna touch him until I return."

Eilidh saw the sense in that. Bhaltair's pain might overwhelm her. Or the healer's sleeping potion might have muted his pain to a level she could tolerate. But she would wait for the healer to return to find out.

Caitrin came in. "Eilidh, dear God," she cried. "At last, ye are awake. Tell me what happened."

"Bhaltair was burned saving me," Eilidh rasped. The smoke she'd inhaled still roughened her voice.

"The healer sent me to sit with ye until she returns. I checked on ye earlier, but she wanted to let both of ye rest. She said ye are to eat and drink more. Eilidh, ye look as though ye need care, too."

"I can wait. Bhaltair canna."

"He can wait for ye to be stronger," Caitrin admonished. "Here," she added and handed Eilidh the bowl of stew she'd sampled. "Eat."

Eilidh obediently took another bite, and another. "I canna eat any more. Cider, please."

Her stomach had nearly rebelled once. What would it do

once she touched his hands? She'd rather spew only cider than a meal. The healer came back as she finished another cup of cider.

"Here 'tis," she said and laid the blade next to Eilidh's hand. "And laird, if ye will find another jug of whisky, I think our lass is ready to begin."

Eilidh nodded, took a seat next to Bhaltair and touched his arm, reddened and blistered, the hair burned off, but not hurt as badly as his hands. She took a breath and summoned her talent, relieved, yet anxious, as her awareness of pooled blood and ruptured tissues grew and pain sharpened into agony. She could feel some burns on his chest but they were not as dire. His arm would heal over time on its own, but she would not allow him to suffer. She left it for now and held her hand above his ruined one.

Ye can do this, she told herself and touched the flesh. There was no pain. Not yet. Ruined flesh extended in a few areas nearly all the way to the bone, but his hands were as heavily muscled as the rest of him, and that meant while the surface looked bad, the flames had not done as much damage as she'd feared. She trimmed away blackened skin and reached for living tissue, using it to grow and spread into more badly damaged areas, building up from within. As she did, pain grew with it. She gritted her teeth and kept going, pulling tissue and fluids from the rest of his body to support her efforts. Until everything went black.

She woke up again in the cot where she'd first come awake.

"Back with us? Good. Drink this." Strong fingers touched her hand, but didn't hold a cup.

Caitrin's voice demanded compliance. It wasn't the same as the Voice Eilidh shared with her mother, but the Fletcher laird's tone had the same effect.

Eilidh raised her muzzy head as a strong arm slid under her shoulders and lifted her up enough for her to drink. Bhaltair? Nay, Uncle Jamie. This time, Caitrin held a cup to her lips, a finger against Eilidh's cheek to steady it. She drank.

"I canna see," she announced when the cup was empty and

she had a chance to take a breath. She was still too spent to summon the fear that the lack should evoke. It proved she was only her mother's echo, her talent fading away into nothing.

"Ye are exhausted. I'm surprised ye can do anything," Caitrin said. "Sleep now. Bhaltair is well enough to wait a few more hours until ye are better."

There had been something in what Caitrin gave her. Eilidh noticed the aftertaste just before she slipped back into the warm, dark place.

$\approx$

BHALTAIR CAME AWAKE SLOWLY, with a sense of heat and the vestiges of a nightmare, Eilidh burning as a witch. He opened his eyes, but everything was a blur. Where was Eilidh? Where was he?

"Bhaltair." Caitrin's voice came from close beside him.

"Eilidh?" He said her name in a raspy whisper. What was wrong with him?

"Here," she said and moved to his head, her hand never leaving his body as it skimmed up his arm to his shoulder to cup his face. He felt the air stir as Caitrin stepped back out of her way.

"What happened?"

"Ye were burned saving me," Eilidh whispered. "I am healing ye, but 'tis taking time."

"How bad?"

"Bad enough."

He fought to focus on her face, but his eyes wouldn't clear. "Why canna I see ye?"

"'Tis the potion the healer gave ye," Caitrin said. "To make ye sleep. Yer vision will clear when it wears off."

"I want to see ye now," he complained. "Eilidh, what do ye mean, bad enough? How badly have I hurt ye?"

"That doesna matter." She left his head and moved back to his left hand.

"It matters to me."

"I'm so sorry, Bhaltair. I healed Orla. I shouldha slept instead of going outside. Pritchard wouldna have found me. Ye wouldna be hurt. I've been too spent to heal ye... I can only do a little at a time."

"Stop it, Eilidh. Caitrin, tell her to stop. She must obey the laird."

"She is, Bhaltair. She must finish—for both yer sakes—no matter how long it takes."

"Send for Aileana." He blinked hard and was rewarded with a clear glimpse of Eilidh's face, thin and pallid, tears on the lashes of her closed eyes. She held his hand. "What has happened to ye, love? I am nay worth killing yerself!"

"I must do this. I owe it to ye."

Bhaltair tried to push up to sitting, but strong hands held him down. "Jamie, damn ye, help me up."

"Ye will stay where ye are until the healers—both of them— say ye may rise."

"God's bones, Jamie, ye are supposed to care for her. Ye are her family."

"There are many ways to care for me. The Fletchers are doing what I need them to do." Eilidh's voice betrayed her exhaustion and despair. Her brave words didn't satisfy him at all.

Suddenly, Eilidh was gone, and both Jamie and Caitrin scrambled to reach her as she fell.

Bhaltair rolled to his side and put a hand down to push himself up. Agony fired from his hand to his shoulder, nearly stopping his heart. He fell back, helpless. Furious. Desperate to care for Eilidh.

"What happened?" He ground out the demand with all the pain and fury in him.

"She fainted," Caitrin said. "We've got her."

"Why?"

"Why did she faint? She's pushed herself to her limits and beyond, for Orla, ye, and others. She needs to sleep for days and eat an entire stag by herself, but she willna abandon yer burns to become putrid."

Terror sent a cold frisson through Bhaltair's chest. Putrid wounds killed. That's what the archer had tried to do to him. He held up his hands and looked at them as best he could through the fog of the Fletcher healer's potion. The right one was mostly red, the left both red and areas of black, little resembling the strong, healthy hands that he used for everything.

"The black is the worst," Caitrin told him. "The red is either lesser burns and the skin is new, or where Eilidh has been repairing the worst of it. She has had to cut some of that black tissue away. She isna finished."

"She was burned, too," Bhaltair managed to ground out around the boulder blocking this throat.

"Aye, but she hasna had the strength to deal with hers, and our healer judged they are not as bad as yers."

"So, she bears her own pain and takes mine as well? And ye wonder why she's spent?"

"Nay, we dinna wonder at all. We make her eat and drink and rest as much as she will, before she returns to ye. And in between, we make ye drink, as well."

Caitrin came to him with a cup. Jamie lifted him to sitting, but stayed behind him, supporting him. Bhaltair realized without Jamie's support, he would not be able to stay upright. His head swam, but he drank down what Caitrin gave him.

"Another," she said.

He drank again. And another, until she was satisfied.

"How long will she sleep?"

"'Tis never long. Sometimes only a few minutes, sometimes an hour or several. She wakes and reaches for ye."

Bhaltair felt as close to breaking down into tears as he had in his life. Eilidh was killing herself to save him. "What can I do?" He had to help her.

"Stay with her," Caitrin said. "Jamie told me about something that happened at Lathan during the Gathering. Ye may be able to lend her yer strength. Even injured, ye have more than she. Yer right hand is healed enough that ye willna disturb her if ye touch her with it."

"I'll get some men to move her cot closer to ye," Jamie offered.

Bhaltair nodded. "I will speak with her when she wakes. She was able to share strength with her mother to save Donal MacNabb—MacKyrie—when he was stabbed at Lathan. Perhaps the others must be healers like her, or with talents like yers, laird."

"I hope they may simply be people she is very close to. Ye ken her better than anyone else here."

"There's another. Cole. They are friends. He might be able to help."

"I'll fetch him," Jamie said and ran from the chamber.

18

Eilidh came awake quickly, took a breath and opened her eyes to candle light, and the sight of Bhaltair sleeping close by, his right arm draped across the gap between their cots and his healed hand splayed on her stomach.

Lending her his strength? No wonder she felt a little better. Nay, he needed it for his own healing!

She sat up, disturbing him and dropping his hand to her thighs. Heat rushed from her chest to her face. He had touched her there, but no one knew save the two of them.

She took his hand in both of hers. The skin was losing its new growth pinkness. She curled each finger, then straightened them again, satisfied with the range of motion and the feel of each well-muscled digit. His palm was again plump and strong. The skin was tender, but it would thicken and strengthen in the next day or two. Her father would not lose his strong right arm, chief of his guards and future arms master.

Her healing sense was still crippled. She could not sense much below the surface of his skin. A cold sweat broke out on hers. If her talent burned out, would it ever come back fully? What kind of future would she have if her echo of her mother's talent had truly died away? She prayed she was only still suffering from exhaustion. If not, Bhaltair would be left in pain and half crippled until they returned home, for Aileana to treat him.

Dear God, her mother would be brokenhearted if she had ruined her talent, even if she had done so to save Bhaltair. When she healed Orla, Eilidh thought she had faced down her worst fear—that of failure. But if she had burned out her talent, she was worse than a failure. She had let down the man she loved when he needed her most. Despair weighed her down again. How could she overcome this?

A glance aside showed her Cole, asleep in a chair by the hearth. What was he doing here?

Someone knocked on the door. Eilidh took a breath. "Enter," she called out, grateful for the distraction. She couldn't bear the thought of the look of shock on Bhaltair's face when he found out she could do no more for him. But he had to know what he would be dealing with until they returned home. She would do everything she could to mute his pain, but her efforts might not help much.

Caitrin came in with a tray laden with food, and was followed by three serving girls carrying pitchers and cups. "I brought water and cider, Eilidh. I hope that is what ye want."

"That is perfect. Thank ye. Please stay with me. Bhaltair still sleeps. Cole, too. Why is he here?"

"How do ye feel?" Caitrin asked rather than answering her question.

Eilidh thought for a moment. "Better. A little better. But my talent is still—" She put a hand over her mouth, too frightened to say it and make it real.

"If ye feel better, that's a good sign. Yer talent will strengthen as ye do."

"Do ye think so?" Hope flared, and died just as quickly. How long would that take?

"I ken it. I have suffered the same in the past. Mine returned when I made the time to care for myself." She gestured at the food and drink. "The rest of the clan is breaking their fast. 'Tis time ye did, as well."

Caitrin's words let Eilidh breathe. She was still recovering. The laird had to be right. "I slept the night through?"

"Ye did. Cole and Bhaltair lent ye their strength. Or perhaps it was just Bhaltair. Cole said he felt nothing, but he stayed with ye, holding yer hand, for hours, in case he was helping. Bhaltair said he is yer friend."

Eilidh nodded as she absorbed that information with a sense of wonder—and shame—as she recalled her touch lending her strength to her mother in the Lathan great hall after Kilgore stabbed Donal in the back. And earlier, she, her twin Tavish and his soon-to-be bride Yvaine, the MacKyrie Seer, and her mother had held hands in her mother's herbal to strengthen the Seers' vision of the threat against the MacKyries. If only she had called on the others here at Fletcher to help her. "I was so intent on proving myself, I failed to ask for help ye might have been able to provide. If I had, both of us would be better by now."

"Bhaltair told us how ye worked together during the Gathering to save Donal, and to help identify the threat. But if I understand it, having others with talents, or those closest to them, touch the healer to lend their strength is a new idea. Dinna blame yerself for not thinking of it when ye, too, were harmed. Eat." Caitrin handed her a full platter.

Eilidh took it and did as the laird bade. Before long, her belly full, she stood, moved to Cole and touched his shoulder. After a moment, she turned to Caitrin. 'Twasn't him. I feel naught. He'll be disappointed."

"So dinna tell him."

"I must. He deserves the truth."

Caitrin nodded, approval in her smile. Of course, the woman who sensed lies would value her determination to tell the truth.

"Ye are awake!" Cole's voice startled Eilidh into spinning to face him. For a change, the room did not continue turning when she stopped.

"I am. Thank ye for what ye did."

"Did it help?"

She hesitated. "A little. Not as much as ye hoped, but kenning that ye tried makes me feel better. I am grateful."

He nodded, stood and stretched, apparently accepting the limits of his role. "I'm sorry I couldna do more."

"Go break yer fast," Caitrin said. "Ye can tell the rest of yer men how these two fare. 'Twillna be much longer before they are both well and ready to return to Lathan."

Cole nodded and, with a smile for Eilidh, left them.

"And ye, my fine lass, will sleep until the midday meal. Ye will eat again before ye do anything else for Bhaltair. I order ye to behave." Caitrin softened her command with a smile.

"Yes, m'laird," Eilidh answered soberly. Caitrin was right. She must recover before she tried to do anything else for Bhaltair. She did not want him to have to continue to suffer with his injuries until they reached the Aerie. It was up to her to make sure that did not happen.

The next time she woke up, she felt more like herself. She was alone with Bhaltair, and the temptation was strong to go immediately to him. But Caitrin had left more food and drink, so she did as the laird had directed and ate before she attempted anything else.

This time, her talent seemed stronger, though not entirely restored. She laid a light healing sleep on Bhaltair, certain that by now, he'd drunk more of the Fletcher healer's potion than he should have. She worked quickly, doing what must be done to heal Bhaltair's left hand. She sensed less serious burns on his chest as well, but chose to leave them for tomorrow, when she would be stronger. Then she checked the condition of his right hand, and satisfied with its progress, settled in the chair Cole had vacated earlier and finished the food and drink Caitrin left for her. She would get more for Bhaltair when he woke up.

Caitrin's entry woke her from a doze. "Ach, I'm sorry, I hoped to check on both of ye without waking ye."

"*Dinna fash*. We're both fine. I've finished what I can do for Bhaltair until tomorrow. He's in a healing sleep, but he should wake soon. He'll need food and drink." She gestured at the empty platter on the small table beside her. "I fell asleep after eating all ye left."

"That's good. All is well."

Was it? Eilidh thought back to what she felt from him as he pulled her from the fire. Bhaltair's fury frightened her, and she had feared he would blame her for what happened to him. Her face must have reflected the change in her thoughts, because Caitrin came to her and took her hand.

"Tell me what is wrong."

Eilidh knew she could not lie—even by omission. Caitrin would sense it. "I fear we canna be together. Ye dinna ken. He hides..." She shook her head, searching for the words she needed to make Caitrin understand. To help herself understand. "His emotions are too strong, I dinna ken whether I have power enough to stand up to him. There is so much violence in him." She held up her free hand to forestall Caitrin's objection. "I ken he is a warrior. I've watched him training with the other Lathan men most of my life. But the things he wanted to do to LeClair, and to Pritchard—both times—horrified me, and not just because of what I might have to deal with when he finished. What I felt when he pulled me from the flames... the way I can feel his emotions—good and bad—through my talent makes it worse. I dinna ken if I am strong enough to love a man with such fierce fury inside him. But telling him so will hurt him."

Caitrin released her and shook her head. "Have ye never heard that a woman's love can tame the wildest man?"

"I dinna think I have it in me to tame Bhaltair. Or to save him from himself." She wrapped her arms around herself and hung her head. "I gave him my heart. Years ago. But now I think I should take what's left of it back."

Caitrin again reached for her hand and squeezed it. "I feel yer pain, I do," she said and lifted their joined hands. "But I think ye are wrong. Perhaps, save in the heat of battle when berserk violence is required to save himself or his men, Bhaltair would never act on those feelings. Yet imagining how he would use them, speaking the words, is his way of letting go of his anger. Ye ken that battle lust is a real and dangerous state men inhabit when they must fight. I've seen Jamie in its throes, and he terrified me, even though I kenned he would never turn it against me. How do ye think they escape it? Calm from it? Some men drink themselves into a stupor, or pick a fight with another man. By speaking it aloud, I think Bhaltair rids his mind and body of feelings he canna act on, and they're worse when he finds that someone plans to harm the woman he loves. Ye."

Caitrin's words gave Eilidh much to think about. "If only ye are right," she told her. "But how will I ever ken, if I canna bear to be around him? Or ken if I am safe with him."

"Has he ever threatened ye?"

"Nay."

"Harmed ye or any of yer family?"

"Nay."

"Has he fought with all he has to protect ye and keep ye safe? To save ye from harm? From that witch-fire yesterday?"

"Aye." Eilidh sighed. How could she be so wrong about him? So conflicted? "He has done all those things. He has never done violence save to protect me and my family."

"Give it time, lass. Healing a heart 'tis like the healing ye do. Both of ye will have to be willing to do the work. Both of ye will have to give some, as well as take, and bear the pain together."

Eilidh wanted to believe her. To believe she and Bhaltair might have a future together.

"I see ye still have doubts. Lass, ye are still tired. Go to yer chamber. I'll have a tub and hot water sent up to ye. 'Tis time to care for yerself. I will also have food and drink left for Bhaltair when he wakes," she added when Eilidh's mouth opened at the same time her gaze strayed to the big man. "He kens he has been well cared for, and he will likely want much the same. Ye can see him at supper."

Eilidh knew better than to argue with the laird. "Thank ye for yer care of both of us," she told her and left the chamber.

KELLINA CAME TO HER LATER, after she'd had time for a bath and to change into clean clothes. "I ken how it is between ye and Bhaltair. Ye are upset with him, and I think I can help."

"How?" Eilidh would not have believed for a moment that Kellina would pass up the chance to take advantage of a rift between her and Bhaltair, but her presence here gave the lie to that assumption. She stepped back and let Kellina enter her chamber, but she left the door open. She didn't want trouble, and she didn't know what kind of help Kellina had in mind.

"Let me tell ye about my life with my husband," Kellina said after they settled in chairs by the small hearth. "I miss him so much, 'tis as if he was my heart and he was ripped from my chest the day I learned he had died. I wasna even with him. I didna learn of it until days after he was gone." She made a fist and pounded her chest. "There's a hole in here that he used to fill. A hole that even Orla canna begin to heal. They brought his body home, but they wouldna let me see him." She stopped for a moment and swallowed.

Eilidh could tell that her emotions were genuine. She was still in pain, nearly two years after her husband was killed. "How did he die?"

"In a battle. Where else? He fought for me and our bairn. For our clan. He was injured so badly, they feared to show him to me. And now he's gone. Forever." She stopped again and took a breath, gathering herself. "Despite all the pain I've suffered since then, I wouldna trade a day I had with him. I would kill for more. He wasna always a good man. He was a warrior, too. But he loved me and he loved Orla. I never doubted him. Her father was the one man I will ever love with my whole heart."

"I'm so sorry for what ye have been through."

Kellina waved her comment away with a flick of one hand. "'Tis in the past. Ye are giving me a future with my daughter that I despaired of ever having. I lived in fear for her, because she is my daughter, and because she is the only thing I have left of my husband. I grieved for her as if she was already dead. I owe ye for saving her, which is why I came to ye."

"Ye didna need to—"

"Ye need to see the good in Bhaltair," Kellina said, stopping Eilidh from speaking. "Aye, he is handsome, and a fearsome warrior, but that isna what makes him the man he is. If ye see only how he behaves when he's terrified for ye and furious that someone hurt ye—well, ye canna do that. Venting his fury with words instead of actions should prove to ye that he kens the difference between the time to fight and the time to rid himself of his feelings. He would never hurt ye. He loves ye and wants to care for ye."

Eilidh nodded, despair filling her. Could she get past her fears?

"And perhaps he's never known a true love in his life," Kellina continued. She reached for Eilidh's hand and squeezed it. "I think ye mean more to him than ye realize. Ye could be exactly what he needs to find peace." Kellina stopped.

Eilidh sensed Kellina's earnestness and sympathy through their link. She was sincere, Eilidh had no doubt. The emotions swamping her made Eilidh's heart hurt. She pulled her hand from Kellina's grasp. "Yer mother sent ye, aye?"

"Of course. How else would I ken how much ye are hurting right now? Ye must heed me. Dinna throw away a good man's love because he expressed his fear for ye in a way ye find hard to accept. Give him the chance to show ye he can be the man ye believe he is."

Eilidh suspected what she meant was that she shared her mother's talent for detecting lies and knew Eilidh was sincere. She took Kellina's words to heart. Eilidh had seen how she suffered without the husband she loved and lost.

And Eilidh did love Bhaltair. How could she consider turning her back on him? She couldn't bear to live without him, or worse, to live at Lathan, seeing him every day and knowing he could have been hers if she'd been strong enough to match his passion and yet, be his opposite. To be soft to his hardness, calm to his fury, confident to his fear. More than anything, she wanted to do that for him, and let him do the same for her.

"Thank ye, Kellina. I ken it was hard for ye to bring up old memories, and to share the pain of yer loss. I understand what ye have told me. Ye are right, I dinna want to throw love away."

"That is the most important decision ye will ever make, Eilidh. Please, think on what I have said. I canna predict what will happen to the both of ye in the future if ye give him another chance, but if ye dinna try? That, I can predict."

"So can I," Eilidh told her. And to do it, she did not need to possess her brother Tavish's talent for seeing the future.

BHALTAIR WOKE aware that he felt better. He clenched his fists, then rubbed his chest. It hurt a little at his touch, but nothing else did. Encouraged, he sat up. Light from the solar's window told him it was late afternoon. He was alone, but food and drink had been left for him on a hearthside table.

He stood and took a tentative step toward it, and another,

relieved that he seemed to have regained some strength. He picked up a cup and studied the fingers curled around it. They looked the same as they always had. Nay, the skin lacked scars that had been there. He held the other hand up to the light and studied it. Eilidh had succeeded in healing his hands. They were better than before he'd burned them, trying to smother the fire in her skirts. His shirt was open, and the skin looked a little red, but all the old scars were still there. His chest had not been burned as badly as his hands.

Satisfied that he was well, or would soon be, he drank most of one pitcher of cider before beginning on the platter of bread, cheese, fresh butter and honey cakes. He should get cleaned up before supper. Despite what he had just eaten, he knew a hot meal would finish putting him to rights. That and seeing Eilidh.

He had vague memories—unless they were dreams—of hearing her talk about her fear of him. Of the fury that lived in him. Had she been speaking to him, assuming he was deeply asleep? Or speaking to someone else? If any of that was real, he wasn't surprised that she had left him alone. But he strongly suspected Caitrin's hand in that, as well. Likely she'd been ordered to take care of herself now that he was out of danger. He hoped so.

Should he go to her now?

It wasn't like him to be reluctant to fight for what he wanted, but Eilidh had made it clear she feared his capacity for violence. Fighting for her seemed like the wrong approach, yet fighting was what he did best. He would never harm her. He would die before he would do such a thing. But perhaps she didn't know that.

So, he judged the wiser course was to give her some time, and to take some time for himself to figure out how to reassure her. How to convince her that his love for her would keep them together, and that he would do everything in his power to keep her safe for as long as they lived.

After a bath and change of clothes in the barracks he some-times shared with his men, he felt more like himself. The men stayed nearby in case he needed anything, and once he was clean and dressed, he called them together to talk about what had happened during the trip. They knew about Jamie's offer. Those who had heard Jamie make it had told the others. They assured him they never believed he would leave Lathan for Fletcher's offer. Happily, he was able to assure them he never intended to. With the air cleared, Cole admitted Eilidh had asked him about what she'd overheard, and he confirmed the offer. Bhaltair's heart sank, certain she would never trust him again, until Cole reminded him of when that had taken place. Long before he had declared himself to her. She had to know he would not leave her. He had told her so.

He heard the bell ring for the evening meal and knew if he didn't speak to Eilidh now, he might never be able to again. She would go on avoiding him as she had all her life. And there would never be a time when the events of this trip didn't come between them. He had to erase her memory of that fearsome man, and replace it with the man who loved her and was not afraid to prove it.

He crossed the great hall and climbed the stairs without speaking to anyone, went to her door and knocked. "Come," he heard her call. She probably didn't expect him to be at her door. No matter. He opened it, stepped in and closed it behind him.

"Bhaltair!" She had changed her clothes and looked more rested, but still worn from fighting for him.

"I've come to apologize," he said. "Ye were terrified, and hurt-ing, and I made ye feel worse."

"What do ye mean?"

"After I pulled ye from the fire. What ye felt in me."

"Bhaltair? How?"

"I heard some of what ye said when ye thought I slept."

"Dear God." Eilidh paled. "I didna mean to hurt ye."

"I fought to save ye. I will never hurt ye, but I will not make excuses. I just want ye to ken that I am deeply sorry."

Eilidh studied him for a long moment.

Bhaltair held his breath. If she threw him out now, she would never be his, and all the time spent loving her, wanting her, would have been wasted. But if she forgave him, they could have a future. One they would have to work for. He would have to do the most work. He had no illusions about that. But he would, and gladly.

She crossed her arms and his heart gave a hard punch to the inside of his chest. She was defending herself, walling herself away from his reaction to the hurtful words she would say to him. His eyes moistened, a sensation he associated only with death and grieving. He had survived much in his life, but standing there, watching Eilidh search for the words to tell him she did not love him, was the worst pain he'd ever known.

"If ye can forgive me—nay, forget that. I do forgive ye. Of course, I do."

He stared at her, uncertain that he'd heard her correctly. "Ye do?" His heart gave another powerful thump that felt like a blow from a war hammer, then resumed beating. He lifted a hand to rub his chest, fighting to understand what had just happened.

"I do, Bhaltair." She took a step toward him, then stopped, as if uncertain how he would react. "I forgive ye. And I hope ye forgive me. I want to be yers. I ken that ye always thought of me as shy and weak, but I am strong enough to stand up to ye. And with ye. To fight for myself. To be yer opposite, yer strength where ye are weak. And I need ye to be my strength where I am weak."

She held out her arms. He noticed the purple bruises marking them, then she pulled aside the neckline of her dress to bare one shoulder.

"I fought for myself when Pritchard captured me. I injured him, but I couldna get a hand on him long enough to control him. Or the other man. There was another man helping him prepare the fire."

"I ken it, love. And that's another debt I owe ye. We caught him the first time we encountered the archer's men. Pritchard wasna with them, but that man seemed to ken something. My men got nothing from him, so let him go with the rest."

"It doesna matter. He did naught but help Pritchard. Pritchard was the one who beat me senseless before he tied me to that tree. I never touched him long enough to stop him. He tied my arms behind me." She took another step. "There are more bruises, ones I canna show ye without undressing. Nay," she said and held up a hand, "not there. He was too afraid of the witch he imagined to try to rape me. He believed he could only destroy the witch by burning me." She glanced at the marks on her arm. "I would have healed them before now, but I wanted ye to see that I fought him."

"Eilidh." His voice broke.

She held up a hand when he shifted his weight to step toward her. "At first, I didna understand yer urge to fight, to do terrible damage, but now I do. If I had found a way to stop him, even kill him, I wouldha done so. I kenned I was fighting for my life. I wasna strong enough. But ye are. I ken I can lean on ye. And that ye need a better way to release yer worst feelings, one I can give ye."

She moved into his arms, and Bhaltair's first-ever tears of joy fell into her hair.

19

The next morning, Eilidh assured the Fletchers that Orla was healthy and strong for the first time since she started eating the clan's food. Jamie and Caitlin admitted to Bhaltair and to her that they'd sent Fletcher scouts to shadow the archer and his men, and that they'd seen no sign of any of them remembering what really happened here, so they agreed that the steps they'd taken with them had been effective, and it would be as safe as could be expected for the Lathans to travel home.

They had learned very little about LeClair and his men, but one thing she was sure of—they would never cross into the Highlands again. She had saved their lives and made them forget the madness that had brought them north, hunting witches. They now believed there were none, except in tales for children on All Hallows Eve. If she'd done her job as well as she hoped, they would tell their friends at home they had found only a few scraggly wolves, no witches, and perhaps some of the witch-hunting fervor of the Lowlands would ease.

Eilidh was happy to hear the Lathans would soon go home. Packing took little time. She needed only her clothes and the few personal belongings she'd brought with her. She left the bounty of healing supplies she'd brought with the Fletcher healer, who thanked her profusely for the gift. By midday, they made their farewells to the Fletchers and the Lathan contingent headed back to the Aerie with an empty wagon and a full Fletcher escort.

"I dinna want to upset my parents," Eilidh told Bhaltair as they rode toward home, "but how do we explain the witch-hunters, the archer and the others, without my father sending men to find and kill them? We were harmed, aye, but not permanently."

Bhaltair kept his gaze on the far distance as he pondered what she'd said. She loved looking at him, even at his profile, the strong line of his jaw, the blade of his nose, and his tawny blond hair that brushed his shoulders. She also loved that he gave serious thought to her questions. Except when he was fighting to save his or his men's lives, he was more contemplative than she had ever realized. She'd always seen him as quiet, which added to his air of menace, but she'd been wrong about that. He was quiet because he thought. He had impressed her with his beauty and his caring, but this intellect that she had become aware of during this trip impressed her even more.

"We *were* harmed," he insisted, "and someone without yer talents would still be suffering. I might have died from the injuries the archer inflicted. Had I not found ye when I did, before the fire grew any greater, ye would have died a horrible death—"

"I ken it, and I'm so sorry ye suffered the wounds ye did," she said, stopping him. "Ye took more harm than I in saving me from the fire."

Bhaltair gave her a frown that told her he wanted to argue that point.

"And I didna die. I dinna wish to tell them about that."

"Eilidh, what do ye think is in the letter we carry from Jamie to yer da? The size of the Fletcher harvest?"

She huffed out a breath and frowned. "Ye have a point."

"Jamie will tell him. If not in the letter, then in another after he deems we have had time to return and relate what we did at Fletcher. So ye may as well tell them the truth—the whole truth —before he does. It will go over better coming from ye, sitting with them, whole and apparently unharmed, than if they first read what Jamie writes."

Eilidh sighed. Bhaltair was right. "I will. We will. They must see the same of ye—that ye are whole and well."

"Very well. But first, I will speak to yer father about us. I want ye to marry me, Eilidh. Soon. I dinna want to live another day without ye in my life."

"I've been in yer life for years, and ye in mine."

"Not as a couple. Not as married lovers. We have much to explore and learn in this life. I want to do all of it with ye."

She reached for his hand. "I want the same with ye."

"Then 'tis settled."

The rest of the trip went without incident and Eilidh was happy to see the Aerie on its high tor when they crested the last hill before reaching it. She was glad to be home, even if it meant there would be more people watching her and Bhaltair. She was not the same person she'd been when they left. She was, after all, home safe and sound, but loving Bhaltair, and knowing he loved her, too, made all the difference.

AFTER THE EVENING meal celebrating their return, Bhaltair followed Toran to the solar to ask for Eilidh's hand. "I ken this is sudden," he said, standing before the laird's desk after refusing the seat Toran gestured him to, "but perhaps ye will want Aileana and Eilidh here, as well."

Toran straightened in his seat behind the desk. "Did something happen while ye were away?"

"Aye, well," Bhaltair said, paused and cleared his throat, making Toran's brow crinkle. He never hesitated, so that pause had likely told Toran to be alert. "Many things happened. Ye may as well hear about them together, from both of us."

Toran shook his head. "Before I send for them, is there aught ye want to tell me before they come in?"

Bhaltair nodded, acknowledging his laird's wisdom. Toran had helped train him and had seen to his upbringing in the clan once he returned from fostering at MacKyrie. The laird knew him well enough to know there were things best discussed among men. "'Tis less something to tell ye than to ask ye—for Eilidh's hand."

Toran laughed, but stopped when Bhaltair's expression remained sober. Bhaltair saw the light flare in his eyes as he realized his question was serious. He steeled himself for Toran to tell him that Eilidh would never be his. That she must make a match that would bring an ally into Lathan as her husband. All his fears burned anew in his chest, making it ache. But after the cut-off laugh, Toran's response was not what Bhaltair expected.

"'Tis about time. Her mother and I hoped ye two might one day be together."

Bhaltair found he could breathe after all. He sank into the chair Toran had indicated.

"For a while I thought Lianna might catch yer eye," Toran continued, clearly giving him time to collect himself. "Until David MacDhai came back into her life. Was it hard, going with them to MacDhai?"

Bhaltair shook his head and let his shoulders drop. "Lianna and I were never more than friends. So, nay, 'twasna. The only worry I had was keeping her safe, and being certain that MacDhai wouldna hurt her again."

Toran nodded, got up, and sent someone to fetch the women. "Let's move to the chairs by the hearth. We'll all be more comfortable there," he told Bhaltair while they waited.

Aileana and Eilidh came in together, making Bhaltair wonder if Eilidh had been preparing her mother for what she would hear.

Toran held out his hand to Aileana, so she came to him and sat on the chair next to his. "Bhaltair has something to tell us, love."

"Aye?"

She turned to him, her expression expectant, confirming his suspicion that Eilidh had warned her what he would ask.

"I have asked the laird for his permission for yer daughter and I to wed," he said, smiled at Eilidh and reached for her hand.

She took his and settled on the arm of his chair. "'Tis what I want," Eilidh told her mother, then turned her gaze to her father and narrowed her eyes. "I dinna ken what plans ye might have had for me, but—"

"None that ye would not approve, daughter," Toran said, interrupting her. "Yer mother and I are quite content with this match."

"What yer da means to say," Aileana added, "is that we are both thrilled and happy. We hoped for ye to make a match within Lathan, with a man good enough for ye. And ye have." She reached across and squeezed her daughter's hand, glanced at her husband, then she turned to Bhaltair. "Now, tell me, what else happened to my daughter while ye were gone?"

EILIDH KNEW her father would care little, and Bhaltair knew the tale, but she took her time relating her suspicions about Orla's condition, what she'd done to heal her for the near term, and asked her mother to consider what else they might be able to do for her.

"'Twillna be an easy problem to solve," Aileana said thoughtfully, and her gaze seemed to go inward.

"There is more," Eilidh warned her, pulling her attention back to their presence. She glanced at her father, then said, "I was attacked on the way there, and again before we left."

"What?" Toran stood.

Bhaltair stood, too, and Eilidh risked his ire to put a hand on his arm while she stared at her father. "Da, sit down. 'Twasna Bhaltair's fault. 'Twas my own bad luck the first time and my fault the second."

"Ye were attacked twice?" Toran frowned, but sat, so Bhaltair did, too.

Eilidh glanced at her mother, who was frowning at her husband, then took a relieved breath and told them everything.

"We might have spared ye some of the details," Bhaltair said when she wound down, "but we carry a letter to ye from Jamie that will probably repeat much of this, so we judged it better for ye to hear it from us. We are well. Eilidh is safe."

"I wasna harmed. Bhaltair was burned in saving me, but of course, I took care of him. It took some time."

"Of course," Aileana echoed. She appeared a little shocked, wide-eyed and pale. "And ye are well?" At Eilidh's nod, she continued. "Witch hunters in the Highlands. Will there be more?"

"Likely." Toran's answer was gruff but honest. "We must keep the secret of yer abilities among the clan and our allies. I willna tolerate having any of my family threatened again."

"We canna be certain others, who shouldna, dinna already ken."

"Nay, we canna be certain. But what ye did to those witch-hunters can be done again. 'Tis a more elegant solution than killing them. They dinna disappear. They go home with tales of finding nothing. If they are believed—"

"Tales of strange abilities, strange creatures, fill Highland myths," Aileana interjected. "We will never silence all the specu-lation. The fear."

"As long as we keep it away from our people, I will be satisfied," Toran said. "Highlanders have been accepting the tales—most of them—for generations. This Lowland threat canna be allowed to spread here."

Aileana frowned. "But think on this. I came from the Lowlands with Colbridge's army. I brought my talent to the Highlands. Perhaps there are others like me where I came from. What will happen to them?"

Toran shook his head. "We canna ken. We can only control what we control. I will send missives warning our allies to keep their women safe, especially their healers."

"I hope it helps," Eilidh said.

"We all do," Toran said in agreement. "I'll enlist Fletcher to help spread the word with our allies closer to them. We will do all we can."

"I ken ye will. Let's forget this for now," Aileana said, brightening. "We have another wedding to plan. That is very good news. Ye are home, safe, sound, and strong. Despite the troubles ye faced, or perhaps because of them, ye discovered yer love for each other."

"Let's drink to love," Toran said and fetched a bottle of MacKyrie whisky and four cups from the solar's cabinet. "And a happy future for us all."

20

E ilidh had watched her siblings go through the nerves that seemed to accompany this day. They had been filled with doubts and anxiety, but also anticipation and joy. She felt surprisingly calm. Determined. Because she'd known Bhaltair all her life? Because of the battles they'd fought together at Fletcher? Or simply because they loved each other? No matter. With her mother, Morven, Yvaine and Lianna's help, she was dressed and ready. The seamstress, Moina, had created a lovely gown that rivaled what she'd made for previous Lathan brides. Eilidh had never felt so beautiful. She hoped Bhaltair agreed. "Let's do this," she told them.

"I'll tell yer da ye are ready," Aileana said, kissed her cheek and left the younger women.

Eilidh heard her shifting the men around at the top of the stairs.

"*Dinna fash*," Lianna told her. "Mother will sort them out."

Eilidh grinned and left her chamber ahead of all of them.

Her parents, brothers, and brother-by-marriage met them at the top of the stairs. Eilidh spared a glance for Drummond and

David MacDhai, but they seemed to have called a truce for the day, so she dismissed them from her mind.

Eilidh didn't want to stop, but she knew the protocol. Drummond escorted his wife, and Tavish his. David and Lianna were the next to the last to go together. Her only sibling missing was the youngest triplet, Jamie. He had sent word that he and his wife Aftyn were dealing with an outbreak of illness and did not want to bring it to the Aerie. He promised they would visit as soon as they could. She missed him, but understood his reason for wanting to keep his family and clan safe.

Instead of watching the others descend the stairs, she kept her gaze on Bhaltair. He smiled at her, looking supremely confident while he waited. She expected nothing less.

Her father caught her eye and mouthed *ready*? She smiled and nodded, so he escorted her mother down. She watched them go, both still tall and strong, as beautiful and in love with each other now as they had always been. Of that she had no doubt. She could not have wished for better parents. Or a better family.

It was time. Finally, it was her turn to take this step. To wed the man she loved. She descended alone, for once not minding being the object of everyone's attention, though she hoped she didn't trip and fall down the stairs. At the bottom, she took her father's proffered arm. Her mother walked on her other side as they made their way through the crowd of Lathans, then Aileana took a seat and Toran took her to where Bhaltair waited near the hearth with the priest. Someone had set up a makeshift altar. Makeshift in name only. It was beautiful, made of garlands of autumn-turning leaves, and probably half of the herbs in the kitchen garden. The scents were lovely and green. She hoped Cook intended to dry and use them later.

They knelt before the priest, who droned on. Eilidh paid him little attention, keeping her gaze lowered and responding only after she heard Bhaltair's voice. A towering, solid presence next to her, she knew she could lean on him. He would defend her, care for her and love her until his dying day. She offered up a silent prayer that such a day did not arrive for many years to come.

Finally, the priest was done. Bhaltair took her hand and helped her to her feet and tilted up her chin with a gentle finger. "We are wed," he told her with a smile that lit his whole face.

"We are," she agreed and pulled his head down for a kiss. The gathered clan cheered at that, so Bhaltair pulled her up on her toes and kissed her back, then turned them both to face the clan.

"My wife, Eilidh Lathan." When they cheering abated, he continued. "We are Lathans and always will be. We will serve this clan with honor for as long as we live."

Eilidh didn't know what to say to follow that, so she simply smiled until inspiration struck. "Our marriage within the clan strengthens our bonds to ye and to this place. We are proud to have ye help us celebrate our love. So let us begin!" She waved a hand for the ceilidh to start.

Everyone found a place at a table and the food came out. And ale, lots of ale. Bhaltair took a sip now and again, but Eilidh was pleased he remained sober.

Once again, she found she didn't like being the center of attention. She never had, but for his sake, today, she would tolerate it. He must have had a word with his men, because no one called out ribald comments, though there were many calls to "kiss the bride." That, she didn't mind. She could kiss Bhaltair for hours and never tire of him, though she would rather not have an audience for the best ones. But those kisses would wait until later.

After the meal and some dancing, Eilidh had enough. "I'm ready to go," she told him.

"I'm surprised ye lasted this long," he said and gave her a gentle hug, then released her. "Go on up. I'll wait a wee so we dinna appear too eager."

"Anyone who knows me will ken I dinna like being stared at, so they willna be surprised if I leave."

"Even if I'm the one doing the staring?"

"That's different." She stood and bent to give him a kiss. "Dinna wait too long," she whispered in his ear.

He gave her a heated look that fired her blood and warmed her all the way to their chamber.

EILIDH PACED IN THEIR CHAMBER, waiting eagerly for Bhaltair to arrive. Moina had made a beautiful night rail for her to seduce him with, but she was too eager to bother to change into it. She would save it for another night when she wasn't so anxious. So impatient.

He would soon be hers, in all ways. She knew there would be pain. All of Bhaltair was huge. But she was tall, and she would adjust. They would fit together. She would spend the rest of her life wrapped in his arms and in his love.

If only he would open the door. Where was he? She continued to pace, kicking her skirt hem out of her way as she walked from one side of the chamber to the other and back again.

A slight noise in the hallway alerted her. She stopped and faced the door, surprised to find herself breathless as it opened and her husband stepped inside. Seeing her, he smiled, closed and barred the door. "Eilidh, have I told ye how beautiful ye are?"

She stepped up to him and reached up to brush aside his hair and stroke his face. "Ye flatter me, Husband. I dinna need sweet words. I need ye."

His head dipped and he kissed her, gently at first, moving his lips over hers, nipping her bottom lip, and using his tongue to soothe away the wee pain.

She opened to him and the kiss deepened. His tongue invaded, and she met him stroke for stroke, all the while feeling his manhood hard against her belly. He wanted her, and she wanted him. But despite the heat she felt growing in his blood, he seemed in no hurry to move.

He might be the warrior, but she knew how to fight, too. She broke the kiss and grabbed his hand, then pulled him to stand by the bed. "This is our field of battle, my husband, where ye will conquer me. But I will also conquer ye."

"I hope so," he murmured into her ear. His tongue followed his words, teasing the swirl of its shell, nibbling her lobe, then he picked her up and dropped her in the middle of the bed. Before she could cry out in surprise, he stretched out beside her and continued his sweet assault.

Eilidh rolled to face him, draped one leg over his hip and encouraged him closer with her foot on his tightly muscled arse. "I've waited years for this," she told him.

"We will make up for lost time."

"All in one night?" Suddenly she wasn't entirely sure her tactics were wise.

Bhaltair laughed, and the deep rumble in his chest made her bones vibrate and fully awoke her healing sense. She felt the blood coursing through his veins and filling his cock, the tension in his muscles as he stroked her, his touch firm but gentle, and the desire that filled him. For her. "If only ye could feel what I feel," she told him.

"Yer talent?"

"And yer body. Yer need to have me. How it makes me need ye even more."

He groaned and pulled her closer. "I want to take this slowly, Eilidh. I want ye to enjoy yer first time—and every time."

"I dinna think I can wait. I need ye to make me yers. Ye forget, I can heal any damage we do."

He stroked her face, the look in his eyes betraying his desire. "We have all night, lass. Yet ye tempt me past reason."

"Good." She pushed him onto his back and rolled on top of

him. Her damn skirt was in the way, as was his kilt. She tugged at both until Bhaltair grabbed her hands.

"Not quite that fast, love," he told her and sat up, forcing her to roll off him. He stood and pulled her from the bed. "First, I want to see all of ye before I go about making ye mine."

"I want the same." She reached for the pin at his shoulder and undid the clasp and pulled the wool down his arm. Next, she reached for his belt. Once that fell to the floor, so did the yards of his woolen great kilt.

He held up a finger and kicked off his boots, then turned back to her, clad only in his léine. The fine fabric was thin enough for her to see the shape of his muscles and the size of the cock straining toward her. She ran her hands over his chest, enjoying how solid and sculpted he was. He sucked in a breath, so she went lower, trailing her fingertips over the rippled muscles of his belly. Then she wrapped one hand around him.

He growled, low in his throat, and sensation spiked so intensely in her own body that, surprised, she released him.

He unlaced her kirtle before she could reach for him again, pulled it off her shoulders, and let it slide into a puddle of silk at her feet. Her fine silk chemise left nothing to the imagination, and Bhaltair studied her hungrily, ran his hands down her arms, and plucked the hem up and over her head. In moments she was bare.

"Ye, too," she said and did the same to him. God, he was beautiful, all slabs of muscle, and everywhere, tight, sun-bronzed skin, and scars. Light colored hair furred his chest and trailed down his belly to curl, slightly darker where she'd held him, then lighter again down his thighs and legs. She licked her lips in appreciation.

"Ach, nay, my love. I'll have ye first," he told her.

She wasn't sure what he meant by that.

He picked her up and lay her on the bed, then joined her and braced himself over her. "Ye may think ye are ready, but ye are not. I will make certain ye are," he told her, then kissed her. She wrapped her arms around his neck and tried to capture him with her legs, but he shifted down.

When he suckled her breast, she arched up, sensations shooting from the tip through her chest and belly to her core. "I never kenned that felt so good," she gasped.

"There's more," he promised and kissed his way down to her thighs. Heat followed the trail his mouth made, then he blew cool air over her belly, making her skin pebble at the contrast in sensations.

She shrieked in protest.

He laughed and went back to kissing her thighs. She had let them fall open, but he pushed them wider, licked and nibbled up one, then the other. When his tongue teased her center, she reared up.

"What are ye doin'?"

"Lie back and let me pleasure ye. I promise ye willna regret it."

She eyed him, dubious, but he'd been right so far, so she did as he asked. In moments, his masterful tongue had her writhing and begging for release. When it came it was stronger and brighter than any pleasure she'd ever experienced. Bhaltair entered her with one finger, then two, stretching her. She was so wet, she barely felt it until he entered the third.

"Ah, lass, now ye are ready."

"Then take me."

He moved up and nudged her opening with the heavy head of his cock.

She held her breath until he shook his head.

"Breathe, lass. If ye tense up, ye will undo all I have done for ye."

She took a deep breath and he entered her, stretching her body in a way that was at first uncomfortable, then something else. The sense of fullness was right, comforting, enticing. She wanted more. When she adjusted to him, he pushed in a bit farther, again, until he reached her barrier. "I ken this will sting," she jested, nervous but eager.

"So I've been told," he answered and pushed through.

Eilidh bit down on a scream against his shoulder, then remembered his advice and breathed, deep and slow. As before, her body adjusted to his size. Bhaltair was thankful for that. He was a big man, and he couldn't imagine hurting her every time he tried to make love to her.

"I'm healing it," she said, surprising him, "to remain like this, so that each time ye breach me, ye dinna have to..."

"Breach yer barrier and hurt ye all over again. Good thinking, love. I can wait."

He felt something. Some extra warmth, a tingle he'd never experienced in that area. It felt good. Invigorating. He withdrew a bit, then pushed deeper. "How is that?"

"I dinna have words to describe it," she said, wrapped her legs around him and lifted her hips.

He took the hint and plunged into her to the hilt, withdrew, and did it again and again. Being in Eilidh was the most incredible feeling he'd ever experienced. Worth every moment of waiting. Of loving her from a distance. She was right. They would make up for lost time, and he would love her until the day he died, which, if being inside her always felt this good, might happen sooner than he wished.

His climax hit with surprising force and duration. He clung to her while he rode it out, needing her touch, her scent, her heat surrounding him, to make it through.

"Ye're killing me, lass," he said when it was over. He was breathing as hard as if he'd fought a battle against a skilled opponent, not a lass half his weight.

"Nay!"

"I didna mean it literally, Eilidh," he added and chuckled to reassure her.

"Does it always feel that good?"

"It never has before. Ye gave me that gift. I am yers forever."

"And ye made me yers forever. Bhaltair, I've never been this happy. I dinna ken what to do."

Tears leaked from the corners of her eyes. He bent and kissed them away. "Love me, lass, and never stop."

"How could I not? I've never done anything else but love ye."

EPILOGUE
FIVE YEARS LATER, 1544

Eilidh stood with her mother Aileana, her sisters-by-marriage Morven, Aftyn, and Yvaine, and her older sister Lianna, watching their bairns, ages from two to eleven, chase butterflies through the glen below the Aerie.

"I wish I still had their energy," Lianna complained, hand on her aching back. She was with child again, due in a few weeks, which was sufficient reason for the entire family to gather. Her last babe was born after hard labor, despite Aileana's presence at MacDhai to help her. Eilidh hated to think how it would have gone without their mother's healing talents. Lianna had chosen to return home for this delivery where her mother and sister could care for her more conveniently. The other siblings had taken her news as an excuse to come, too, knowing that their parents would enjoy having the whole family together, and that opportunities for all of the young cousins to spend time getting to know each other were few.

"'Twill not be long, now," Aileana said, soothing her with a warm hand on her back.

Lianna's eyes widened. "Today? 'Tis too soon!"

Aileana laughed at her daughter's dismay. "Nay, I didna mean today."

"Damn, I'd like to get this over with," Lianna groused.

Morven and Yvaine smiled in sympathy. They'd both become mothers since marrying into the Lathan clan.

Eilidh shared their sympathy, too. Her time was coming sooner than anyone knew. She looked forward to the future, though things were changing.

The last few years had been relatively peaceful at the Aerie, but not outside the Highlands. Scotland had gained an infant queen in the last year, and Henry VIII of England was determined to marry one of his sons to her and unite the two countries under English rule. When the Scottish parliament rebuffed him, he sent ships. They'd burned Edinburgh and fought in Glasgow in the spring. The violence had not yet reached the Highlands, but Eilidh knew her father and the other lairds who'd signed his treaty would stand together. How that would help them if war with England reached them remained to be seen.

In the meantime, Aileana gave her more and more responsibility as the clan's healer. That meant many sleepless nights caring for sick or injured clan members, helping new bairns come into the world, and easing the way for the old and dying.

Toran had named Bhaltair the clan's arms master four summers ago when old Duncan was injured during training, and he realized he was getting too slow to safely continue with that responsibility. Bhaltair took to the challenge eagerly, making Eilidh proud. In addition to being the chief guard, he was responsible for training the younger lads to become warriors as fierce as he. He handled both with apparent ease.

She watched him ride the perimeter he had set, checking in with each of the guards, making sure they stayed alert and were ready in case there was any trouble. All the husbands stood guard around the close perimeter Bhaltair had set to allow the wee ones to run free, and more Lathan guards stood watch farther out, from the tree line of the nearby woods down to the burn that cut across the glen. Toran, the Lathan laird, Eilidh's father, would take no chances with the future of his family. And all of it was present in the glen. They didn't expect any trouble of the human kind, but predators roamed the woods nearby, and ten small children might tempt a pack of wolves beyond sense. So Bhaltair stayed alert and ensured their circle of protection was solid.

During all the years she thought herself in love with Bhaltair, Eilidh fantasized about what life would be like with him as her husband. In the years since they wed, she learned that she never understood what it would truly be like. How happy she would be, and how happy they would be together. Not that everything was perfect, but they worked through their disagreements and always turned back to each other for comfort. She and Bhaltair complemented each other's strengths and weaknesses, just as she'd hoped and promised.

"What are they doing now?"

The question came from Morven, Drummond's wife, and pulled Eilidh's attention from her husband back to the children they were supposed to be watching. The ten of them had gathered together in a circle in the middle of the meadow and appeared to be studying something.

They only looked studious. Knowing the eldest two, Drummond and Morven's Rory, and Lianna and David's Mirielle, she suspected they were conspiring, and using the other children, mostly two- to four-year-olds, as a shield from the watchful eyes of the adults.

Eilidh glanced aside at her elder sister and her mother. "What do ye think? Should we go find out what they're doing?"

Lianna nodded. "Look at them. They're up to something. Aye, we should."

Aileana, more willing to give her grandchildren the benefit of the doubt, shook her head. "What trouble can they get into with all their parents nearby?"

Lianna and Eilidh laughed. "Ye do recall yer own bairns, aye? And those are ours."

Aileana nodded. "Well, in that case, I suppose ye should see what they're about."

Lianna gathered the other mothers with a tilt of her head. Morven, Yvaine and Aftyn joined them and they walked together across the glen. "I'm glad we came," Aftyn said as they went. "'Tis the first visit we've made in much too long. Our lasses needed to meet their cousins, and Jamie needed to renew his bond with his brothers and sisters."

"I wish ye didna live so far away," Eilidh told her. "We see ye too seldom."

Aftyn nodded, but Eilidh guessed she had more to say, though she stayed silent for a few paces.

"That may change soon," Aftyn announced.

"How?" Lianna was quick to ask. Jamie was the youngest triplet, born after Drummond and her.

"The abbey hospital is well established. Jamie has worked hard to ensure they ken how to care for their patients. But it is getting harder to keep his talent hidden. Over time, enough people see a wee bit here or there and start asking questions. After yer encounter with the witch hunters at Fletcher a few years ago, it has been on our minds. And news has traveled to the Scottish abbeys of Cromwell's attacks on Catholic cathedrals and abbeys in England. Everyone is on edge. To keep our lasses safe, Jamie wants us to move to the Aerie before winter sets in."

"They would be safer here. We are not aware of any encounters with the English nearby," Eilidh told her.

"Exactly. We are much closer to the troubled areas, and Jamie thinks our association with the abbey willna protect us when the abbey is at risk."

"Then come," Lianna said. "In fact, dinna go back. Or leave the lasses here, go retrieve what ye need and make yer peace with leaving, then return. Dinna wait for winter."

"That is sound advice," Morven, ever the practical one, told her. "Ye should do as Lianna suggests."

"Neither Tavish nor I have had any visions related to ye, but I will speak to him and we will try," Yvaine told her. "These are unsettled times. Ye must keep safe."

Once they reached the children, Eilidh's heart beat faster as she saw one of the young girls sitting on the ground, one leg extended. Together, the mothers rushed toward their children. Eilidh stayed back, realizing the children had instinctively closed in around the hurt child, holding hands in a circle of protection.

"What is going on here?"

Eilidh suspected she knew, but she couldn't believe it.

Morven looked to her son Rory, the eldest, to explain what they found.

Rory shrugged. "Those two," he said, indicating Yvaine's girls, "told her," and he nodded to the lass on the ground, "not to run this way after a butterfly. She did anyway, stepped in a hole and hurt her ankle. The rest of us joined hands and made a chain with all the healer's bairns closest to her, and one touched her ankle and fixed it. Him," he said and nodded to one of Lianna's twin boys.

"Ye did what?" Incredulity filled Lianna's voice.

"It can be done. It has been done. Here," Eilidh told her, then waved to her mother and beckoned her. "Mother will want to see this."

"Are we in trouble?" Rory looked uncertain. So did Morven.

"Nay," Eilidh assured him, and smiled at all the other children. "Ye have done very well."

Aileana strode up, moving quickly, as if her daughters' worst fears had been confirmed, and she had to come help solve whatever troubled her family.

"Wait till ye hear this," Eilidh told her. "Rory, tell yer gran what ye just told us."

Rory repeated the tale. Aileana's smile grew with each detail he added. Then she knelt by the lass whose ankle had twisted, touched her leg, and smiled again. She pushed to her feet, helped up the lass, and held her arms wide. "Come to me, weans. All of ye have done well today."

"Really?" Mirielle's face made it clear she expected trouble.

"Really." Aileana couldn't get her arms around ten children at once, but she hugged them all before she was done.

"Astounding," she murmured when she'd touched each child. "Now, go play. The sun is still high."

They scattered in ten different directions, and Aileana turned to her daughters and daughters-by-marriage. "My gift did not appear until after my first moon-blood, but Jamie healed a butterfly's broken wing when he was just four, here, in this very glen." She smiled at each of them. "Ye have done well. Yer talents, or yer husband's, or mine, have passed to yer children. All who carry my blood. And ye may not realize it, but on their own, they just did the most extraordinary thing, clasping hands and sharing the strengths of their various talents so that even the youngest of them could help heal their injured cousin. 'Tis a skill we adults learned only a few years ago, this sharing of strength to help a healer." She turned her gaze to her elder daughter. "Yer sons. More male healers! I dinna ken why talents manifest earlier or later in some, but we have seen that they do." She raised her arms to the sky and threw her head back. "What a wonderful day!"

LATER THAT EVENING, after all the bairns had gone or been put to bed in the nursery, the adults gathered in the great hall near the hearth to discuss the day's revelation. Aileana had sworn the women to secrecy until after supper, when they would tell their menfolk together.

"We're all here," Toran told her when the last set of parents came down the stairs and settled by the hearth with the rest.

"What news do ye have that is so important ye call everyone together to share it?"

Aileana stood and repeated what had happened in the glen that afternoon. Eilidh enjoyed the reactions on her brothers and her and Lianna's husband's faces. At first, David MacDhai and Bhaltair didn't seem to understand the significance, but as Toran, Drummond, Jamie and Tavish all burst into whoops of delight, they caught on and grinned.

"So, the talents continue to spread," Toran said, stood and hugged Aileana to him. "Look what we, nay, *ye*, have created!"

"We, my love," she told him with a proud smile. "And our children. And someday, their children will share their gifts, too."

Bhaltair's expression sobered. "The more these talents spread, the more difficult it will be to protect those who carry them," he said.

His smile had told Eilidh he shared in the joy of Aileana's announcement, but as usual, he thought immediately of their well-being. She loved him for himself, but also for the care and concern he showed her immediate family and the rest of the Lathan clan.

Her brother Jamie's wife Aftyn spoke up. "Perhaps the day will come when they have spread far enough to be common and not something that has to be hidden, their wielders protected."

Jamie nodded. "We are not at that point yet, still, I am hopeful that day will come. I have found the healers at the abbey, none of whom have a talent like mine, welcome the sometimes "miraculous" cures that occur in their patients. They, however, are not the problem. The patients themselves can be highly superstitious, and the fear of witchcraft is greater in the south than here. So that future ye long for will take time. Perhaps many generations."

"Not all talents are healing," Drummond reminded them. "Ye all still come to me when ye have lost something. Or someone," he said with a fond smile at Morven. "And Tavish, ye and Yvaine must do what ye can with yer sight to guide us."

Tavish nodded and took Yvaine's hand. "We will, of course."

"So, Mother, what did ye learn from the weans about their abilities?" Eilidh asked her. "Ye made certain to touch each of them."

Aileana shook her head. "I'm still thinking about what I learned—or didna learn. I will tell ye when I am able. And Morven? David? I wish Rory and Marielle could share in the gifts the other children have—or will have. As those talents become more apparent, ye must remember to make those two feel special in their own ways. Because they are and always will be."

"Always," David said, his voice gruff with unspoken emotion. Lianna squeezed his hand.

"Aye, always," Morven echoed with a smile for Drummond.

Eilidh smiled at the obvious love those couples shared. As she swept her gaze back to Bhaltair, Aileana caught her eye and nodded.

She knew!

Well, of course she did.

BACK IN THEIR CHAMBER LATER, Eilidh gave Bhaltair the news she'd been saving for a special moment. After the events of the day, this seemed the perfect time.

"What did ye think about Mother's revelation?" She began there, wanting to be certain he understood what had happened.

"'Tis wonderful news," he told her as he wrapped her in his arms. "If I hadna seen what ye did to strengthen the Seers visions, with the weans now doing it, I might not have believed it, but ye proved it can be done. Still, for the talents to have begun in bairns so young!"

She leaned back and looked him in the eye. "And what would ye think if we were to be part of all of that?"

Fine lines appeared between his brows, crinkling the tanned

skin and giving him a fierce expression. "What do ye mean, part of all that? We are. Ye are."

"I mean, by summer, ye will be the father of twins. Twins who, by all we saw today, will probably carry some special talent, like mine, my mother's, and apparently the majority of the rest of the family."

His brow lifted and his mouth widened into a grin. "Do ye mean it? Twins?"

"Aye, a lad and a lass, I think. 'Tis still a wee early to be certain."

"I dinna care which they are, my love. Though one of each will be fun."

"And likely more to follow, if that is what ye wish, love," Eilidh told him.

"What we both wish, ye mean," he insisted. "Ye must be happy about each bairn, too."

"I will, and we'll have all the help we need with Drummond and Morven here—and Aftyn told me she and Jamie are planning to move back here before winter sets in."

"I think that's wise. All the discord with England will raise tempers and make trouble like we had at Fletcher all the more likely. I want all of ye safe. David can protect Lianna and their bairns. Tavish and Yvaine will be safe at MacKyrie. I do worry for the Fletchers. If yer brother Jamie does move back here, the Fletchers will be the ones left most exposed."

"But we canna keep all the talents confined forever. If they stay true from generation to generation, members of our clans will move to other parts of the Highlands, or to towns and villages in all directions."

"In their own time, aye. But Eilidh, love, this is our time. And these," he said, putting a gentle hand on her lower belly, "will be our bairns. I swear to ye I will love them and protect and care for them as I do ye."

"I ken ye will, Bhaltair. As will I." She stepped back and held out her hand to him. "Now, perhaps 'tis time for ye to care for me."

His expression cleared and his gaze darkened as it traveled from her face down her body and back up again. "Gladly. But who will take care of me?"

"Wait yer turn, my *muckle* man. Ye willna be forgotten."

"*Muckle*, aye. I'm too big to forget." He laughed and scooped her up, then dropped her on their huge bed.

Giggling, she rolled to the middle. "Come and get me," she taunted.

With a roar, he was on her, covering her in kisses and stroking her face, her throat, her breasts, and running a hand down her body. "As usual, ye have on too many clothes, Wife,"

She lifted a hand to her forehead, palm out. "Dear me, what can we do about that?"

He reached for her and she shrieked. "Dinna tear my dress! Moina is tired of having to repair everything I wear."

"'Tis my wish to keep her busy," he said. "Surely ye dinna want her to be bored?"

"How could she be, when she kens I'm always bringing her the last set of clothes ye tore in yer eagerness to..."

"Aye?" He rolled off her and lay on his side, one hand supporting his head as he studied her.

She rolled off the other side of the bed, out of his reach. "She thinks this is all we do! Ye willna tear any more of my clothes, Bhaltair!" She quickly divested herself of her garments, then dove under the covers before he could grab her. "Ye can join me when ye are similarly undressed," she told him.

Accepting her challenge, he stood and stripped, then tossed the covers aside, baring her.

"Ye are mine, now, Wife."

She opened her arms in welcome. "And ye are mine."

Later, happily tired and replete from their love making, Eilidh curled against Bhaltair's side, her head on his massive shoulder, and contemplated the future. "How many bairns do ye want?"

"As many as ye do, love."

"We'll take them one at a time—or two—and see how it goes. And love them all."

"As much as I love ye, Eilidh. For as long as I live."

With a happy sigh, Eilidh cuddled closer, and let Bhaltair love her.

AUTHOR'S NOTE

Surprise! Look for the first book in a new series in late 2023! Want to know more?

So do I! I have several projects started. It's a matter of picking which to finish first. Keep an eye on my website at www.will-ablair.com to find out more. As I know, so will you.

A Historical Note

The major witch hunts of the 17th century happened after the time period of this book, but despite the fact that the Highlands were always more accepting of the idea of special talents, wise women, healers and such, than the Lowlands and Borders, the threat was beginning to make its way north much earlier.

The other looming threat was the Protestant movement, which also spread via trade from the Low Countries, and from England, north into the Lowlands. The history of Catholicism versus Protestantism and the rulers of England and Scotland is well known. But what may not be understood is how early the hints of looming trouble appeared. As early as 1428, the Bishop of St. Andrews had 24-year-old Protestant Patrick Hamilton burned at the stake outside St. Salvator's Chapel, and in 1546, George

Wishart was hanged, then burned at the stake outside the St. Andrews castle by the next Bishop of St. Andrews.

By the early 1500s, tensions were rising. In his attempt to gain power with Henry VIII, Thomas Cromwell set about wiping Catholic Churches and monasteries from England and taking their wealth to the Crown. His Protestant fervor helped carry that torch (sometimes literally) north to Scotland. Protestants were much less accepting of the old ways, and of Catholic rituals, even to the point of eliminating the open celebration of Christmas in Scotland for over 400 years.

Mary Queen of Scots was still an infant when Henry VIII tried to force her marriage to his son Edward in order to weaken Scotland's ties to France. When the Scots rejected the Treaties of Greenwich that sealed the union in 1543, he began what became known as the Rough Wooing, that would continue for eight bloody years of battle and led to Mary being taken to France to marry the Dauphin. After her return to Scotland and subsequent marriages, in 1567, Mary's son, became James VI of Scotland. He took the throne of England as James I in 1603, inherited from Elizabeth I, Mary's cousin, uniting the two countries— temporarily. But that's a subject for another time.

AFTERWORD

The ailment Orla suffered from was what we now call Celiac Sprue, a reaction to the proteins in wheat, barley and rye that cause the immune system to attack the lining of the small intestine, damaging it and making it unable to absorb nutrients from food, which is doubly dangerous in infants and children. I'd like to imagine it was rare in the 16th century, but today it affects around one out of 100 people, including me. There's no medicine to treat it. The only "cure" that allows the gut to heal is to permanently eliminate those three proteins from the diet. For celiacs, going gluten free is not a fad or a lifestyle choice. It's a medical necessity, and a challenge in today's world of packaged foods and restaurant meals, many of which contain wheat gluten in some form or another, either inherently or by cross-contamination during preparation. It has no taste or smell. There's no reliable way to test the food before consumption. Accidental exposure is common and can be devastating.

ALSO BY WILLA BLAIR

ABOUT THE AUTHOR

Willa Blair is an award-wining Amazon and Barnes & Noble #1 bestselling author of Scottish historical, light paranormal and contemporary romance filled with men in kilts, psi talents, and plenty of spice. Her books have won numerous accolades, including the Marlene, the Merritt, National Readers' Choice Award Finalist, Reader's Crown finalist, InD'Tale Magazine's RONE Award Honorable Mention, and NightOwl Reviews Top Picks. She loves scouting new settings for books, and thinks being an author is the best job she's ever had.

Willa loves hearing from readers!
Contact her:
www.willablair.com
authorwillablair@gmail.com

Sign up for my Newsletter
Find links to the rest of my books